BONE WARRIORS

Bone Warriors

Bron Bahlmann

Sweetwater Books
Springville, Utah

© 2009 Brian Bahlmann

All rights reserved.

The views expressed within this work are the sole responsibility of the author and do not necessarily reflect the position of Cedar Fort, Inc., or any other entity.

This is a work of fiction. The characters, names, incidents, places, and dialogue are products of the author's imagination, and are not to be construed as real.

No part of this book may be reproduced in any form whatsoever, whether by graphic, visual, electronic, film, microfilm, tape recording, or any other means, without prior written permission of the publisher, except in the case of brief passages embodied in critical reviews and articles.

ISBN 13: 978-1-59955-322-1

Published by Sweetwater Books, an imprint of Cedar Fort, Inc.
2373 W. 700 S., Springville, UT 84663
Distributed by Cedar Fort, Inc., www.cedarfort.com

LIBRARY OF CONGRESS CATALOGING-IN-PUBLICATION DATA

Bahlmann, Brian Abraham, 1993-
  Bone warriors / Brian Abraham Bahlmann.
    p. cm.
  ISBN 978-1-59955-322-1 (acid-free paper)
  1. Magicians--Fiction. 2. Bones--Fiction. I. Title.
  PS3602.A435B66 2009
  813'.6--dc22

                                                            2009008771

Cover design by Angela D. Olsen
Cover design © 2009 by Lyle Mortimer
Edited and typeset by Heidi J. Doxey

Printed in the United States of America

10 9 8 7 6 5 4 3 2

Printed on acid-free paper

Contents

Acknowledgments xi
Chapter 1—Body Count 1
Chapter 2—Don't Go in the Woods 6
Chapter 3—The Day the Dremi Flew 11
Chapter 4—City of the Missing 18
Chapter 5—Orphan Makers 23
Chapter 6—Going in the Woods 30
Chapter 7—The Green Thing 34
Chapter 8—Under a Rock 39
Chapter 9—Prisoner 44
Chapter 10—A Place to Sleep 47
Chapter 11—Tree of Fire 51
Chapter 12—Strange Alliance 54
Chapter 13—Something in The Woods 59
Chapter 14—Cow Cavalry 63
Chapter 15—Strange Black Rocks 70
Chapter 16—Dead Nor Alive 75
Chapter 17—Hang the Boat 79
Chapter 18—Too High 84
Chapter 19—Splinters 90
Chapter 20—Missing 96
Chapter 21—Log 100
Chapter 22—Stowaway 105
Chapter 23—Beached 113

Contents

Chapter 24—Lizard Village 116
Chapter 25—Boars 127
Chapter 26—Bird Men 139
Chapter 27—Nightmares 150
Chapter 28—Magnus 157
Chapter 29—Rigor Mortis 160
Chapter 30—Sinking 172
Chapter 31—Scalies and Furries 182
Chapter 32—Badlands 186
Chapter 33—Sharp Spires 193
Chapter 34—Blumpers 197
Chapter 35—Dreaming Awake 202
Chapter 36—No Way Out 207
Chapter 37—The First Terror 213
Chapter 38—The Second Terror 219
Chapter 39—Dungeons 228
Chapter 40—Traitor 233
Chapter 41—Followed 240
Chapter 42—Piles of Bones 244
Chapter 43—The Necromancer 252
Chapter 44—A Good Place to Be 257
Glossary 265
Book Club Questions 267
About the Author 271

Dedication

I have no favorites, so I dedicate this book to all five of my brothers, who also proofread this book for me: Andy for being brave enough to be the oldest brother, Jeff for letting me crawl in his bed when I was a scared little kid in the night, Scott for sharing my love of fantasy, Zack for being my boxing trainer (you made me tough) and for the hanging boat and help with the names in this book, and Michael for being the best little brother on earth.

Acknowledgments

Thanks to my proofreaders C. L. Beck, who never forgets my birthday, T. R. Ransom, who acts like an idiot with me, Greg Anderson for cleaning my teeth, Marianne Olson for always being there, Darla and Kristen Nielson whom I don't even know, but my mom found to read for me.

Thanks to my middle school English teacher Mrs. Eicher for being the first outsider to read the book.

Thanks to Dad for understanding that this is my basketball. (Although I still like playing basketball, too.)

Thanks to Mom for letting me inherit her crazy love for writing and for her editing skills.

Thanks also to Robin Williams for inspiring me to laugh and live like a kid all the time.

Thanks to Grandma Ruth and Aunt Carolyn Anderson, Aunt Rebecca and cousins Daniel, Jacob, Jessica, Jennifer, and Jacquelyn McGarry for the pizza, cake, and support in small envelopes. I'll always remember the surprise first-book celebration you gave me.

Thanks to Christopher Greenhalgh for being my friend since before we were born.

And finally, thanks to all my enemies for making me stronger.

1
Body Count

"Fight us now! We will bloody your beards!"

The threat rose on rancid breath from a red-bearded man in stained leather breeches. His bloodshot eyes sent hateful glances up the hill toward the enemy while his ragged warriors stamped their impatient dirty feet at the edge of a meadow.

The necromancer sneered at the barbarians' wretched disorder, his cold eyes focused through two slits in a silver mask etched with the ghostly outlines of a skull. His nose twitched, his dry lips curled in disgust at the barbarians' stinking flesh.

Red Beard took a dozen steps into the meadow. His men followed, leaving gaps between the trees that were quickly filled by more barbarians. Their muscled arms raised a forest of spears and broadswords, flashing sunlight. Spiked maces swung from thick wooden handles and axes practiced head-cutting sweeps while gruff voices raised more insults.

"You're nothing but worthless swine!"

"We'll cut your heads off for trophies, you armored weaklings!"

"Come to the slaughter! This day, you die."

Hate rose with the taunts, gap-toothed mouths slapping together as though anxious to taste blood. The only thing that held them back was the necromancer's advantage of higher ground.

A broad-shouldered knight strode out from the necromancer's troops and dropped to one knee before his commander. He bowed his head, showing a grinning skull etched on top of his helmet. The quiver of arrows he carried on his back was destined for the enemies' stinking bodies. Raising his head, he squinted in a patch of reflected light from the silver mask. "The troops are ready, sir."

Strange black designs swirled around the necromancer's dark blue robe, changing shape, stretching and curling their way through the folds like living things. He turned his lean body and saw his troops assembled in perfect lines, according to experience, with swords and javelins at their sides. They were clearly outnumbered.

Good.

The necromancer wasn't interested in winning. He only wanted bodies, and his own fallen men would be easier to claim. The enemy usually carried off their dead, the fools, and sometimes burned them, making the bones completely unusable. Broken bones were worthless too, but sometimes that couldn't be helped, especially in war.

The necromancer gave a single flick of his black-gloved hand. The knight rose to his feet. "Remember," the necromancer said, his voice low. "No matter what happens, you and your brother must stay close to me."

"Yes, sir." The first knight bowed while another huge knight stepped in beside him and nodded agreement. The bodyguards were there to carry out the necromancer's deadly orders because he never killed with his own hands. Killing took power from the soul, and he needed all his power. It took strong magic to work the spell that would make all the difference.

Slowly he raised his gloved hands and pointed to his armored soldiers. Loud cries arose from the waiting barbarians, their decaying teeth gnashing in frenzy. Then the necromancer spoke the deadly words. "Begin the slaughter."

His knights grabbed the halters of two young dremi, their snake-like bodies squirming in the grass behind them. The dremi's triangular heads tossed gray-blue manes over powerful shoulders, held up by two forelegs, each as tall as a man. The rest of their bodies slipped behind them in a column of muscle ending in a pointed tail. The knights swung their armored legs up behind the dreami's large pair of leathery wings while the dremi stepped impatiently, their knees locking and unlocking, long toes sifting the grass. A smaller pair of wings flapped further back along each of their dark, scaly bodies.

Then the necromancer flung his gloved finger forward, pointing across the meadow, his robe fluttering.

"Attack!" cried the knights, pressing the smooth, glossy scaled dremi's necks with urgent hands. The long creatures came to attention and opened their wide mouths to show teeth as sharp as pointed daggers. They surged forward, dragging their writhing tails with powerful strides of their forelegs, forming a protective barrier before the necromancer. Two glistening streams of liquid shot out from the backs of their throats. When the liquids touched in front of their pointed noses, two bursts of bright orange flame rose into the air.

At this signal, the front lines of the necromancer's army lowered their javelins, raised their swords, and marched down the hillside. The barbarians let out a wild roar and pounded toward their enemies, flattening grass and flowers into a morbid carpet beneath their filthy feet. When the necromancer's warriors reached flat ground, they released a volley of javelins. The first row of barbarians fell, screaming, but more swarmed forward to replace them with wide open mouths and raised weapons. A few seconds later, the two armies crashed together in the meadow. The necromancer watched the furious battle from the hilltop, his wrinkled heart leaping every time a soldier fell. So many lovely dead bodies.

When the battle ended, the victorious barbarians gathered their fallen leaders, leaving the rest to their fate. The enemy retreated just ahead of sunset, Red Beard bobbing lifeless above the heads of his warriors until he disappeared into the dark shadows beneath the trees.

The necromancer looked out over the corpse-covered meadow where barbarians sprawled alongside his own armored men. A few survivors contorted their wounded bodies or raised weak arms, begging for help. His dry lips set in a line as grim as the mask he wore. He would most certainly help them with their suffering. He turned to the knight standing nearest to him. "Bring in the wounded," he said. "Leave the dead."

The knight gave the order, which was carried out by the dozen soldiers who'd escaped serious injury. They carried their bleeding and broken comrades into a tent set up for their care. With skin walls too thin to shut out the moans and cries of distress, the tent could not keep the irritating sounds from squeezing inside the necromancer's withered ears, filling his head until there was no room to think. He strode away, the black designs chasing each other around his dark robe. Both of his bodyguard knights followed at a respectful distance.

Suddenly the necromancer whirled, stabbed his finger at the tent, and roared, "Leave me! Go see to them!"

The knights bowed. "Yes, commander," they answered, and then left to oversee the administration of the poisonous medicine they mistakenly thought would help their broken comrades. Only the necromancer knew that none of the wounded were expected to survive.

The necromancer turned away and walked alone. Once the cries of pain were far enough away to be of no consequence, he stopped and looked at the bodies, stained blood red from the dying sun. There were so many, more than he'd hoped for. He slowly raised his black-gloved hands above his head, his hard heart pumping with dark excitement as he moved his curved fingers in slow circles. "A los morte com ta corpus," he chanted.

Two huge figures lumbered out from a copse of dark trees. Each walked into the meadow on two thin legs beneath bodies that were twice as tall as a man and three times as broad. The bone golems appeared to be scarlet lacework gone horribly wrong, with wide spaces between woven sections. Wobbling skulls sat on top of the bone skeletons and turned with quick jerks to find bodies to stack in their giant arms like sodden firewood. Only when the sun buried itself beneath the horizon did the monstrous bodies gleam sickly white in the moonlight. The bone golems' jerky movements came from a random attachment of bones. Never stopping, they used their strangely fitted joints to silently carry out the grisly task until not a single body was left in the trampled meadow. Then the golems deserted the bloody battlefield, disappearing beneath the dark trees with their grisly burdens.

The necromancer clasped his black-gloved hands behind him and headed back toward the tent, where a final feeble cry shot up toward the dark sky. Then all was silent.

It had been a very worthwhile battle.

2
Don't Go in the Woods

"Derrik!" Tweaks yelled, jumping up and down like a freckled grasshopper. "I did it!"

Derrik put his big, square hand on Tweaks's head, forcing his friend to stand still, but that didn't stop Tweaks's ears from wiggling up and down as if trying to break free of his head. "Stop that," Derrik said. "You look like a stupid mooncalf."

Tweaks ducked out from under Derrik's hand, his short red curls springing out in all directions. "But this is the best thing I've ever made!"

"What is it?"

"A machine to collect dit eggs."

Derrik snorted.

"Come on, Derrik, this could free kids everywhere from having to gather eggs. Besides, when have my inventions ever failed?" Derrik opened his mouth, but Tweaks quickly added, "And the time my water heating machine exploded doesn't count. There was a newt in the water."

"All right," Derrik said, crossing his arms. "Show me your wonderful invention."

"Okay, but it's not here," Tweaks explained. He started down the road, his eager face turned back over his shoulder. "Come on."

Before Derrik could follow, the front door of his rough board house popped open and his mother, Mali Sparks, stood in the doorway. Her intense tawny eyes looked at the boys through tendrils of soft brown hair that were forever escaping the braid around her head. She sent a puff of breath through rounded lips, sending the hair dancing over her upturned nose. She was small enough that Derrik could have picked her up and sat her on a shelf, but he would never dare try. Her temper would have her serving him dry bread and scummy water for a week if he did.

"What are you doing out here?" She looked from Derrik to Tweaks, then broke into a smile. "Gerret, is that you?" she asked, using Tweaks's given name.

"I came to see Derrik," Tweaks admitted in a voice that sounded like an apology. His blue eyes dropped from Mali to study the unremarkable ground.

"Good," Mali said, her voice light. "You can help Derrik bring in water. Two buckets, please. And be quick about it." Then she flapped her small hand at them and shut the door.

"Great," Derrik said.

"Let's hurry so we can see my invention," Tweaks urged, trotting ahead. Tweaks had barely disappeared around the corner of the house when he suddenly bounced back and tumbled to the patchy grass. Derrik heard an, "Oof!" Then his father staggered around the corner, his hand pressed over the leather blacksmith apron he wore across his stomach. "For such a small guy, you are solid as stone," Willan Sparks said, sticking out a large hand to help Tweaks up.

"Sorry, sir," Tweaks whispered. He stared at the big hand a moment before raising his own hand to meet it.

Willan glanced at his son over the top of Tweaks's head. Except for the beard and lines by his father's eyes, fifteen-year-old Derrik may as well be staring at his own reflection. Wavy brown hair hung nearly to their shoulders, and dark eyes sat under eyebrows that drew two straight somber lines. Both had noses a little longer than most, although they weren't out of proportion, and their full mouths were set in jaws strong enough to crack bones.

Willan's biceps bulged as he easily pulled Tweaks to his feet.

"Are you headed for the forge, Da?" Derrik glanced at the

blacksmith shop sitting a hundred yards from the house.

Willan nodded.

"Do you need my help?"

"No, son, it's just a small repair job on your mother's stove," Willan said. "Won't take but a few minutes."

Derrik's eyes grew wide with hope. "Will she be frying scones for supper then?"

Willan snorted. "You and your always empty belly." He nodded toward Tweaks. "You ought to be sharing your food with your friend so he can grow taller." Willan ruffled Tweaks's hair and said with a smile, "You could help yourself by standing up straight, young man."

"Yes, sir," Tweaks murmured, keeping his eyes down.

"Tweaks and I were going off," Derrik said.

Willan's voice was firm when he said, "Not to the woods."

Derrik sighed. "I know, Da, you keep telling me that."

"And I'll keep on telling you."

"What's really so bad about the woods?" Derrik asked.

Willan shook his head. "Your mother wouldn't want me to say."

Derrik pushed back his shoulders. "I'm practically a grown man, Da."

"Even grown men don't go there," Willan replied.

Tweaks looked back and forth between Willan and Derrik, chewing his lip.

"I've seen men cutting trees in the woods," Derrik protested.

"They don't go in the woods," Willan corrected him. "They pick at the edges, working in groups, removing one layer of trees at a time as quickly as they can." Willan popped his knuckles and gazed into the distance beyond his forge. "I wouldn't want to be there on the day they finally reach the center of those woods."

"Why?"

Willan looked at his son with clouded eyes. "Because there's something in there."

"Wh-what kind of thing?" Tweaks whispered.

Willan sighed. He looked toward the house, and then back at the boys. "Are you sure you want to hear this?"

"Yes," Derrik said. Tweaks merely dropped his chin, a sign that Willan took for assent.

"No one who's come out alive knows for sure," Willan said.

Tweaks shivered.

"But it wasn't always so," Willan added, as if that would soothe Tweaks. "Those who built the village a hundred fifty years ago floated downriver in boats, studying the shadowed depths between the forest tree trunks with worried eyes for any sign of wild animals. If that was all that ever lived there, they should have been glad. They cleared trees, built homes, fenced fields, and when they went into the woods after wandering livestock, they discovered sink grass."

"Sink grass?" Derrik asked.

Willan nodded. "A place that looks firm and fine until a body steps on it, then they sink and drown, quick as you can whistle. My granda told me of times he went in the woods with his da for good hunting, fat birds and four-legged beasts a-plenty, and no troubles besides sink grass. But something strange happened about a hundred years ago. An able-minded villager, gone so long he was feared dead, came out addle-headed, claiming to have seen horrible creatures deep in the forest. Other villagers never came out. Strange cries rang through the trees at odd hours. Travelers were turned around, walking and walking without getting where they thought they were going. A few survived, some walked themselves to death or landed in the sink grass, which amounts to the same thing."

Willan's dark eyes blazed as though flames twisted through them. "So no one ventures into those wild trees alone any more. Especially not my son."

The air hung thick with Willan's warning. Then Tweaks spoke in a thin voice, "Sir, may we get the water now?"

"What water?" Willan asked, blinking as though the daylight caught him by surprise.

"Mama sent us to fetch water," Derrik answered.

Willan's eyes flew open in mock fear. "Get going then," he urged. "Don't keep your mother waiting, or there will be no scones for any of us. Shoo, shoo!" He waved his big hands toward the well.

The boys moved past him at a trot. Then Willan called, "Be home before dark."

Derrik asked, "What's to be afraid of in Bylon after dark?"

"Me!" Willan roared, his beard split with a grin.

3
The Day the Dremi Flew

Derrik and Tweaks bent sideways, arms held out for balance and water buckets sagging. They waded toward the house through Mali's flock of dits, the knee-high birds skittering around on thin orange legs that made up half their height. With black feathers long enough to cover their dark, round eyes, the only way to tell their fronts from their backs was to find their thin orange beaks poking out. Round, brown dit eggs tasted good, and their feathers made the softest pillows you'd ever hope to lay your head on. Mali didn't like to cook her birds, saying the meat was too greasy, but Derrik thought it was really because she was so fond of the silly birds.

Derrik lifted the back door latch and staggered inside. His mother stood up from the potato bin, new red potatoes clutched in her small hands. "Where's Gerret?" she asked.

Derrik turned in time to see a thin arm push the water bucket into the house, scraping it across the wood plank floor with a stuttering sound. Before Derrik could answer his mother, Mali dropped the potatoes into her apron and, holding the apron in a knot with one hand, marched past her son. She grabbed Tweaks by the ear with her free hand and pulled him inside.

"Gerret Manning," she scolded, "when will you learn that you're as good as family in this house?" Mali turned Tweaks loose.

"I already know," Tweaks said, rubbing his ear. "I just don't much like the indoors."

"Not since you got that baby brother, you mean," Mali said, giving her lumpy apron a shake.

Tweaks looked down at his scuffed leather boots. "Skippy's so noisy I can't think things through," he mumbled.

"Skippy? Your mama told me he was called Soren. Why do you call him Skippy?"

Tweaks pinched his thin lips together.

"She won't stop asking 'til you tell her," Derrik warned. But Tweaks only shook his head, so Derrik blurted, "He'd like to skip having that baby altogether."

Tweaks shot Derrik a wounded look.

Mali stared at Tweaks a moment, bouncing her apron. Then she said, "It's that loft you sleep in, the way it's open to everything. Get your father to build on a room for you, with a door that closes."

"Mama, Tweaks has his own mother to give him advice," Derrik reminded her.

"Maybe if she'd look up from her new child once in awhile, she'd remember her old one," Mali muttered.

"Mama!" Derrik said.

Mali turned to the table and emptied the potatoes out with a thump.

"I'm going out with Tweaks now," Derrik said.

Mali spun around. "You won't be out past dark."

"No."

Mali pointed her finger at Tweaks. "When you get back, you'll eat with us."

Tweaks nodded so hard his curls bobbed. "Thank you. I will."

"And we eat at the table," Mali said, swinging her finger toward the polished wooden table so Tweaks would clearly understand. "Not outside."

"Yes, thank you," Tweaks said.

Mali turned to Derrik, reached up, pulled his head down,

and gave him a sound kiss on the cheek. Then she turned toward Tweaks, her hands outstretched. Tweaks scuttled backwards out the door. Mali dropped her hands, and Derrik hurried out after his friend. Before they'd walked ten paces, Mali was at the door, calling out, "Boys." They stopped and turned toward her. "Don't go in the woods."

There it was again, the advice Derrik heard so often, it sounded like one word, *dontgointhewoods*. Mali stood waiting for her son's reply, as she always did.

"I already told Da we wouldn't," Derrik answered.

"Then tell me," Mali insisted.

"We won't go in the woods," Derrik said. Mali smiled, waved, and disappeared into the house.

Tweaks's head barely reached Derrik's shoulder as they walked down the road. "She wouldn't really have . . . you know . . . kissed me, right?" Tweaks hurried to keep up with Derrik's stride.

"She would if she could've reached you." Derrik answered, rubbing the back of his hand against his kissed cheek.

"Your mother is nice and everything," Tweaks said. "But that would be . . . that would be . . ."

"Too much?" Derrik offered.

Tweaks nodded.

"Once I tried to sneak away," Derrik said, "but she chased me down the road. That was more embarrassing than just letting her kiss me in the house where no one could see."

Tweaks stared up at Derrik, his mouth open. "She chased you?"

Derrik nodded. "Yelling all the way."

"Scary." Tweaks wiggled his ears.

"Mooncalf!"

Tweaks grinned and then reached into a pocket and fished around with his fingers, the tip of his tongue showing. He pulled out a strange contraption of wire with loops at both ends and a clear piece of fossil lightning wrapped in the center. He set one wire loop over an ear and the other loop, which was bent long at the end, alongside his nose so that the lightning glass was positioned in front of one eye.

Derrik didn't look twice at the apparatus on Tweaks's face. He'd seen it often enough. He was there when Tweaks stumbled across the fossil on the white beach by the lake. It was a rare formation, created by a bolt of lightning hot enough to melt sand and create a rough tube of glass. Over time, a small piece broke off the tube and tumbled in waves, rolling it over and over, polishing it smooth with repeated washings of gritty sand.

Tweaks didn't have good enough eyesight to see the clear glass on the white beach, so he'd found the fossil the hard way, by stubbing his toe on it. When he held it to his eye to make out what it was, he yelled in excitement. The circle of glass made things much clearer. Clever boy that he was, Tweaks put it in his pocket.

Later, he fastened it to wire that sat on his face so his hands were free. Since his lucky find, Tweaks had made a lot of things that no one ever saw or thought of before.

The two friends crossed fields of fresh green grass, stirring up colorful little creatures that fluttered away on sparkling wings. They passed an orchard with long ubella fruits, not quite ripe, but the promise of their goodness was carried by the sweet-tart smell on the breeze.

"Do you think you could have built your wondrous machine any further from town?" Derrik asked.

Tweaks straightened up with indignation, but he was still shorter than Derrik. "I didn't see any point in building an entire dit coop when there was a perfectly good one not being used."

Derrik didn't bother asking Tweaks why he didn't use a coop closer to town. He knew the water-heating incident was still fairly recent and far too public for Tweaks's liking.

At last Tweaks stopped in front of a sagging shed set at the edge of an abandoned farm. The faint odor of dit droppings wafted out of the doorway.

"Okay, Derrik," Tweaks said, looking up at his friend, one eye enlarged behind the glass, the other eye looking impossibly small beside it. "Believe me, this really works, but let me make sure it's set up right before you say a word. Oh, and don't touch anything. Got it?"

Derrik shrugged. "Should I wait here while you clear out the dit poop?"

"No, you can come in," Tweaks said.

Tweaks stepped in and Derrik followed, ducking to fit. Light snuck in through the doorway, showing a cramped interior with a roof of weathered gray wood slanting to one side. Stained boards where dit nests used to rest lay cracked and tipped along the walls. Somehow Tweaks had managed to stuff an odd-looking machine into one corner. Four long tubes led to the remains of four old dit nests sitting on the only flat board in the building.

Tweaks crouched by one nest and carefully moved the moldy hay aside. "I didn't have any real eggs," he explained. His nose wrinkled and then he sneezed. He reached into the pile of hay and pulled out a small blob of brown matter that looked suspiciously like animal poop. "I made these out of straw with a thin covering of mud to mimic the weight of actual eggs."

"Those don't look anything like real dit eggs," Derrik said. "In fact, those are the ugliest eggs I've ever seen."

"Well, I had to make these to practice with so I wouldn't keep breaking real ones," Tweaks explained.

"No self-respecting dit would ever mistake those for real eggs," Derrik said.

"They'll never have to see them," Tweaks answered mildly. "And they work." He set the brown blob back in the nest. "The tubes are positioned so they don't interfere with the laying bird, yet they're close enough to do the job of collecting." Tweaks made tiny adjustments to the position of the nearest tube. "The process is triggered when the dit—"

Suddenly, without warning, Derrik toppled over. A sharp "crack" made his ears ring as he stumbled, threw his arms out, and caught himself against the wall. A sliver of wood dug into his palm. Tweaks fell hunch-shouldered into the broken shelves, letting loose a loud yelp. Mud eggs rolled on top of him, cracking and spilling brown chunks of mud everywhere.

Derrik would have laughed if he weren't so scared.

"What happened?" Derrik yelled.

Just then, he felt himself tipping the other way. A loud "bang" threw him back, and he crashed into the shuddering walls of the old coop.

Tweaks relaxed onto the center of the floor and lay there for a moment before pushing himself to his hands and feet. "I think the coop tipped." Tweaks grabbed his glass from where it hung off one ear and stuffed it into his pocket.

"What kind of stupid invention did you make?" Derrik asked.

"My invention didn't do this," Tweaks insisted. "Something happened outside."

Derrik staggered the three steps it took him to cross the coop and ducked his head out the doorway.

Sun shone on an innocent landscape, offering no clue as to what had just happened. Derrik looked from side to side. He could see nothing wrong, but uneasiness settled on his shoulders like a heavy cape in the heat of summer. He became aware of a strange whooshing sound vibrating through the air. Something touched his back. He jumped with a yelp, bumping his head on the doorframe.

"Sorry," Tweaks said, moving back a step. "I didn't know how close I was."

"Then put your glass back on," Derrik grumbled, rubbing his head.

"It's too valuable," Tweaks said. "I don't want to lose it if there's something out there waiting to get us."

"Do you want to go first?"

"That's all right," Tweaks answered. "You go ahead."

Derrik took a cautious step outside. Tall grass whispered in surprise and swallowed his feet. A dangerous breeze blew across his face. Without walls or a roof, anything could come at him from any direction, even from behind.

He glanced over his shoulder. Tweaks blinked back at him with innocent blue eyes.

Derrik turned and snuck around a corner of the coop on the balls of his feet. He made sure to flash a glance in all directions, wondering if there was someone, or something, watching him. Whoever it was could be hiding in the orchard. With frequent upward glances at the blue sky, Derrik knelt to examine the ground. Undisturbed weeds and grass grew tangled among a few bright flowers. Nothing had passed this way recently. Everything appeared normal, yet worry touched the back of Derrik's neck like an annoying insect. What happened to them in the dit coop wasn't from anything natural. Something was terribly wrong.

When Derrik glanced up again, he saw a sight that made his heart feel like it was falling down stairs. He stood and backed up, craning his neck to make sure that what he saw was real. A huge crack scarred the slanted roof of the coop. It hadn't been there when they arrived. He was sure of it. What could have hit the shed hard enough to break the roof and nearly tip the whole thing over? A shiver of alarm made Derrik suddenly want to go home.

"Derrik!" Tweaks yelled from the opposite side of the coop. "Hurry!"

Derrik dashed around to where his friend stood and pointing a shaking arm upward. Derrik followed the direction of Tweaks's finger.

At first he thought it was the bump on his head making him see things, but the flying snake shapes undulating through the air, growing smaller and smaller as they drew further and further away, were all too real. It was a small flock of dremi. Derrik was hypnotized by the way they beat each pair of wings one after the other in a beautiful waving motion. Derrik stared, unable to focus on anything but the repeated pattern of dremi wing beats.

Tweaks shook Derrik's shoulder and screamed, "Derrik! What's wrong with you? They're headed for town!"

4
CITY OF THE MISSING

Derrik ran past ripening orchards and through greening fields, waving arms through startled clouds of sparkling insects and dodging ground-nesting birds whose anxious flight didn't even slow him down. His lungs burned and his legs ached, but still he ran, stumbled, and ran again. He slowed in aching disbelief when he spied a column of smoke rising up from behind the spreading limbs of an ancient tree covered all over with trembling leaves.

"No, no, no," Derrik gasped. He made his tired legs carry him onward and forced his lungs to suck in another breath. He loped past the tree and through another field until at last he saw his hometown.

He stopped and bent over, pulling in great gasps of air tainted with smoke. He told himself the smoke could be from a burning ditch or someone's cooking fire run amok. It had to be a small tragedy, something that could be set right with a few buckets of water.

Then running footsteps overtook him. He ignored the urge to turn around, knowing it was Tweaks. His friend skidded to a stop, gasping for air like a drowning man. They both stared silently at the town. Then, without a word, they walked side by side toward the smoke and a life that neither one of them could have imagined that morning.

Broken buildings that had sheltered families the night

before now spilled brick and timber guts across the road. With wide eyes and sickened hearts, the boys saw the town gathering hall ablaze, orange claws of flame reaching through the windows and scaring up the column of smoke they'd seen spiraling to the sky. Snapped trees leaned like dying men over spot fires that burned wooden crates, an overturned cart, and stuffing spilled from mattresses.

"What happened?" Tweaks's eyelids blinked rapidly.

"I don't know." Derrik shook his head and then swallowed hard. "But we've got find out."

The boys made their way closer to the heart of town, stepping around obstacles that peppered the street and coughing on plumes of drifting smoke. Besides the wicked crackle of fire, the town was strangely silent. No children screamed with laughter or shouted arguments. No animal noises rode the air. No tools were at work, sawing or chopping. No cart wheels rumbled on the packed dirt roads.

"Can you see anybody?" Tweaks whispered.

Derrik didn't answer. His throat was tight with horror. What if they were the only two survivors?

Then something moved. Tensing, Derrik whirled to face whatever it was, not knowing if he should run or attack. But his muscles turned to jelly when he saw Bruit Kalra, a farmer who lived on the edge of town, stumbling along with a bucket half full of water, headed for the town gathering hall.

"Bruit," Derrik called, his voice cracking with relief.

Bruit seemed not to hear. Derrik moved closer with Tweaks right behind him.

"Bruit," Derrik called again, tripping over a broken fence in his hurry. Bruit's eyes stared straight ahead, and he kept to his course. Finally Derrik drew close enough to touch the farmer's homespun sleeve. Bruit shrugged Derrik's hand off without even looking at him and kept walking. Derrik's heart wrung out like a limp dishrag as he watched Bruit totter away through a ribbon of smoke. What was wrong with him?

Then a sudden, suffocating fear rose in his chest. He whirled to face Tweaks. Grabbing his friends' shoulders, he shouted, "Why can't he hear us?"

Tweaks tried to step back, his mouth open in surprise, his eyes on Derrik. "I don't know."

Derrik let out a heavy breath, released Tweaks, and then darted a look around. "We've got to find someone else." He grabbed Tweaks's arm and drew him along.

Tweaks pulled back. "I can walk."

"Sorry," Derrik mumbled, letting go of his friend.

They walked further into the horror of their broken village. It was worse than a graveyard because everything broken and dead lay on top of the ground. Moving slowly through the rubble, Derrik saw movement and whirled to find a limping rovo, an animal that many villagers kept as pets. "Come here," Derrik called, squatting down on his heels.

The little animal turned its woolly head toward him and cocked its round ears. Derrik's eyes filled with pity when he saw one of the animal's ears torn and bleeding. Derrik patted his thighs. "Come here, boy, come on." The rovo tucked its long tail closer to its woolly body and limped away on toes flexible enough to work as hands when it climbed trees. A thin splinter of something stuck out from the rovo's hind leg.

"I just want to help you," Derrik said.

"Derrik, I think I see someone," Tweaks said, slapping Derrik on the shoulder.

Derrik jumped to his feet so fast he was lightheaded for a moment. "Where?"

"Over there." Tweaks pointed to the corner of the cobbler's shop that had broken and spilled over the bench where the little man had sat working just this morning. Someone was sitting on the ground with his back against a section of wall that still stood. "Come on, Tweaks," Derrik said. "Say something to him."

Tweaks took a tentative step forward. "Hello?" he called.

The man slowly turned his head and looked at the two boys.

"Diggen!" Derrik yelled. He hurried to Diggen's side and

crouched beside him. The man's face sagged. Derrik couldn't help noticing its disturbing shade of gray, except for one eye that was bruised black. Diggen's lips showed a single line of crusted blood where they met.

"Can you hear me?" Derrik asked.

The voice of the village guard came out raspy and slow. "Yes." One of his front teeth flashed with a jagged diagonal split from gum line to biting edge. He coughed, his breath spewing out like swamp air. He pressed a dirty hand to his throat and fell silent except for the occasional rasp of his tortured breathing.

"What happened here?" Derrik felt tears pushing up to his eyes.

"Where is everybody?" Tweaks added.

The guard stared at them for so long that Derrik was afraid he wouldn't answer. Finally, Diggen said in a gravelly voice, "Boys . . . where have you been hiding?"

"In the old fields," Derrik said. "We ran back when we saw the dremi."

"Good thing . . . you can't run faster," Diggen whispered, and then he coughed long and hard until the front of his shirt was spattered red. Derrik put an arm around the man's shoulders, and Tweaks patted his leg. When the coughing fit ended, Diggen took in a rattling breath and said, "They took most of the villagers. We don't know where, but they took them and we tried to stop . . . we couldn't . . ."

"Who took them? The dremi?" Derrik asked urgently.

"Rode on . . . no . . . we killed one . . . there." Diggen pointed with a trembling arm to the corner of the bakery, now only a pile of timbers and stones.

Derrik stood to face the ruined building. A pair of scuffed black boots, toes up, stuck out from behind the debris. Legs covered in dark fabric disappeared behind the broken rock wall. "Are you sure he's dead?" Derrik asked.

There was no answer.

"Diggen, are you sure he's . . ."

"Dead," Tweaks's fearful voice said.

Derrik turned and saw Diggen tipped over on the ground. The guard's chest was still, his chin spattered with blood, his good eye closed, and his ruined eye slightly open. Yet Diggen's face was peaceful.

Tweaks stood up on shaking legs, his horrified eyes on the guard. After a moment, Derrik said, "Come on, Tweaks."

Tweaks stared up at Derrik. "You mean . . . just leave him?"

"We can't help him any more." Derrik ran the back of his hand over his forehead. "Come on." Derrik put a shaking arm around Tweaks's shoulders. "Let's go see who did this."

The two boys walked closer to the scuffed boots. Derrik took small steps, watching for a twitch or kick, but the boots remained still. The boys slowly rounded the corner. The first thing they saw was a wooden spear shaft sticking out of the enemy's chest at an angle, pointing like an accusing finger at the gathering hall. A waft of smoke skidded across the ground, blurring their view of the enemy's face. Derrik blinked. The enemy soldier's head appeared deformed, like he had some kind of head injury. Derrik swallowed. He hoped it wasn't too terrible. He wanted to be able to sleep nights.

Then the smoke cleared, and Derrik stared in horror at the enemy's face. He'd never seen anything like it before, not even in his nightmares.

5
Orphan Makers

The creature's clothing fit the body of a man, but the head sticking out from the top of the soft woven tunic turned Derrik's stomach. It was twisted to one side, facing the boys with slitted yellow eyes set in scaly brown flesh. Sickly yellow stripes ran into the collar from the corners of the lipless mouth, which was open slightly, showing needle-like fangs hanging from the top jaw. A thin tongue with a forked end lay in the dirt. There was no hair. Instead, a repulsive tail long enough to reach the creature's ankles grew out of the back of its head.

"What's wrong with his head?" Tweaks whispered. He reached into his pocket, pulled out his eyeglass, and held it up to his eye. "Augh!" he yelled.

"Stop!" Derrik said, grabbing Tweaks and turning him away. A shudder rippled through him. He didn't want to turn his back on the enemy in case it wasn't really dead, but he couldn't bear to look at it anymore. As he hurried his friend away, the skin on Derrik's back tingled with fear as though the dead snake man might suddenly rise up and shoot an arrow into his flesh.

A sudden thought made Derrik stumble. "My parents!" he yelled, breaking away from Tweaks and running toward home, and he dodged debris and hot spots in headlong flight. He heard Tweaks's shorter legs pounding along behind him. When Derrik's house came into view, he saw that it was still standing. Derrik let out a breath that sounded like a sob. He let himself hope, even though the front door was clearly missing and the doorway was blasted black with scorch marks radiating from the opening, the black rays still smoking. Derrik dodged past his front door, which lay like an oversized wooden cobblestone on the ground. He burst inside, the sudden darkness after sunlight causing him to stumble on a broken chair and bruise his leg. He absently rubbed the sore spot while his eyes took in the scene. The kitchen table was lying on its side, a puff of white scone dough rising like a giant mushroom on the floor beside it. Broken scraps of Mali's favorite blue pottery bowl fanned out from the table to the far side of the room where black scorch lines climbed the wall as if in fear of the blue shards.

"Mama!" Derrik screamed, side stepping the chair and limping through the house to the back door, which was hanging open on its hinges. "Da!" he called out into the quiet yard.

No one answered. He ran into the yard and crossed the distance to the forge with desperate strides, his pounding feet avoiding dead dits dotting the spotty grass. He burst into the forge. "Da!"

No answer.

Derrik checked every corner, looked behind barrels, and threw leather tack strips from the cupboard, but it was no use. There was no one there. Derrik stood slumped in the middle of his father's blacksmith shop, frozen with hopelessness.

"Derrik?" Tweaks called.

Derrik didn't move. "They're gone," he said, his voice cracking.

After a moment, a hand touched his arm. "Maybe they're at my house," Tweaks said. "Come on, Derrik."

Derrik looked at Tweaks. He'd looped his glass wires around his head and stood staring at Derrik with a large, worried eye.

Derrik nodded.

The boys made their way to Tweaks's house with less enthusiasm. Every second it took to arrive was another second they could hope that their parents were really there. Tweaks lived nearby, but now the familiar path was strange. Caught up in a search for missing landmarks and trying to decipher the rubble left behind, Derrik would have hurried right past Tweaks's house if his friend hadn't tugged on his arm.

Derrik turned to see a place he barely recognized. The house stood crippled, its roof missing, along with Tweaks's sleeping loft. The front door hung open like a broken tooth. The yard was pitted with craters as though some demented thing had dug with no purpose and then scattered bare flower stems over it all.

Tweaks led the way inside. His voice was small inside the four wrecked walls. "Ma? Da?" He blinked his magnified eye, which suddenly filled with tears. "Skippy?" Tweaks left the room, still calling, but Derrik didn't join him. He already knew they would find no one.

Derrik bent his head back and stared at the sky through what had once been the ceiling. Sick and dizzy, he sunk into a chair beside Skippy's overturned cradle, stuck his head between his knees, and began to cry. He had never, ever imagined that something this terrible could happen. He closed his eyes, telling himself that when he opened them, he would be home and his mother and father would be waiting for him at breakfast.

Derrik heard a small noise. He opened his eyes and sat up. Tweaks stood in the doorway holding a charred piece of cloth that had once been a baby blanket. Tweaks's thin body trembled, his reddened eyes staring at Derrik while tears dripped off his chin.

Derrik set his jaw and wiped his fists over his cheeks.

"What now?" Tweaks whispered, rubbing his hand beneath his nose.

Derrik stood up so fast his chair tipped back and crashed to the floor. "I'm going to find my parents!" he said.

"But, Derrik!" Tweaks left the charred blanket on his shoulder and spread his hands, rolling his eyes upward to take in the sky where the ceiling used to be. "Look what they can do. How could we—?"

"What else can we do?" Derrik interrupted, fury breaking through his sadness. "We can't just sit here the rest of our lives without trying to help them!" He imagined his father wrapped in chains, for that's the only way he could be kept from his son, comforting Mama with the words, "It's all right, Mali. Derrik will come."

Tweaks broke into Derrik's thoughts. "Derrik, we don't even know where they went. How could we ever find them? Besides, we haven't killed anything bigger than a drunf." Tweaks swallowed and touched his eyeglass. "From what we saw, this enemy is vicious and powerful."

A shudder passed through Derrik at the thought of the snake man, but his resolve was firm. "I'm going," he declared. "If I can kill a drunf as big as you with one shot, I'll just use two shots for each of them. Besides, I'd rather die trying than just sit here."

"Derrik!" Tweaks's voice rose in desperation. "They had at least seven dremi, maybe more!"

"I don't care," Derrik answered. "I'm going. You can stay if you want to."

Tweaks lowered his head and rubbed his curls with his hand. Then he raised his eyes to Derrik. "Even if you go, you don't know where they took them."

"I figure the dremi would head back the way they came. Anyone along the way could help me. Dremi aren't hard to miss."

"It's late."

"I'll go first thing in the morning."

"But there's so much to do here." Tweaks spread his hands. "What if our families come back? We need to make things right for them."

Derrik remained silent, breathing hard.

Tweaks tried again. "I wish you'd stay and help."

"We don't always get what we wish for," Derrik said. "I wish you'd come with me."

Tweaks's eyes blinked several times, but a tear escaped anyway. He ducked his head and whispered, "I'm too afraid."

Derrik swallowed a lump in his throat. He didn't want to go alone. But he wouldn't stay. Without another word, Derrik turned and hurried away, leaving Tweaks standing slump-shouldered in the ruins of his house.

Derrik passed the charred body of a rovo, leaped over a pile of broken bricks, and dodged a hole in the ground. When he reached home, he ignored the open doorway and headed to his father's forge. Grabbing three arrows he'd tipped and fletched the day before, he slid them into his quiver and leaned it against the wall by the door. He sat at his father's workbench and grabbed a knife. Laying a straight shaft of wood against the work surface, he pushed against the knife to shape the end for an arrow point. "Ow!" he gasped, dropping the knife and spreading his palm.

A dark sliver of wood from the dit coop lay slant-wise in his palm. It wouldn't help anything if he got an infection. So he picked up the knife with his other hand and, gritting his teeth, dug out the sliver.

Derrik smeared salve on the wound and bound his hand with a strip of cloth from a collection his father kept for handling hot iron. Then Derrik's shaking fingers fastened his four new arrowheads to wooden shafts. He laid them aside and picked up the single arrowhead he hadn't finished. One edge of the point was not as sharp as the other. It would be better with another heating and pounding flat on Da's anvil. Was it worth the time and effort to fire up the forge? Would one more arrow make a difference to win his family's freedom?

Derrik's gaze wandered to the open door. It was late afternoon, and the light was fading fast. As he watched the dusk deepen, fear of the coming night grew big in Derrik's heart. Yet in a strange way, he welcomed the darkness, too. The passing night would bring him closer to leaving this place of horror—this place still stamped with warm memories of his family.

Derrik decided there was no time to improve the arrowhead. It was still a weapon that could do damage. He picked up another straight shaft and feverishly fixed the arrowhead onto it. Then Derrik pushed himself to his feet and stormed out into the yard. He knelt by a dead dit, yanking out handfuls of feathers. His teeth clenched and his eyes blinked away tears. When he had enough, he returned to the forge and carefully added the feathers to his arrows for fletching.

After sliding the new arrows into his quiver, he took down his bow. Raising it in his left fist, his arm straight, he aimed it out the forge doorway and pulled back the string to test the spring in the limbs. He held the string back, taut, until the pressure hurt his fingers. He imagined one of those snake men creatures in his yard, the one who took his mother and father away. His teeth bared, and his arm shook. He would kill every snake man he saw.

Slowly, he eased the bowstring back into place. He hung his bow on the wall and walked out into the dark evening. He stopped and looked at his empty house, dark against the night sky. There was no one there for him now. It was up to him to find them and bring them home.

When Derrik walked inside, he nearly tripped on an overturned kettle. A dark stain spread beneath it like blood. Derrik hesitated, his heart hammering in his chest. Then he bent and turned the kettle over. His hands came away slick with oil for frying scones. Derrik picked up a wad of cloth to wipe his hands. Then he recognized it as his mother's apron. He clutched it tight in his fists and glared at the destruction around him. He felt like crying again, but instead he jumped up and kicked out in anger, sending a chair skidding across the floor. He bent over, grabbed the edge of the table, and hoisted it up in one mighty heave. The table crashed onto four legs. Mama wouldn't be happy with the way her house looked. He would have to do something about it before he brought her home.

Derrik lit a lamp, then cleaned up the sticky dough, swept the floor, and set everything that he could back in its place. He found some bread, a couple of ubella fruits, three unbroken dit eggs, and an old pan. He wrapped the eggs in straw and put everything into a big leather bag. Then he stood in the middle of the house, the circle of lamplight pitifully small.

A strange sound started above Derrik's head, and he tensed, his scalp tingling with fear. *Pat. Pattapat. Pat. Pat. Pattapattapattapat.* Derrik identified the tiny sounds as rain hitting the roof. It grew steadily until a loud drumming filled the house.

On leaden feet, Derrik moved to his bed in the smaller of two bedrooms built off the main living area. He put out the lamp and lay on his bed, staring into the darkness.

6
Going in the Woods

Derrik opened his eyes to dark and eerie silence. A sudden, vague fear gripped him so hard that he shot up in bed, his eyes wide, seeing nothing in the deep darkness. Nothing leapt out at him, and nothing sunk fangs into him. There was no sound.

Gradually his heartbeat slowed, and his breathing returned to normal. The silence only meant the rain had stopped. Scorched mattress odor filled his nostrils, proving that every nightmare from the day before was terribly real.

It was time to go.

Derrik swung his feet out of bed and slung the leather sack over his shoulder. He stood up and made his way through the kitchen, straight out into the yard. Breathing in the wet scent of rain-washed grass, a surge of hope coursed through him. He could do this. He had to.

He turned his face toward the sky to see a thin band of faint gray lying against the horizon. He shivered and then turned and pressed his shoulder into the back door, forcing it up against the doorframe. The front door would have to wait for his father to get home.

The food sack bumped against Derrik's back as he made his way across the dark yard to the forge. He stepped over dead dits, their feathers flattened by rain. He tried to talk himself out of cleaning them up. Marauding animals would be glad to have them. But as Derrik set his sack down inside the forge, he realized that no matter how big of a hurry he was in, he didn't want his mother coming home to a yard full of decomposing birds.

Derrik hurried through the yard, kicking the dits into a sorry looking pile of feathers stitched with thin orange legs sticking out every which way. The scent of death wafted up to his nose from the soggy pile of carcasses. Derrik balled his fists in frustration. He'd have to bury them.

He grabbed a shovel and then went to work prying heavy, wet clumps of earth from the ground behind the forge. Derrik's muscles strained as his determination drove the shovel into the heavy dirt again and again. When the hole was deep enough, Derrik kicked all the birds in. Then he shoved mud on top of them, creating a sticky mound. It had to be good enough.

In the light of approaching dawn, Derrik hurried to the forge and grabbed his bow and quiver. He dipped his water skin into the rain barrel until it bulged. After fastening it to his belt, he lifted the leather food sack onto his shoulder and left town without a backward glance.

Derrik headed in the direction the dremi had taken into town. He walked on until the sun rose. It warmed him through and lit up the sparkling insects fluttering along on either side of him. Sometimes they pulled ahead like miniature cart horses leading the way. Derrik relaxed. What bad thing could happen when you were surrounded by such light-hearted company?

When Derrik reached the edge of the fields, he stopped at the first row of trees marking the beginning of woods. The insects circled over his head in a shining flurry and then headed back toward town, leaving the damp woods behind. Derrik watched them go, wishing he could go with them. But he had to move on.

He turned and looked down the wall of trees in one direction and then the other. A dank breeze puffed out of the woods, running its chill fingers around the back of Derrik's neck. He shrugged his shoulders high and stiff, willing the cold tremors of warning to pass. If he knew of any quick way around this wooded obstacle, he would take it. The river meandered around in too many time-consuming loops, and he wasn't sure it led to the far side of the woods anyway. Perhaps the monstrous snake men held his parents captive somewhere in these trees, where they waited for him to come and rescue them.

Don't go in the woods.

Derrik breathed in the sharp smell of pine needles and the musty odor of rotting leaves that trailed out of the woods, warning him to turn around and go back. The small of his neck prickled, and he dug the toe of his shoe into the ground. He did not want to enter the forbidding woods, but there was no more time to waste. His parents would understand that he needed to go in the woods to save them. Derrik pulled the bow from his back and drew an arrow from his quiver. He fitted the arrow to the string and held his bow at the ready. Taking a deep breath, Derrik walked in among the trees.

The first thing he noticed was the surprising cold. He couldn't think of any reason for it except for the leafy branches blocking the sun overhead. His shoes squished on damp ground, and an occasional overhead drip let him know the leaves hadn't completely dried from last night's rain. Derrik moved on with no clear path to follow. Without the sun to guide him, he worried that he might not be headed in the right direction. He walked on, unsure of how much time passed. He kept his bow ready, always suspecting one of his worst nightmares to jump out in the flesh and attack him. But nothing happened. The forest was as silent as a grave.

When he crept toward an oak tree as wide as a church's double doors, he caught a whiff of a familiar pungent odor. He cautiously walked around the huge tree and found himself at the edge of a rough clearing. Scattered trees looked as if they'd been pushed off to the side by some tremendous force that left dirt clinging to their roots. A few logs formed several rugged circles scattered around the clearing.

Alarmed that someone had been here before him, Derrik stopped still. He listened so hard his head hurt, but he couldn't hear any hissing or other snake men sounds. There were no footsteps, no clank of weapons, and no breathing except his own. His eyes darted from broken trees to deep shadows and back again, searching for danger.

Satisfied there was no immediate threat, Derrik took a cautious step into the clearing. All was still. As he inspected the area, he came across a fire pit of black ash in the center of a ring of fallen trunks. Another set of trunk benches surrounded a separate pit, more sinister because of the pile of bones beside it. A sick feeling rose up in Derrik. He forced his feet to take him closer until he could examine the bones. When he saw they were from drunfs, the queasy ache in his stomach eased.

Derrik stopped at the center of the large clearing where a huge stake of rough green wood had been driven into the ground. Stamped all around in the damp soil were human footprints. Derrik found strange tracks of overlapping feet at the far edge of the circle, pebbly imprints mixed in with shoe marks. Derrik bent closer and put his finger to the cold soil. Chains had lain here. This had to be where the snake men kept their captives when they stopped overnight. Derrik forced his fear down. He was headed the right way. Human tracks meant that his parents still lived. He wouldn't let himself believe anything else.

Derrik moved around the clearing again, stopping with a catch in his heart when he noticed two giant lizard-like hands imprinted in the mud. Dremi feet. His eyes followed the long stretch of flattened grass leading away from the footprints where the serpentine body must have dragged itself along.

Derrik raised his head. His family seemed so close. He had to keep going—had to catch up to them and save them. He glanced around the tree line. Frowning, he turned in a slow circle, searching for landmarks. His eyes darted around in disbelief. There were several trees as wide as chapel doors. Which one had he passed to enter this place? His excitement shrank to a sudden stab of fear. Every tree in the hastily cleared circle looked pretty much like the others. He didn't know which way to go.

7
THE GREEN THING

Derrik was about to circle the whole clearing again when he noticed a waver in the air above the trees. He raised his hand and shaded his eyes for a better look. Thin wafts of smoke pulsed into the air at odd intervals. It had to be from Bylon. Even though last night's rain was enough to drown a dremi and certainly stop the town fires, Derrik imagined that those left behind, like Tweaks, would be burning debris now, clearing the way for the future.

Derrik turned his back to Bylon so he was headed the right way. He was excited to go on, but before he'd gone more than a dozen steps, he suddenly folded over with a cramp in his gut. The severe hunger pang reminded him that he hadn't eaten since last night. Even though he longed to continue the search, he'd be a poor rescuer if he collapsed from hunger.

Derrik made sure to face the way he wanted to leave the clearing. Then he sat on a log beside the nearest fire pit. He dug into his leather sack and quickly tore off a crust of bread. He stuffed it into his mouth and chewed while he wrestled to pull the pan free. His foot scuffed against the ground, his toe landing in the fire pit. A puff of smoke rose in protest from the heart of ashes.

Derrik stared at the smoke for a moment, hardly daring to believe his luck. Then he quickly dug under a nearby pile of sodden leaves until his fingers touched the old dry ones at the bottom. He scraped them out and crumpled them into tiny pieces on top of the ash, watching closely and scarcely breathing. The shreds curled and darkened and then offered up a tiny flame. Derrik quickly added more leaves, then slivers of bark. His hunger motivated him to build up the fire carefully, until at last he had a cheerful blaze. He didn't need such a big fire for cooking, but it was his only companion, and it gave him a feeling of safety.

Derrik cooked all three eggs and then piled the golden yellow puff on top of a chunk of bread. He ate it quickly to appease his growling stomach. Then he slowly ate one of the ubella fruits, the tangy flesh energizing him. He put the last of the bread and the remaining fruit in his food sack. He didn't know how far he'd have to go, so he decided to watch for more food. He drank half the water in his pouch and then fastened it back on his belt.

Reluctantly, Derrik left the fire behind, pushing his way between the dark trees. The forest settled in around him, strangely quiet. He hadn't seen any animals, although he'd heard scurrying in the underbrush and the beat of wings when birds took flight. This silence was unnerving. He found himself straining his eyes, trying to spot the cause of such unusual quiet.

A sudden shriek from overhead jolted Derrik's heart into a quick trot. His arms flew up, bow drawn, ready to send the arrow flying as he sighted up into the tree. A little brown and yellow bird no bigger than his fist sat framed in glossy green leaves, staring down at him from its perch. It opened its shiny black beak, let out another blood-curdling shriek, and flew away.

Derrik went limp with relief. He loosened his grip on the bow and eased the string forward. Then something slammed into his back, knocking him face-first onto the forest floor. He landed with such force that moss and mud pushed into his mouth and nose. He jerked his head back and turned it to one side, snorting his nostrils clear before taking in a strangled breath. A sudden needle-like pain stabbed into his right shoulder. He let out a garbled scream and forced himself up onto his knees and left arm. He reached back to grab whatever it was that had him in a death grip.

Before he could get hold of it, sharp teeth clamped on his hand, shooting pain down his arm. Derrik threw himself backward, intent on crushing the thing between himself and the ground. While he was in the air, a green blur leapt off his shoulder, trailing the bandage it had ripped from his hand. The green thing landed on tiptoe while Derrik hit the ground so hard, his vision blurred. Feeling stupid and angry, he flung himself upward so fast that darkness crept in the sides of his vision.

Crouching on the ground before him was a cat-like creature, shaking loose Derrik's bandage and bristling all over with mottled green fur that matched the leaves overhead. Two pure brown eyes stared at him with malice, narrowing when the beast hissed like a steam kettle about to explode. Gray teeth, half an inch long and no thicker than his mother's sewing needles, popped out of mossy green gums. The creature whipped its two tails back and forth, the ends tipped with sharp, gray curved points. It lifted a padded foot that had more than its share of toes, which were curved in a half moon around the front of the paw and studded with sharp hooks as gray as death. Derrik's shoulder still stung fiercely from those punishing claws.

The beast let out another evil hiss that ran fingers of ice up Derrik's back. Derrik darted his eyes beyond the green demon's wicked claws to where his bow lay in the dirt. He couldn't get to his weapon without going through the creature.

Before Derrik could think of any defense, the cat creature sprang again. Derrik fell back, his hands thrown up, useless against the onslaught. The two tails came at him from both sides, whipping him hard enough to shred his shirt and gouge the flesh underneath. Claws raked his hands away and then sunk into the flesh on both sides of his neck in a burning agony of pain. Derrik screamed. The creature flattened its ears and ducked its head under Derrik's chin. Its mouth was open, ready to puncture his throat.

Suddenly, the creature jerked left. Its claws pulled free, leaving tiny rivers of hot blood running down Derrik's neck. The green thing snarled at something beyond Derrik's line of sight. Derrik turned his head, drawing in a fearful breath and tensing for whatever new horror awaited him.

To his immense relief, the familiar form of Tweaks appeared, although he was sideways from Derrik's point of view. Tweaks waved his arms like a madman and yelled in a high, warbling voice, "Get out of here!" With his eyes still on the green cat, Tweaks bent and felt around the forest floor, finally coming up with a stick about an inch wide and twelve inches long. "Shoo! Shoo!" Tweaks called, poking the stick toward the animal.

Derrik wanted to laugh at Tweaks's attempt to be scary. But the green cat had different ideas. It stepped back on paws stained red with Derrik's blood. With a final snarl, showing its needle gray teeth, it turned and ran, disappearing into the shadows of the forest.

Tweaks dropped the branch and hurried over to Derrik. He knelt beside his friend, sliding a hand under his head. "You're bleeding," he said, helping Derrik sit up.

"I thought you weren't coming," Derrik gasped. "How'd you find me?"

Tweaks tapped his eyeglass. "I followed your tracks. I changed my mind this morning and went to your house, but you were gone. I knew you'd be heading for the woods, so I hurried, hoping I would find you." He fumbled at his waist and pulled his water skin free. Uncapping it, he offered it to Derrik. "It took an attack to slow you down long enough for me to catch up."

"I'm glad you did," Derrik said. He rinsed the mud from his mouth. Tweaks took the water skin back, used it to wet a corner of his shirt, and then dabbed at Derrik's bleeding neck. "I'm not sure I'm getting it very clean."

"Use your eyeglass," Derrik suggested.

Tweaks stopped and blinked at Derrik. "I can't. I threw it at that thing."

Derrik sat up straighter. "How did you hit it?"

"I don't know." Tweaks gave Derrik a shaky grin. "I couldn't see after I took it off."

"You could have wiggled your ears at it, you know," Derrik said. "That would have scared it away." Derrik rolled over to his hands and knees, searching for the glass. Before long, he spied an ear wire sticking up from a patch of weeds. When he tugged on it, the rest of the contraption followed. He handed it to Tweaks. "It's bent," he said.

Tweaks fitted it to his face, readjusting the wires until the glass sat over one eye. He looked at Derrik with his big eye, and then he whipped the glass off and stuffed it into his pocket.

"What's the matter?" Derrik asked, casting a worried look over his shoulder.

"You look worse when I can see better."

Tweaks finished helping Derrik clean his wounds, using most of the water in Derrik's water skin, too. Then they started off through the forest.

"Did you bring any food?" Derrik asked.

"Yes." Tweaks rummaged in the leather pouch at his waist. "Half a loaf of bread and some lettuce."

"Lettuce?"

Tweaks nodded, patting his pouch with pride.

"How much water is left?" Derrik asked.

Tweaks shook his water skin. "All but gone."

Even though Derrik's wounds no longer bled, he felt light headed. He did his best to go on, leaving no excuse for stopping as they made their way beneath a canopy of leaves. The forest grew steadily darker.

"Derrik," Tweaks said. "Don't you think we ought to stop for the night?"

Before Derrik could answer, they heard a sound that would change their lives forever.

8
Under a Rock

"Uhhhssssuhhh." The sigh was soft, yet sinister.

Derrik stopped suddenly. "What's that sound?" he asked, pressing a hand to his head.

Tweaks's voice shook. "I d-don't know."

Derrik staggered. "We have to find out."

"But you're hurt."

"If we don't look, we could be dead." Derrik readied his bow with trembling hands and then slowly moved forward, his eyes fighting the dusk and his neck wounds throbbing with pain. Navigating around a couple of trunks brought Derrik onto a strip of treeless land that spread before him. About twenty feet away stood an outcropping of dark volcanic rock. At the base of the rock was the last thing Derrik expected to see.

A snake man lay flat on the ground, his green eyes closed to scaly slits, his chest rising and falling with the strange moaning hiss that had warned the boys he was there.

"What is it?" Tweaks asked, his fingers fumbling at his pocket.

"Something that should crawl back under the rock it came from," Derrik whispered. He clenched his hands on the bow and raised it to fire, string drawn back to his shoulder, arrow nocked.

Tweaks quit fishing for his eyeglass and touched Derrik's arm. "Wait!"

"Let go," Derrik snapped, shaking Tweaks's hand off.

Tweaks gasped. "What are you doing?"

"Shooting him." The string slid through Derrik's fingers.

"No!" Tweaks shouted, too late. The arrow sped toward its target. But something went terribly wrong. The arrow curved wide of its mark, its tattered fletching trailing as it rattled off the rock and rolled to the ground beside the snake man.

"What?" Derrik growled his disappointment through a haze of pain. He studied his enemy. The creature didn't move, except for the breath that moaned and hissed in and out, in and out of his revolting body.

"That stupid green thing shredded my fletching!" Derrik shouted. Spinning around, he grabbed Tweaks's shoulder with iron fingers. "Why did you tell me not to shoot?"

Tweaks winced. "Think about it, Derrik. If we capture him, he can tell us where our families are." Tweaks swallowed. "After that we can . . . kill him."

Derrik's jaw tensed, then relaxed. When he finally released Tweaks, his friend sagged and brought up a hand to rub the sore spot where Derrik had squeezed too hard.

"Sorry," Derrik said. "It's just that . . ."

"No," Tweaks said, putting his palm out. "Don't say anything."

Derrik was silent for a moment. Then he cleared his throat. "I think you're right."

Tweaks gave Derrik a sideways glance.

"I think we should capture the snake man."

Tweaks didn't reply.

"Did you bring any rope?" Derrik asked.

"No."

Derrik looked around, his eyes on the ground as though he expected to find what he wanted there. "We need something to use as rope." Derrik threw his head back and scanned the trees, even though stretching his sore neck was painful. There was nothing. "Come on, Tweaks, put your glass on and help me find something to tie up that . . . thing." Derrik turned his head to glare at the snake man. He lay where they'd first seen him, still unconscious. But this time Derrik noticed something he hadn't seen before. A ribbon of tan appeared in patches among the greenery.

"Tweaks," Derrik said, waving his hand for Tweaks to come nearer. "Look over there." He pointed. "Is that rope?"

Tweaks studied it through his glass, his large eye shifting from one end of the coil to the other. "Either that, or a very thin, very still snake," Tweaks said.

Derrik shivered. It had to be rope. And if the snake man was unconscious, then Derrik could sneak over there, grab that rope, and tie him up before he even knew a thing about it.

"I'm going to get it," Derrik said.

"But, Derrik, he could wake up."

"That would be bad for him." Derrik dropped his sack, bow, and quiver so he could move freely. He took a step closer to the snake man, then stopped and said, "Tweaks, if he moves, run."

"But, Derrik—"

"Do it!" Derrik whispered fiercely. Then he took another step and another. The snake man moaned and hissed his alien breath through a fanged mouth. "Aaahhhsssssahh." His eyes remained shut.

When Derrik stepped closer, the ground squished beneath his feet. Another half dozen steps along the deep green expanse that he'd thought was grass had him moving through calf-high water. He glanced back at Tweaks to see his friend's enlarged eye staring back at him beneath worried brows.

Derrik felt strangely disjointed, yet there was nothing to do but keep on going.

A thought tickled the back of his mind. It was a pleasant thought, so Derrik struggled to coax it forward. Finally, it came. He was waist deep in water, the cold numbing his scratched skin. It was just what they needed to fill their canteens.

A current hit Derrik's legs, strong enough to wrap wet strands of grass around him like thin fingers tugging him down. Derrik clutched the tangle of grass rising above the water, bracing himself against the relentless pull. He knew with sudden, sobering clarity that if he lost his footing and fell into this strange grass river, he'd never get his face above water again. He would drown, trapped forever in the interwoven mesh of water roots that doubtless held the bones of those forest-goers who'd never returned to Bylon. This had to be the mysterious sink grass his father had warned him about.

Derrik cast a desperate look ahead. He was nearly to where the snake man lay on firm ground. Now he could see weapons scattered around the enemy's body—a scimitar with a handle curved into the shape of a snake, a weird looking helmet covered in scales that was far too narrow at the crown, and an odd wooden item made of four stout sticks forming an "X" shape. A single taut sinew appeared to hold the contraption together. Then Derrik saw a quiver of about a dozen foot-long bolts lying nearby, giving him a clue that this last strange weapon must be some kind of bow.

Clutching the slippery grass blades, Derrik pushed forward. He didn't know if he could make it three more yards, but if not, he would die trying. He kept his steps small, his feet planted wide apart, digging in the roots with his toes. If the sink grass was going to take him, it would not be by surprise. A few more labored steps took Derrik into thigh-deep water. Now he was close enough to grab the rope if he leaned forward. He measured the distance to the snake man, who was even more hideous up close. Every exposed part of his body was covered with dark green scales the color of vomit. One of his palms was turned up and open, showing a grinning skull branded deep into the scales. One fang was streaked dark with blood. The forked tongue had crumbs of dirt clinging to it, and looked as dried out as a strip of tanned leather. The thought of touching this monster was repulsive, but he had to do it.

Derrik leaned forward and reached out a trembling hand for the rope. His fingers were only few inches away when the snake man's black tongue flickered, then shot back into its dreadful mouth. Derrik gasped and stumbled, grabbing at stalks of grass to keep from falling into the water. Fear danced with sharp feet down his spine. His father had told him that snakes smelled with their tongues. Had this snake man smelled him? Did he know someone was there?

Derrik studied the figure, his heart thumping so hard it was sure to give him away, but the enemy's eyes remained closed. A deep scratch ran from one eye to the corner of his mouth, cutting through a few scales and pushing others aside. His snake breath rasped in and out. The forked tongue stayed inside his mouth. A shiver ran through Derrik hard enough to threaten his risky footing. It wasn't the cold current battling for right of burial that made him shiver. It was a horrible thought that exploded into his brain, raising an ache deeper than his fresh wounds. What if he was walking into a trap?

Derrik narrowed his eyes and clenched his teeth. If the snake man thought he could trap the son of Willan Sparks so easily, he would be mighty surprised when Derrik turned his own trap back on him and buried him under a slimy rock where he belonged.

Derrik's gaze traveled down the snake man's body, noting a dark brown water skin at his belt. One pant leg was torn, and it looked as if the creature had tried using one end of the rope to tie a patch of red-stained cloth over the tear. Apparently he'd passed out before finishing the job. Too bad it hadn't killed him.

Derrik didn't dare take his eyes off the enemy to check on Tweaks. He slowly climbed out of the grass river. Pant legs dripping into his shoes, he reached for the rope again more slowly than before. Nothing happened. He took hold of the cold coils and drew them toward him.

The snake man shifted. Derrik froze. He stared at the creature for a long minute. Only the chest moved up and down, up and down. Teeth clenched, Derrik slowly pulled the rope closer.

Then, with a movement too quick for Derrik to follow, the snake man darted a scaly hand into his boot and whipped out a knife.

Derrik jerked backward. His wet shoes slipped on the bank, dangerously close to sending him back into the sink grass. The snake man grabbed Derrik's arm and yanked him backward, the knife blade flashing as it aimed for his throat.

9
Prisoner

The snake man hissed, his tongue flailing wildly. The scream rising from Tweaks's throat was nearly drowned out by the terrifying screech of a fist-sized brown and yellow bird on a leafy branch. Before Derrik could blink, the bird beat its way out of the tree as a green blob of fur smacked into the snake man, forcing his grip on Derrik to tear loose. Derrik stumbled backward, his feet splashing in the water while the two-tailed cat creature opened its mouth in a needle-toothed hiss and clawed the snake man.

Derrik splashed over to the snake man's strange bow and picked it up. It was surprisingly heavy. He lugged it under one arm and went to claim the scimitar. The two creatures hissed and fought desperately as Derrik lifted the broad bladed sword from the ground—its snake-shaped handle fit nicely in his hand.

The snake man scrambled back from the gray needle-like claws aimed at his neck, leaving Derrik clear to scoop up the quiver of bolts. Derrik then put more distance between him and the combat.

"Derrik! Come on!" Tweaks hollered.

Derrik pushed his hand out toward Tweaks to silence him, and then bent his head to the strange bow. He tried different ways of fitting bolts onto the sinew string. Soon he discovered that threading the bolt through a hole partially concealed by a carved snakehead seemed to give it the best aim. He tried pulling back the wooden bar on the back of the bow, but was only able to stretch the sinew part way. He dropped to the ground so fast that Tweaks cried out, "Are you hit?"

Derrik shook his head and braced the X frame against his feet, pulling back on the bar with his hands until the bolt was well cocked. Confident that he was ready to defend himself, Derrik let the tension loose and watched the two struggling creatures.

At first the cat seemed about to kill the snake man, but it turned out to be only the advantage of surprise. When the snake man threw the cat off him with a sharp hiss and drew his sword, the cat creature screamed with frustration. It managed to dodge the blade and attack with teeth and claws, yet it seemed a harder job to puncture snake man scales than human flesh. Still, the cat creature's red-tipped claws proved it was doing damage.

Derrik gently touched the wounds at his neck, watching the fighters quick-jab, dodge, and strike with incredible speed. Derrik let out a hard breath. If Tweaks hadn't come along when he did, Derrik was sure he would have been shredded to death.

The combatants rolled over and over on the ground, the cat using its tails to whip the snake man's limbs, and claws to snag his clothing.

The snake man grabbed for the tails, missed, and slashed at the cat with his knife. The battle seemed to be a draw until the tail on the back of the snake man's head rose up and wrapped itself around the cat, squeezing and lifting it into the air.

The cat twisted and swung its hooked tails at the snake man's face. The snake man's tail yanked the snarling beast further away. The two green hooked tails lashed at the snake tail, which jerked, then swung the raging ball of green fur around once before slamming it down on the ground. Blades of grass whipped back and forth in a frenzy as a gargled screech ripped the air. The scream shook and bubbled, dying away to silence. The grass swayed and then stilled, standing upright once again.

The snake man stood staring at the grass, his shoulders hunched. He turned cold yellow eyes on Derrik. Derrik felt icy fear crawl up from his belly as he pulled back the wooden bar, aiming a bolt right at the snake man's face. The snake man blinked once and then swayed from side to side. One of his knees gave out, dropping him crookedly to the ground. He knelt with one knee up and one down for a second before his eyes rolled back and he toppled over into an unconscious heap on the ground.

10
A Place to Sleep

Early the next morning, the snake man stretched his arms out against their bindings. He slowly opened his yellow eyes and surveyed his hands, bound with his own rope. He reached up to touch the coil tied tight around his neck.

"No, you don't!" Derrik said, waving the scimitar.

The snake man slowly dropped his hands and turned his yellow eyes on Derrik and Tweaks, studying them where they sat huddled together like two monkeys sheltering under the same leaf.

"What will you do?" the snake man asked. In spite of the hint of "s" on every word, his voice was unnervingly normal.

"Kill you eventually," Derrik snapped.

The snake man nodded. "Until then?" His tone was too pleasant for facing imminent death.

Tweaks jumped to his feet. "Show us where our families are!"

The snake man struggled to stand, favoring his wounded leg. Derrik rose to stand beside Tweaks. The snake man's shirt-sleeves hung in tatters when he raised his bound hands to point through the trees. "They've been taken to the necromancer's palace."

"What's a necromancer?" Derrik asked.

"One with powers to raise the dead," the snake man explained.

"But my parents aren't dead," Tweaks said. "What would he want with them?"

The snake man sighed. "The necromancer's intentions are to raise a different kind of dead, the ones he creates himself."

"Quit wasting time," Derrik said, holding the scimitar up as if daring the snake man to make a move.

"It's this way," the snake man said.

Derrik made sure the prisoner stayed in front, his heart unmoved by his captive's obvious limp. If the snake man ever slowed enough to allow slack in his rope, Derrik shouted, "Keep up, there!" and poked the scimitar in his general direction. His intention was to keep the snake man far enough ahead so he couldn't suddenly whip around and grab a weapon. Derrik was pretty proud of the fact that their prisoner never even tried.

Tweaks followed Derrik, cradling the heavy bow against his chest like an awkward sleeping child. Soon he and Derrik would trade places and weapons.

"May I have some water?" The snake man's gentle words were easy to listen to. He didn't seem angry and didn't struggle against his bonds, which made Derrik even more suspicious.

Derrik stopped, so the snake man did, too. Tweaks fished a water skin from Derrik's leather bag. "Just watch it," Derrik said, brandishing the sword. Tweaks lay the water skin on the ground. Then the boys backed up several steps, drawing the limping snake man back until he reached the water skin. He bent and picked it up with his bound hands. "Thank you," he said. His head tail swung forward to hold the skin steady while he pulled the cork with his fingers. Then the tail lifted the water to his lipless mouth and poured while he swallowed.

With one eye on his captive, Derrik took a quick drink himself. The grass river water was surprisingly sweet and good. While their prisoner was unconscious, they'd filled every container they could find, including the enemy's. Derrik had also retrieved his faulty arrow with the broken fletching, which prevented it from flying straight.

The snake man lowered his water skin. "Do you have any food?" he asked.

Derrik made a show of digging in his bag, knowing full well

that he and Tweaks had eaten everything but a few lettuce leaves the night before. "Sorry," he said. "Nothing but some lettuce."

The snake man stared at Derrik, his yellow eyes flickering gold. Derrik shifted his feet, trying a more aggressive stance. Tweaks twisted his hands.

"I could hunt." The snake man's voice was quiet, yet the words carried clear and strong.

"No!" Derrik said. "You'll not get your scaly hands on any of these weapons." He waved the scimitar for emphasis. The snake man's tongue darted into view and then disappeared back into his mouth.

"What are we going to do, Derrik?" Tweaks asked.

"We'll find our own food," Derrik said.

"He's got to eat, too."

Derrik dug out the remaining soggy lettuce leaves and tossed them to the prisoner. The snake man left them lying on the ground.

The travelers made another water stop late in the afternoon, at which time they dug for roots and snacked on berries. After the snake man finished drinking, he said, "It's getting dark. Don't you think we should stop for the night?"

Derrik bristled. "You're not in charge here! Put that skin down and walk on."

The snake man sagged.

"Get going," Derrik barked.

The snake man laid the skin on the ground and moved on between the trees. Derrik passed the skin, eyes on his enemy's back. Tweaks stopped, picked up the water skin, and tucked it into his waistband.

"Derrik," Tweaks said softly. "I'm pretty tired."

Derrik stared straight ahead for a moment and said, "All right, we'll find a place soon."

Tweaks trudged along behind Derrik. Suddenly, he pointed and cried, "Hey, Derrik, how about that?" Ahead of them, the snake man stepped into a clearing with strange but beautiful blue-green grass, as thick and curly as wool. The trees surrounding the clearing wore moss as thick as fur and blacker than evening shadows. When Derrik and Tweaks stepped on the woolly grass, its softness pressed the bottom of their shoes and triggered every tired bone in Derrik's body.

"We'll stop here," Derrik announced loud enough for the snake man to hear. The prisoner leaned against the nearest trunk, sliding his back down along the moss and sinking into the grass with a moan. His eyes closed.

"Move over," Derrik commanded, swinging his sword toward a tree with a wider trunk.

The snake man looked up with weary eyes. "I thought it would be easier to tie me to a small tree," he said.

"You're not doing the thinking," Derrik roared. "Now move!"

The snake man struggled, gasps bursting from his fanged mouth as he got himself to his feet with awkward jerks. He let out an explosive hiss and then stumbled to the tree that Derrik indicated. He collapsed beside the trunk, falling over onto his side.

"Sit up," Derrik commanded.

The snake man didn't move.

"Get up!" Derrik yelled, stiffening his arm and pointing it at the enemy.

"Derrik," Tweaks said. "I think he's unconscious."

Derrik glanced at Tweaks, but Tweaks's gaze was fixed on the snake man. Derrik turned to see the snake man barely breathing. Even his head tail lay limp. Derrik moved closer and kicked the snake man's boot. It wobbled, but the rest of the creature was still.

"I don't like it," Derrik said. "We can't tie him properly."

"He's close to the trunk," Tweaks said. "We'll put the knots on the far side of the tree. He won't be able to reach them. Even if he tries, we'll hear him moving around and stop him."

"I'll stand guard," Derrik said.

Tweaks nodded. "I'll help you."

11
Tree of Fire

Blip—fizz—whoosh

Derrik struggled to open his eyes. He only managed to pry them apart to slits. Warmth from a small fire just two feet from his face radiated out in gentle waves, backing off to let cool night air slip in around him before pulsing out another breath of heat. Just beyond the flame he saw the snake man's yellow eyes widened in alarm, flame reflected in the yellow depths.

What was this? Had Tweaks somehow built a fire to make this reptile more comfortable? It would be much better to hold a match to the enemy's ragged sleeve. But when would Tweaks have done this? Derrik could feel Tweaks leaning against his shoulder. Derrik rested his head against the soft trunk of the tree where he and Tweaks sat guard, wondering about this odd turn of events. His body was unusually heavy, too tired to move, like he was in a dream.

Blip—fizz—whoosh

The snake man turned his head and narrowed his yellow eyes at another fire burning just behind him. Strange. Derrik was sure that Tweaks hadn't set that one. Something was very odd about this whole thing. But that was the way with dreams.

Blip—fizz—whoosh

"Ow!" the snake man hissed and jerked his hands back from searing heat. He whipped his head around and stared at a fire that licked at the rope tying him to the tree.

Good. Maybe he would catch on fire and save Derrik the trouble of killing him later.

The snake man tipped his ugly green head to stare up into the branches, apparently searching for the culprit who'd dropped fire on him. Derrik would have laughed, but it took too much energy.

Just then, he noticed something small drip from an overhead limb, something that could have been rain.

Blip

It hit the wooly grass, damp with dew.

Fizz

A spark jumped out.

Whoosh

A small fire burst up from the ground.

The snake man stared in horror at the new blaze and then pulled against his bindings with all his strength. The rope snapped, flame bouncing at its end across the grass. Then the snake man pushed up to his knees, moaning.

Worry brushed Derrick's brain. But this was the way of dreams, wasn't it? The next thing was sure to be frightening, like falling off a cliff.

Blip, fizz, whoosh

The snake man stood, completely free except for the rope around his middle. The tip of his tail got busy working the knots loose.

Blip, fizz, whoosh, blip, fizz, whoosh

The snake man hopped away from a new fire threatening his feet. He looked around the clearing and found Derrik's eyes watching him through the wavering light of dancing flames. His eyes shifted to Tweaks, who leaned against Derrik for support. Tweaks's chin was on his chest and their weapons were safely at their sides. Derrik could feel the weight of his bow and arrow between his knees.

The snake man shrugged out of the loosened ropes and bent to pick up his weapons.

Blip, fizz, whoosh, blip, fizz, whoosh, blip, fizz, whoosh

The strange sap dripped down between Tweaks's shoes, starting a fire. The snake man grabbed the nearest pack and beat out the flame, breadcrumbs spraying out of the top. "Wake up!" the snake man hissed. Derrik blinked, suddenly seeing the face of his father before him. "Hurry," his father said. "We have to get out."

Derrik stirred. It was still so hard to move. "But, why, Father? What's wrong with living here?"

"Get up! Fire!" the snake man shook Tweaks and then Derrik, hard enough to snap his brain awake. Derrik's eyes widened, and he sat up suddenly, reaching for his bow. It was no longer there. His eyes filled with horror when he saw the snake man standing over them, his muscled arms full of weapons.

12
STRANGE ALLIANCE

"It's all right," the snake man said. "We need to go now."

"You're not . . ." Derrik began.

Blip, fizz, whoosh

"Ahhh!" Derrik yelled, jumping to his feet and leaping away from a fire that was too close for comfort.

"We've got to get out from under these trees," the snake man said. "Come on."

Tweaks stood, staring at his previous captive with wide eyes.

Creak

The snake man flung his weapons aside and leaped at the boys, his fangs spread wide in his open mouth, scaly fingers outstretched. The boys screamed as he hit each one in the chest with a hand, knocking them several feet backwards. He dropped to the ground and rolled to one side.

Boom

A branch crashed and splintered on the spot where the boys had just been standing, sending woolly grass flying in all directions amid the boys' yells of terror. The snake man worked his way to his feet, his eyes narrowed in pain. He limped over to the boys and put out a scaly hand. "Come on," he said, his voice urgent. "Let me help you."

Tweaks took hold of the green-scaled fingers and allowed the snake man to pull him to his feet, but Derrik pushed himself up and away, his eyes blazing with fear and anger. The snake man grabbed his weapons and led the smaller boy out of the ring of trees. He kept going deeper into the woods until the drip and hiss of the spontaneous fires was only a memory.

"W-what was that?" Tweaks asked through chattering teeth.

The snake man stopped and let Tweaks go. He leaned forward, wheezing. "Not sure," he said. After a few more breaths, he added, "I can only guess that the tree sap ignited when it hit the forming dew."

"Why?"

"I don't know." The snake man shrugged. "Must be some strange substance in the sap, or perhaps the dew. Maybe the trigger was that strange woolly grass. I've never seen anything like it before." The snake man looked around. "It looks like we're safe for now."

Tweaks took two steps back, suspicious eyes blinking rapidly at the snake man. "What did you do with my friend?"

"Nothing."

"Then where is he?"

A familiar voice spoke from the darkness behind them. "Right here."

Tweaks spun toward Derrik. "Where were you?"

"I wasn't leaving anything behind," Derrik said, dropping a couple of black-spotted sacks and some floppy water bottles beside Tweaks. He pulled the bow off his shoulder and eyed the snake man warily. "Who are you?"

In the gray pre-dawn light, the boys saw the snake man stretch the scales around his mouth a little tighter, which could have been a grin. He gave a little bow, then winced. "My name is Ssaska."

"Why did you save us?" Derrik asked, his voice and body tense.

"I never wanted to hurt you in the first place."

"Liar!" Derrik shrieked. "You killed Diggen! You stole our families and probably killed them, too!"

Ssaska waited, shoulders slumped, for Derrik to stop shouting.

"I did not agree to attack your village," Ssaska said into the tense silence. "I argued with the others, trying to talk them out of it. But they believe the necromancer."

"Who's the necromancer?"

"He's the one who sent us."

"So if you were sent to the village, how did you end up in the woods?"

Ssaska wrapped his arms around his middle. He looked cold and very alone. "They pushed me off a dremi because I wouldn't quit telling them they'd done wrong."

Derrik's heart stuttered. "Who pushed you?" He could just imagine his father's muscles bulging when he gave the repulsive snake man a shove.

"My fellows were responsible."

Derrik couldn't picture it. This . . . Ssaska . . . must be shifting the blame so Derrik wouldn't guess that his father had gotten the better of him. But however he got here, the creature before him was obviously the enemy. The problem was, he didn't act like it. By now, this Ssaska creature could have aimed his strange bow at the boys, he could have slashed them with his sword, or he could have left them to burn under the fire trees.

Tweaks shuffled his feet and then asked, "How did you get out of your bindings?"

Ssaska waved his head tail back and forth. "With this, and a little help from the fires."

Tweaks studied Ssaska's tail a moment, then asked, "Does that mean you could have untied yourself any time you wanted to?"

"Yes, I would say so."

"Liar!" Derrik shouted.

Tweaks asked, "Then why didn't you?"

Ssaska looked down at the boy. "Because you tried so hard to be brave."

"That's ridiculous," Derrik said. "We're not children, you know."

"Derrik," Tweaks said. "I need to tell you something."

"Wait," Derrik said, holding his hand up. "We don't want

him hearing everything." He jerked a thumb at Ssaska.

"I'll stay here," Ssaska said, leaning against a trunk.

Derrik and Tweaks moved away, putting trees between themselves and the snake man until he was out of sight.

Tweaks turned to Derrik. "I think we can trust him."

"Why? Because he saved us once?" Derrik paced back and forth. "We don't know why he saved us. Maybe he eats boys."

Tweaks folded his arms. "Then why hasn't he?"

"Maybe he's not hungry yet."

"Derrik, you're being ridiculous."

Derrik stopped and faced his friend. "No, I'm not. You are. How can you trust him after what he did to our village? How do you know he's not lying? He could be laying a trap!"

Tweaks took out his glass and held it up. "How did I know there were birds in the sky before I got this? How did I know leaves grew on trees?" He placed the glass over his eye and adjusted the wires. "How, Derrik, did I know how to build a dit egg collector when no one ever has before? There's something inside me that tells me what I can do and helps me believe things even when I can't see them." He pointed between the tree trunks. "Ssaska wants to help us."

"I can't believe it." Derrik threw his hands up in the air. "Don't you remember old lady Judisy? She's nice as pansies one day, handing out cookies and compliments. Then another day she throws mud at you and calls you a fool."

"He's not like that," Tweaks said, his arms folding tight against his chest.

"Well, I'm going to keep my arrow trained on him," Derrik declared.

"Do as you like," Tweaks replied, and then turned and started off through the trees.

"Not that way," Derrik said, hurrying after his friend and turning him around. "We came through there." He pointed with his bow.

"No we didn't, Derrik. I would have remembered that scar on the tree."

"How? It's on the far side of the trunk. You can only see it from this side, not the side we came from."

Tweaks walked in a circle, his eyes searching the forest around them. "Derrik, I have a bad feeling about this. I think we're lost."

"We can't be. We didn't go that far."

"Ssaska!" Tweaks yelled.

"Shut up!" Derrik snapped.

"Why?"

"He could sneak in and ambush us!"

Tweaks threw his arms up in the air, "Derrik, he could have killed us plenty of times by now. He's not trying to kill us. Okay?"

Something moved through the trees. Then everything was still. Derrik swung toward it, his bow at the ready, the wounds in his neck throbbing.

"Ssaska?" Tweaks whispered. "Is that you?"

"Well, it's not a giant dit," Ssaska said, coming into view between the trees.

Derrik let the arrow fly.

13

SOMETHING IN THE WOODS

"It's a good thing you're fast," Tweaks said, trotting to keep up with Ssaska. "Otherwise, we'd be lost and you'd be dead."

"He didn't shoot straight," Ssaska said.

Tweaks grinned and looked back over his shoulder at Derrik, his ears wiggling.

"Why do you want to look like such a stupid mooncalf?" Derrik shouted.

It was three days since Ssaska had dodged Derrik's arrow—an arrow Derrik was reluctant to admit he'd shot by accident. Yet Ssaska had said no more about it. He was a good guide, heading with certainty through the trees. Derrik could only hope he was leading them to the far edge of the forest. The snake man's strange sense of smell, with his thin tongue flicking in and out, had saved them from more than one creature intent on jumping them from above or attacking from a thick stand of underbrush. Ssaska showed them how his crossbow worked, complimenting Derrik on figuring out how to load it. Derrik had tried not to smile.

Ssaska managed to catch a large black and brown rodent that would stand knee high to Tweaks. The boys weren't hungry enough to try it, so Ssaska ate it himself. Later that day, he spied a mossy green drunf, its tan spots wavering in the dappled light through the leaves overhead. It was a different color than the brown drunfs around Bylon, yet it placed its round hooves in careful steps just like the drunfs Derrik knew. They watched as it browsed on a shrub, lifting its head often to look for danger. It never saw the bolt coming. The shot was clean and true, and Tweaks and Derrik each had a bellyful that night.

Now their food was gone. Tweaks shook his bulging water skin, shimmering drops flying off into the carpet of leaves. This time Ssaska had warned them of the sink grass before they got their feet wet.

Suddenly, Ssaska stopped, his tongue flicking out and back in.

Derrik came to a stop behind him and craned his neck forward. "What is it?"

"Is it food?" Tweaks asked.

"Sh," Ssaska said, waving them back. He turned his head from side to side, testing the air, and then raised a scaly finger and beckoned them to follow as he headed off into the trees. After walking several yards, Ssaska slowed.

"What's there?" Derrik demanded.

"Can't you smell it?" Ssaska hissed.

Tweaks sniffed. "Smell what?"

"It's delicious," Ssaska said, his eyes half closed as his tongue licked the air.

Then Derrik caught the strange but not unpleasant smell of something smoky, like cooked meat, yet there was also a vague whiff of orange mixed in. When Derrik turned the other way, he found an entirely different smell, a faint stink. He wasn't sure which one Ssaska was following.

"Go slowly," Ssaska said. He led the way, with Tweaks right behind him and Derrik dragging behind. Derrik's face was pinched in disapproval.

Another few steps brought them to the edge of a clearing. In the center stood a young tree. The plump carcass of a black and brown rodent as long as Tweaks's thigh hung from a branch.

Ssaska's tongue flicked faster. "Looks like supper."

"It's a trap," Derrik whispered.

"The trap has already been sprung," Ssaska explained. "That's why this fellow is hanging there, and I can see no use in wasting good food." He turned his head from side to side. "I don't detect any danger. It's just you, me, Tweaks, and dinner."

When Ssaska moved in to claim his banquet, Derrik thought he heard rustling in the trees. His bow was up in an instant, arrow nocked and ready to shoot. Tweaks drew his arm up, brandishing the scimitar. Ssaska stopped, turned, and pulled back his crossbow with the bolt snug against the string. "Come closer," he said. Another rustle sounded behind them as Tweaks and Derrik hurried to join the snake man. Ssaska turned quickly, but there was nothing to see. The game of sounds went on, the rustling growing louder and more frequent. Then came the unmistakable sounds of laughter, punctuated by sharp whistles and short yells. The three travelers stood back to back, forming a triangle of weapons facing out, ready for whatever was out there.

Derrik noticed something strange. He blinked once, then again when he saw a man's shadow fall across a tree trunk. "I've got someone," he whispered.

When Ssasks saw the shadow, he called, "Hello."

Derrik jumped. "What are you doing?" he growled.

"We mean you no harm," Ssaska called again. "We only wish to travel in peace."

A rock the size of a dit body sailed out from the trees, aiming straight for Derrik's head. Ssaska's tail whipped out and batted it away.

"Ow!" Ssaska hissed, waving his tail rapidly back and forth.

Another rock sailed over their heads, narrowly missing Tweaks.

"We've got to hide," Tweaks shouted. "Head for the trees."

The scar on Ssaska's face twitched. "Tweaks, you cover our backs," he hissed, not taking his eyes off the shadow. "Derrik, shoot now." The arrow and the bolt swished through the air, thudding into a tree trunk, dit feathers quivering in the shadow. But there was no cry of alarm.

Thud.

Derrik and Ssaska whirled around and stared in horror at the place where Tweaks was supposed to be. He was gone.

Cold fingers danced up Derrik's spine. "I told you it was a trap!" he shouted.

Thud. Thud.

14

Cow Cavalry

Derrik didn't feel well. His head was full of pressure, like a terrible sinus infection that pounded with each heartbeat. He forced open his swollen eyelids. As soon as he got a look at his surroundings, he quickly shut them again.

"Hey, the one's the middle's awake," a booming voice said. "Opun yer eyeses, little boy." Derrik felt a hard poke in the back, and his eyes flew open again. He was gently swinging upside down, staring up past a tarnished belt buckle and a metal studded leather shirt into the nostrils of a huge man in a pointed hat. The man grinned down at him and hoisted the tree branch in his massive hand.

"Derrik," Tweaks moaned.

Derrik twisted his neck and saw Tweaks's bright red face swinging slowly back and forth beside him. It stopped swinging as soon as Derrik slowed and then hung straight again. "I told you not to trust him," Derrik croaked.

"Do you mean me?"

Derrik turned to see Ssaska's green face staring at him from the other side, his body also bound in the ropes that kept them suspended over the ground.

"They got you, too?" Derrik murmured. "I thought you . . ." Then his voice trailed off. He would have hung his head in shame for suspecting Ssaska if it weren't already hanging upside down.

Nine men stared at them from their seats on the trunks

of felled trees, like birds on a branch, only much closer to the ground. Most wore long hair with ruddy cheeks showing above full beards. The man on the far end held Ssaska's scimitar, which appeared as long as his forearm. Derrik recognized his bow in the hands of another giant, but it looked strange. It was only half the size it was supposed to be. The crossbow was small too and bounced effortlessly from hand to hand of the giant who held it.

"Who are they?" Derrik asked, his tongue feeling strange as it gravitated to the roof of his mouth.

"Cow cavalry," Ssaska answered.

Beyond the men, a dozen cows chewed cuds or nuzzled under leaves. The enormous animals stood seven or eight feet at the shoulders, their shaggy backs nearly reaching the lower branches of the forest trees with black fur fading to gray on their bellies and feet. One pressed its long horns up against a tree trunk and rubbed, closing its eyes in bliss as it scratched its head. Derrik caught a whiff of the strange odor he'd smelled in the clearing, that odd mixture of smoke and oranges. Several of the big beasts wore leather saddles.

"Aroo!" shouted the man with the stick. "Now they're awake we cun asker them wut we wantsa know."

The giants stood up from their tree trunk seats and moved in to circle the three travelers. The broadest one said, "You did good to guard them, Marson."

The man with the stick beamed. Even from upside down, Derrik could see that Marson was the shortest of the giants. "And yous did gooden to pops 'em with rocks. Does you want for me ta pokes 'em agin, Bladden?" Marson thrust out his stick, and Derrik cringed.

"No," Bladden said. "We've got other things to do with them now."

The giant standing beside Bladden rubbed his palms together. "It's not often we catch much more than a sickly carnor in our traps, but today we get three spies!"

"We're not spies!" Tweaks tried to shout, but his voice came out strangled.

Bladden's eyes took in Tweaks. "This little one has a temper," he said. "Tut, tut. And he lies."

"Ah'll pokes himmen for you." Marson moved closer to Tweaks.

"No, I want you to get him down," Bladden said. "Make sure you don't bump his head, or he may not be able to tell us everything we want to know."

Marson dropped his branch and stepped in to grab Tweaks's rope.

"No, no, no," Tweaks moaned, twisting away in a vain effort to avoid the giant.

"Comen on down, you little mans," Marson said, grabbing Tweaks's leg and breaking the rope as easily as if it were a fish bone.

Once Tweaks was loose, Marson carried him by the leg, like a goose to the slaughter. He strode to the nearest saddled cow and pulled a claymore as long as Tweaks's body from a scabbard. The thin blade gleamed as the giant turned.

"No!" Derrik yelled, his blood-filled face growing hot from the effort.

Marson looked at Derrik in surprise. "Settlers down for'n you gits a turn sometime too."

Then Marson sat Tweaks down on a tree stump that looked like a stepping stone next to him. He pointed the claymore at Tweaks's neck, grinned at Bladden, and said, "Is readier for you nows."

"Now then," Bladden said, sitting himself on the ground and leaning forward so he could look into Tweaks's face. "What is your name? Where are you from? Who sent you? Why are you spying on us? What are you doing with the information you gather?"

Tweaks answered the questions he could and said he didn't know on the others.

"This is a waste of time," one of the giants said, jumping up from his seat and striding back and forth in the clearing. The ground shook, making Derrik's eyes jiggle. "Let's get 'em all down and beat it out of them."

The angry giant moved toward Derrik, who suddenly realized things could be worse than hanging upside down by his feet. Just before the giant reached him, a large shining bolt zipped through the air, puncturing the huge man's back. It stuck clear through his chest, the dripping red point aimed straight at Derrik's face. Disbelief filled the giant's eyes. He stared down at the bolt. Then his eyes darkened, and he let out a roar that created an earthquake. He spun around on his kettle-sized shoes, hands clenching and unclenching in the hope of catching his attacker.

More bolts flew through the air. The cow cavalry ducked behind tree trunks, leaving Tweaks alone on the stump.

"Help!' Derrik yelled. "Stop! Don't shoot!"

Cold, scaly hands circled his ankle, and Derrik screamed. A dark purple snake man spun Derrik around to face him. Flashing his black tongue, he raised a knife. Derrik screamed again, his muscles tightening.

Suddenly, the snake man shuddered and crumpled to the ground, showing Marson standing behind him with a tremulous smile. "Youse no stawbed now," he said, and then lumbered off, his red-streaked claymore held high.

Derrik trembled at the sounds of war around him. He glanced to one side and saw Ssaska still hanging from his rope. Ssaska was straining to raise himself halfway up and yelling something Derrik couldn't understand. Derrik tried to find Tweaks, but his vision was limited. It was hard to make things out upside down, and he was at the mercy of his turning rope.

Tweaks had to be all right, he just had to be.

Derrik couldn't follow the battle very well. He saw snake men running. He heard giants bellowing, and screams, moans, and earth shattering booms. His best view of the war was the dead snake man on the ground below him, cold yellow eyes staring up at him from between dark purple lids while his dead mouth opened in a sardonic smile.

Tears rose in Derrik's eyes. He didn't want to cry, but it was all so awful. He missed his home, his parents, and even working at the forge on hot summer days. It was strange to feel tears running up into his hair. He soon discovered that crying made his nose clog, and he couldn't clear it very well while hanging upside down, so he made himself stop.

Gradually, things grew quieter. Derrik looked toward Ssaska, but the snake man was gone, his rope hanging empty. A sense of doom filled Derrik's heart as he searched the ground, but there was no sign of Ssaska.

"Ssaska!" Derrik hollered. "Tweaks!"

In a moment, Ssaska stood before Derrik with his knife in hand. His cold eyes were mirrors reflecting the two snake men standing on either side of him. One was covered in scales as red as blood with orange splotches that made him look messy. The other snake man shone black. When he turned his head, Derrik saw bumps sticking out above his eyes, like he was growing horns.

The hairs on the back of Derrik's neck prickled. The snake men must have won the battle. Worse yet, Ssaska had rejoined his fellows. Keen disappointment stabbed Derrik's gut. Why hadn't the giants won? Their grudge seemed to be a simple misunderstanding, one that could have been explained if given enough time. Derrik couldn't forget how Marson had killed a snake man for him.

"How'd you get loose?" Derrik asked. Pretending he felt no fear, he craned his neck toward the stump. "Where's Tweaks?"

"Hold still," Ssaska warned.

The mottled snake flicked out his black tongue. "What should we do with him, commander?"

"Cut him loose," Ssaska said without a trace of friendship.

Derrik went cold. Ssaska was a clever fiend. After forcing Derrik's guard down with false trust, Ssaska showed his true colors. That was a snake for you. There was no warm beating heart in those scaly bodies. Just cold, cold blood.

The mottled snake flashed a knife and moved to Derrik, slashing at the rope with enough enthusiasm that Derrik truly feared for the safety of his feet. Suddenly, the rope gave way and Derrik landed on the ground with a thump.

"Take him to the others," Ssaska ordered.

Derrik couldn't walk. The two strange snake men held him between them as he stumbled toward a gathering of seven giants sitting in a circle with rope wrapped around their huge torsos and binding their arms behind them. They didn't look quite as big when he saw them right side up. Snake men bodies lay scattered around at the giant's feet. The snake men carried Derrik right over the top of a brown and black snake creature that had a tail with a bump on the end. Derrik's dragging feet caught on the tail and the bump let out a dry rattle. Derrik yelped.

The black snake man grinned, his fangs shining white. "You're afraid of us even when we're dead. That's good. Very, very good."

Another snake man frowned up at Derrik, his dull, dead yellow eyes nearly hidden beneath a bony brow ridge. His body was grotesque—flattened wide in the middle—as though he'd been stepped on. Derrik squeezed his eyes shut.

When his guards spun him around and pushed him backwards, his eyes flew open and his arms shot out, seeking a safe hold. Someone grabbed him and lowered him down to sit on a log. Derrik found himself beside a giant with a bolt sticking out of his leg. The huge man didn't even look at Derrik. No doubt his mind was on other things.

Derrik turned the other way to see the shaggy face of Marson looking down at him through a black eye. His pointed hat was missing. Even though his lip was split and bleeding, Marson spoke. "You's'n almos' falled, but I caughted you."

Derrik swallowed against a dry throat. "Thank you."

Marson's gaze did not waver. A huge tear gathered in his good eye and rolled down his broad cheek. "Youer spieses bringed bad men that hurted us."

"No," Derrik said. "It wasn't me or Tweaks. We didn't know about any of this."

"Shutsup er me kickens you," Marson growled.

Derrik clamped his mouth shut and stared daggers at Ssaska.

"... sent to clear the forest," the mottled snake man was saying. "Need reinforcements, sir."

"How will you get them?" Ssaska asked.

The mottled snake looked at the giant cows. "May have to ride one of those, sir." His lip raised in derision. "I'd rather ride a dremi, but ours died unexpectedly." He drew his sword. "But we have time enough to kill the prisoners, nice and slow."

The black snake man drew his sword and advanced toward the gathering of giants.

"Up close and personal," Derrik heard the mottled snake man say. "That's the way I like it."

When Marson saw the snake men coming, he let out a terrible roar. Derrik squeezed his eyes shut from the pain in his ears. When Marson fell quiet, Derrik opened his eyes to see the mottled snake man face down on the ground, a bolt sticking out of his back. Blood spilled over his orange splotches, making him all one color before darkening the ground.

The black snake man stared at Marson as though he were to blame, his yellow eyes round circles of surprise. Then he fell forward, too, and Derrik saw Ssaska with his crossbow aimed at the prisoners.

15

Strange Black Rocks

Ssaska lowered the crossbow and hurried to the two snake men. He knelt, pressed a hand to each of their necks and waited, head bowed. Then he stood up, his shoulders rounded, his eyes dull. "They're dead," he announced. "Come on, Derrik, let's set everyone free."

Derrik jumped up. "I don't understand you, Ssaska! I thought you were the enemy, then I thought you were our friend, then I thought you had tricked us and turned spy like the cow cavalry said. Now you kill your own kind. Are you crazy?"

Ssaska regarded Derrik for a moment. "No. It's war that's crazy." His head tail swayed. "Those snake men soldiers are from the necromancer's palace. They didn't know I'd been pushed off a dremi, so they thought I still held my rank."

"You're an officer?" Derrik asked, still skeptical.

"Was," Ssaska corrected. He tapped the skull brand on his left palm. "This pod of soldiers was sent to drop failed experiments in the forest. When they lost their dremi, they found me tied up and came to my rescue." He dropped his eyes. "I was grateful and didn't want to kill them, but I couldn't let them torture you. I told them to go, that I would meet them later, but they didn't want me to have all the fun of killing you. They wanted to do it themselves. I couldn't let that happen."

He dropped his head and rubbed a fist across his eyes.

"I am now convinced you are not spies," Bladden said, his

voice slow and dull. "That . . . necromancer . . . has sent others before. They are not always in the form of a man." He narrowed his eyes at the saddled bovines. "One was a cow." His voice broke. "All we want is to be left in our woods to live in peace."

Derrik and Ssaska untied the giants. After a brief search, they found Tweaks huddled beneath the log seat. Tweaks didn't want to believe Derrik when he said it was safe to come out, so Marson reached in and pulled Tweaks out as easy as a grub. With shaking fingers, Tweaks fished out his eyeglass and raised it to his eye. When he saw Marson's grubby face, he quickly pulled it off again.

Bladden stood before Ssaska, whose head reached the giant's waist. "You will take one of our cows to finish your journey to the necromancer. She will carry you to the sea," Bladden said. "She knows the way, and will avoid dangers from the forest's heart, where the necromancer casts horrible spells." Bladden shuddered. "The things that come out of there aren't natural. They're not for laying eyes on, as you'll never sleep the same after." His gaze rested on the treetops, but his mind seemed further away.

"Thank you," Ssaska said, dipping his head in a bow.

Derrik looked up at the giant cows, his panic rising as high as their saddles.

"Once you reach the ocean, let her loose and she will find her way back."

Bladden turned and grabbed a cow by the halter. She looked down at the small humans and the snake man with mild brown eyes. "Tell Portina 'giv' if you want her to go, 'lat' if you want her to stop. 'Gant' will make her go faster and 'lyke' will make her go slower."

"What does she eat?" Derrik asked, trying to mask his nervousness.

"Almost anything green. Our cows have very strong digestive systems," replied the giant.

Portina looked bigger up close. Her stirrup was at the level of Derrik's eyes. He looked up at the saddle. It would easily hold the three of them. But it was so high. He swallowed. How would they get on? And how would they stay on once they got up there?

"Me's'll helpen." Marson grabbed Derrik around the waist and lifted him up on the saddle. Derrik gripped the leather with both hands, not daring to look down. Then Marson did the same for Tweaks and Ssaska, so they sat eye-level with him. Marson blinked at them, his black-eyed lid quivering with the effort. "She's not milken," he said. "Sorry fur thaten." Then he rubbed the cow's shoulder with obvious affection.

"I'm not sorry," Ssaska hissed.

"Why?" Derrik asked.

"How would you like to milk this monster?" Ssaska asked.

Bladden pointed them in the direction of the sea, and Ssaska tasted the air. Then they started on their way, moving through the woods faster than they could walk. Tweaks seemed restless and kept moving around behind Derrik.

"Hey," Derrik said, trying to hold himself rigid. "The ground's a long way away. Quit bumping me."

Tweaks tossed an end of rope over Derrik's shoulder. Derrik flinched and flicked it away. "I'm making a rope ladder," Tweaks said.

"What for?"

"You said yourself it's a long way down. Are you going to spend the rest of your life sitting on a giant cow?"

Derrik shook his head.

What Portina lacked in speed she made up for in her incredibly long strides. With sure footing, she stepped over fallen trees and around rocks. After traveling for a while without falling off, Derrik was able to relax a little. He was surprised to find that the cow's easy gait nearly rocked him to sleep.

"Lat!" Ssaska called. Derrik sat up and rubbed his eyes. He noticed Portina's big head turned to stare at something with deep intensity. Curious, Derrik tried to see what held her rapt attention. They were still surrounded by trees, but they had stopped at the wide end of what looked like a natural corridor. Tree trunks ran down either side of an empty grassy stretch, ending at a huge stack of black rocks reaching as high as the tallest tree. Portina's eyes were fixed on the rocks.

Tweaks fitted the glass to his eye and stared down the corridor. "It looks like a giant cow pie," he said in wonder.

"I don't like it," Ssaska muttered.

Tweaks passed the rope ladder to Ssaska, who looped it over the saddle horn and climbed down. Portina didn't move. The saddle creaked as Derrik and Tweaks followed Ssaska to the ground. Staring up at the giant cow's back, Tweaks asked, "What if she steps on us in the night?"

"She won't," Ssaska said.

"But if she does, it would be too late to do anything about it then," Tweaks said.

Ssaska turned and faced Tweaks. "What do you suggest?"

"We could sleep in the rocks," Tweaks said, pointing down the corridor.

"That should be nice and comfy," Derrik said.

"No," Tweaks said, his voice rising. "We could put down branches or something. Maybe there's a ledge of something soft growing up there. Come on, let's take a look."

Ssaska glanced up at the sky, his tongue flicking in and out twice before he said, "There's enough time to check it out before dark. Let's go."

As soon as the three of them started down the corridor, Portina let out a worried "Moooo," loud enough to stir Tweaks's curls.

Ssaska hesitated. "I don't like the sound of that," he said.

"What?" Tweaks asked.

"I think she's warning us."

"Ha!" Derrik laughed. "She's just a cow."

Ssaska looked down the corridor. All was still. He started moving toward the black rocks again, Derrik and Tweaks right behind him. Portina bellowed again. Ssaska stopped, but Tweaks kept going.

"Tweaks!" Ssaska called.

"It'll be dark soon," Tweaks answered. "I want to see it before it's too late."

Derrik followed a few steps behind Tweaks. Portina mooed again and again. The boys didn't look back. They had nearly reached the rocks when a strange sound came from behind them, like drums pounding a rhythmic beat. Ssaska gave a shout. They turned in time to see Portina galloping toward them, a wild look in her eye, with Ssaska trailing far behind on foot.

"What is wrong with that cow?" Tweaks asked, pulling out his eyeglass and holding it up to his eye.

"I don't know," Derrik said. "And I don't really want to find out." He turned, ran the few remaining steps to the ugly rock, and then jumped up to stand on the lowest lump. That was when he felt the vibrations through his shoes and into his feet. He turned to give Tweaks a puzzled look.

But Tweaks wasn't looking at Derrik. He was looking above Derrik, to the top of the rock. And even if he hadn't had his eyeglass on to magnify his eye, Derrik would have been able to see the terror in it.

16

Dead Nor Alive

"Derrik! Get down!" Tweaks screamed, backing up so fast he fell on his rear end.

Alarmed, Derrik whipped his head around to look up the hill. He began to tremble, and he couldn't tear his eyes away.

Creatures of various sizes and deformities crawled over the top of the rock and tumbled down the lumpy slope toward Derrik. It was hard to define exactly what they were, but they didn't look human. Their faces seemed put together wrong, with a muzzle appearing beneath a feathered forehead, or a set of jaws snapping on both sides of a long nose. Some didn't appear to have any mouths at all. Some had eyelids with pointed lashes that looked lethal. Their limbs appeared generally disproportioned, with long forelegs and short hind legs or, more commonly, a long arm with grasping fingers on one side and a stubby toeless limb on the other. Some of them had skin on their bones, but others did not. Most wore partial skin, either stretched tight between joints where it yawned and closed with a fearfully nightmarish appearance, or skin hanging in tatters from twisted limbs. Some of their bones gleamed white in the dusky light, others were stained gray or streaked brown, like dried blood. A few seemed to lack skin or bone at all, but appeared to be nothing more than a dark, smoky outline of some creature best left unseen.

"Derrik!" Tweaks screamed over his shoulder. "Run!" Tweaks was on his feet, making a dash toward the galloping Portina. He didn't seem to care if the cow ran over him.

Derrik tried to jump off the rock, but it was as though his feet had been fused there. He cast another terrified glance up the black mound, then wished he hadn't. The nightmare creatures were almost upon him. His heart beat painfully, begging him to take it away from this awful sight. Derrik wanted to run, wanted to escape with his life, but with his feet rooted to the ugly rock, he knew he was going to die.

The rock shook beneath him under the onslaught of living nightmares scrambling toward him. A skeletal creature with legs like a spider rolled ahead of its comrades, reaching toward Derrik with deathly white limbs. Derrik drew back, but the cold bones stretched out and touched him, curving around his body like a belt and then tightening their grip. Derrik screamed and pushed against the bones with frantic fingers, his muscles trembling so hard he could have pounded a hole in the rock from shaking. A part skeleton horror had its hand stretched out toward Derrik's face, its shriveled, dry skin hanging like torn fabric from its fingers. Whether it meant to suffocate Derrik or rip his face off, he was just as dead.

Derrik closed his eyes, hoping his end would be fast. He was surprised by a vicious yank at his back. His eyes flew open, and he was in the air, above the horror of creatures that tumbled below him. The monstrosities crowded at the bottom of the rock like spilled toys, reaching toward him, their mouths open, their arms grasping at thin air.

Then Portina swung Derrik around, keeping hold of him with her big soft mouth. His feet swirled out in front of him, bringing the deformed skeleton spider into view. Derrik was horrified that it still had hold of him, clutching his foot with jointed bones. An ovoid head stared up at him with empty eye sockets above a pointy-toothed grin. He gave a shout and a vicious kick, but the thing only clung tighter to his leg. Panic welled up in him. Derrik flew through the air, his shirt tight across his chest. He kicked again at the cluster of bones hanging onto his foot.

Then Portina did a most unexpected thing. Swinging Derrik

sideways into the air, she brushed him against the nearest tree. Derrik yelled and covered his face with his hands. This cow was insane. He would never get near her again if he lived through this day. Once she quit dusting him with tree limbs, Portina galloped straight down the corridor. But this time the bone thing was gone.

When Portina reached Ssaska, she lowered Derrik to the ground and let out a bossy "Moo" that knocked Derrik down.

"Get up the ladder," Ssaska said, his eyes on the rock. Derrik didn't look back, but staggered to his feet and struggled up the ropes. Tweaks was right behind him, his eyes seeming to be permanently fixed in a frozen stare of horror. Ssaska was next, his body bristling with weapons. As soon as he sat in the saddle, Portina took off without a command.

"Are they after us?" Derrik asked through chattering teeth.

"No," Ssaska answered. "It looks like they're stuck to the rock."

Derrik stared at the rushing leaves passing by him in a blur. All of the creatures were stuck to the rock but one.

"What were those things?" Tweaks's voice shook.

"The necromancer's mistakes," Ssaska said grimly.

"What mistakes?" Derrik wasn't sure he really wanted to know but figured the knowledge might come in handy.

"I'm not entirely sure," Ssaska admitted. "I'm captain over drills and new recruits. He uses other captains for things like prisons, war, and soul flame experiments."

"What's soul flame?" Tweaks asked.

"I've only heard rumors," Ssaska said.

"Tell us something," Derrik begged. "Even the smallest idea might help make some sense of those nightmares back there."

Ssaska thought for a moment. He leaned forward, patted the shaggy black fur on Portina's back, and said, "Lyke." Portina slowed to a walk, but only after she turned her big head to look back over first one shoulder and then the other.

Ssaska sat up straight. "I was recruited after the time of humans. The necromancer developed a revulsion for the humans' fleshiness, so he replaced them with lean, scaly snake men. While Captain Friss gave me orientation, he let slip a comment about soul flame. Suddenly, he stopped speaking. He was silent so long that I asked him what a soul flame was. He nearly suffocated me when he covered my mouth with his hands. 'You better hope you never find out,' he snarled, his eyes wild with the strangest look I'd ever seen, 'and you're never to say that again.' But I was curious and asked questions of others. I got bits and pieces of information, but I don't know what's true."

After a long pause, Derrik said, "Tell us. Even rumors start from truth."

Ssaska let out a whispery sigh. "All right. It seems the necromancer has found some kind of everlasting life. He's worked many years, even decades, creating a greenish blue soul flame from spirits of the dying. The flame animates dead things. Early on, he made mistakes, which he banished to the center of these woods, keeping them imprisoned with enchantment."

"The giant cow pie," Derrik said, absently rubbing his leg.

"Yes, that could be an enchanted gateway, but I don't know for sure," Ssaska said.

Tweaks stared at Ssaska. "The necromancer still makes mistakes."

"He does," Ssaska said. "The mistakes those snake men brought in escaped when the dremi died. But the first mistakes have been here long enough that if they still had their own souls, they would be dead."

"They sure looked dead," Derrik said.

"But the soul flame is hard to extinguish. And the soul never dies," Ssaska explained.

17
Hang the Boat

Ssaska handed Derrik his knife. Derrik took it, his hand fitting around the snakehead handle. He looked up at Ssaska with questioning eyes. "Keep it tucked in your belt," Ssaska said. "It appears that you need it more than I do."

"Thank you," Derrik said more casually than he felt. His bravery had gone up considerably with this weapon close at hand. "How much further?" Derrk asked.

"We could reach the ocean tomorrow," Sasska replied.

That night, Derrik woke with a start, the dry sound of clacking fading away into the darkness. He stared up into the black shadow of leaves overhead, wondering if the sound was from a vanishing nightmare or if the skeletal spider was out there somewhere in the night. The thump of heavy feet made him suck in his breath and tense every muscle, but it was only Portina. She bent her huge head and sniffed at Derrik. Then she lowered herself to lie down beside him. He no longer feared that she would crush him in the night. With her warm presence like a huge furry building beside him, he slept.

The next morning, they pressed on. At midday, they reached the edge of the sheltering forest. Portina stopped beneath the final patch of green shade and stared out over a beach that gradually slid into the endless blue of a vast, empty ocean.

Ssaska was the first to climb down the rope ladder. He took a drink from his water skin as Tweaks and Derrik climbed down, and then he led the way out from under the trees into the sunshine. Portina stopped to nuzzle a patch of sand berries and followed them onto a beach of golden sand, her hooves making craters the size of boulders. They stared silently out over the expanse of blue water, broken only by serpentine waves that rose into sparkly scales, opening their frothy mouths wider and wider until they finally smashed themselves to pieces against the shore.

"It's like the end of the world," Tweaks whispered, moving to stand closer to Derrik.

"That's only because you're used to trees," Ssaska said. "The world is full of things far stranger than this."

Derrik shivered in the open space, feeling exposed and vulnerable. "Where do we go now?" he asked.

"This is a wide channel. It took us a long time to fly over on the dremi." Ssaska narrowed his yellow eyes as he watched waves slap the sand. "The necromancer's palace is set in the badlands on an island just over the horizon. We must cross the water."

"How?" Tweaks asked. "Do you have a boat?" He pulled out his eyeglass and turned his head to scan the tree line.

"I have no boat," Ssaska answered. "But we must find a way or our journey ends here."

"It doesn't end," Derrik said. "I'll swim if I have to." He squinted out across the sparkling water, seeking land.

Ssaska shook his head. "It's too far."

Derrik glanced at Tweaks. "Tweaks, build something."

Tweaks turned toward Derrik. "Like what?"

"A boat."

Tweaks eyes went wide. "You expect me to build a whole boat to carry us across an ocean? What about my water heating machine? Do you want us to end up like that newt?"

Derrik's eyes filled with disappointment.

"What of the newt?" Ssaska asked.

"Never mind," Tweaks said.

"But a boat isn't a machine," Derrik argued.

"Then you build it," Tweaks answered. "We're not getting anywhere just standing here."

Portina let out an agreeable, "Moo."

Tweaks pointed toward a jumble of fallen trees at the forest's edge. "We might make a raft from those."

Derrik started toward the fallen trees with Tweaks right behind him. Ssaska used the rope ladder to lead Portina. Tweaks picked up a small log and examined it through his eyeglass. "How much rope do we have?" he asked.

Ssaska's thin tongue lashed out, his eyes measuring the meager tangle of tree trunks. "Not much."

"Enough to build a raft?" Tweaks tossed the small log, then grabbed the end of a larger one.

"Doubtful," Ssaska replied.

"What if we take apart the rope ladder?"

"It wouldn't matter," Ssaska said. "It's still not enough. Besides, that's not enough wood there for a raft that would carry us all."

Derrik pulled on a log, moving it onto the beach a few inches. "That doesn't mean we won't find enough," he said. "Come on, Ssaska, help me straighten these out so we can see how much more we'll need."

While Derrik and Ssaska worked on untangling the logs, Tweaks moved further down the beach, searching for more wood. When he rounded a small grove of ubella trees hung thick with fruit, he looked up through his eyeglass at a most astonishing sight. He blinked, then closed one eye, and stared hard through the glass. Finally, he turned and dashed back through the grove, screaming at the top of his voice, "Derrik! Ssaska!"

Derrik dropped a log and came running. Ssaska dodged over to Portina and reached up to pull his crossbow free. He fitted a bolt to it as he ran to catch up with Derrik. Tweaks hurried ahead of them, rounding the grove of trees once more. As soon as Derrik caught up, he gasped, "What is it?" his eyes darting around to all the shadowy spaces.

Tweaks wiggled his ears and pointed up toward a cliff a little further along the beach. Ssaska skidded to a stop beside them. "Can you see it, too?" Tweaks asked. "Is it what I think it is?"

Derrik was too stunned to call Tweaks a mooncalf. He stared at the cliff face, trying to make himself believe what he saw. It was Ssaska who answered, "It's a ship."

"But why is it hanging off a cliff?" Derrik asked.

"I don't know," Ssaska said. "Let's go find out."

They moved down the beach, unaware of the strange white fingers flexing and straightening in the soft shadows of the grove's branches. Portina raised her big muzzle to take a mouthful of leaves and the white fingers retracted from sight.

The travelers walked the beach slowly, checking the woods and water for any sign of danger. The frequent glances over their shoulders showed nothing but a giant cow grazing on a tree. The cliff ahead was nearly straight up and down at the bottom, rising up past the ship where it angled off on a gentler slope, as if someone had cut a wedge from the top of a cake.

When they first saw it, the ship appeared to be a small sloop. When they reached the bottom of the cliff, they realized a full sized galley swayed slightly in the wind overhead, hanging from three thick ropes that forced it to dangle above the sea. The hull suffered from several holes, like a big rotting tooth. Torn and dirty sails dangled from the yardarms, giving fleeting glimpses of the main mast.

"How did it ever get up there?" Tweaks asked, running his magnified gaze over the ropes and the ship.

"More important is who put it there and why," Ssaska said.

"We'll find out," Derrik said. "Doesn't every ship keep a log?"

"They're supposed to," Tweaks answered. He craned his neck for another look just as the sails flapped up, giving a better glimpse of the ship. "Hey! Is that a dinghy?"

Ssaska's tongue flickered twice. "I think so."

"So we can choose from two boats," Derrik said.

Tweaks jumped up and down, his curls flying. "The dinghy's better. It's smaller and made to navigate shallow water."

Ssaska stared up the steep cliff. "It might be easier to chop down more trees to build a raft."

"That would take too long," Derrik said. "The dinghy's already built. Let's go get it."

"You insist?" Ssaska asked. "Well, then, let's go." With his mouth in a grim line, he put one dark green hand on the rocky cliff face and began climbing.

18

Too High

The climb up the cliff face did not go well. They couldn't get far, because the waves had polished the base of the cliff nearly smooth, leaving all the good toe and finger holds up higher.

"There's got to be another way," Ssaska said. "Let's go inland and see if we can reach it from the back side."

"What about Portina?" Tweaks asked.

Derrik slapped his forehead. "What if she's already taken all our stuff back to the giants?"

"Tweaks, go get her," Ssaska said. "Hurry. Tie her in the shade where she can reach grass and water. Then follow us to the back side of the cliff."

"Sure, send the short guy," Tweaks grumbled. He turned and trotted back down the beach. Before he reached the grove of trees, Portina stuck her head out from between the trunks, her eyes curious, her mouth working in sideways circles over a juicy wad of leaves.

Tweaks grabbed the rope ladder and gave a tug. Unimpressed, Portina swallowed and reached up for another mouthful, dragging Tweaks along the sand. Then she settled into chewing again, but this time she was willing to follow Tweaks onto the beach, her bottom jaw going around and around while her hooves made huge dimples in the sand.

"Good cow," Tweaks said. "Good, good, cow."

He walked her into the forest and tied her rope around a

branch. She regarded his knot with solemn eyes.

"Stay put," Tweaks warned. "There's a boat we've got to get." Then Tweaks scrambled after Derrik and Ssaska. When he reached the bottom of the wooded slope, he closed one eye and peered through the glass, but couldn't see anyone. "Derrik?" he called. "Ssaska?"

"Up here," Derrik's faint voice answered.

Tweaks started up the slope. The higher he went, the thinner the trees grew. By the time Tweaks reached the place where Derrik and Ssaska sat, he was ready to sit down and rest with them. But Ssaska stood up on his long, fluid legs in one motion and strode on up the hillside.

"You okay?" Derrik asked, looking into his friend's sweating face.

"Lead the way," Tweaks answered.

"Grab onto my shirt," Derrik said. Tweaks took hold of the back hem of Derrik's shirt, and the two boys followed Ssaska to the top of the cliff.

A sea wind lifted their hair and cooled the sweat from their faces as they stared down the angled slope covered with small, flat rocks, like fish scales. At the bottom was a complicated system of wooden structures and pulleys sitting on a narrow flat shelf, a reprieve just before going over the edge. Taut rope wove through the mechanism, then disappeared over the side.

Ssaska was the first one to start down the slope. He wove his way around rocks and a few stubborn, scraggly bushes that forced their way up through the loose, flat shale that made this a treacherous place.

Tweaks started off next. After a few steps, he stopped and looked at Derrik. "Come on," he said. "I don't want Portina to get tired of waiting."

Derrik nodded and took a step down the slope. His heart pounded painfully in his chest. This was much worse than sitting safely in the saddle of a giant cow. He stuck his arms out for balance, his hands trembling, and then took another tiny step. His toes pushed against the ends of his shoes as they slid forward. His eyes darted toward the edge of the terrifying cliff. Derrik forced himself to take another step. He had to get the boat, had to go and save his parents. No matter what. Sweat beaded his brow. He didn't dare risk his balance by bringing in a hand to wipe it away. He took another step, wishing he was anywhere but here.

Ssaska was nearly to the flat area, moving as easily as if he walked on level ground. Tweaks was nearly halfway down the slope. Derrik forced himself to move his feet faster. That's when a gust of wind hit Derrik from the side. When he leaned into it for counterbalance, the wind swung around and pushed him from the other side. His feet skittered on the steep slope. As he fell, a nearly paralyzing fear rose up and clogged his throat. He had to stop himself or he would roll right past the flat spot and over the edge of the cliff to certain death. He threw his hands out, fingers curved into claws to grab at anything. Sharp pain cut into his right palm. He drew his hand up and skidded on his stomach. He screamed.

Tweaks stopped and spun around, his mouth open. As soon as he saw Derrik, he darted over to the spot just below him, frantic feet sending stones skittering down the slope. Tweaks dug his toes into the shale, fell forward, and stretched his hands up. Derrik skidded into Tweaks, the force of his body sending them both sliding down, crumpling his friend in half before they finally skidded to a stop. Heart racing, Derrik lay panting for breath. "Are you all right?" he asked.

Tweaks was silent a moment. Then he straightened out and raised his head. "I think so." His skin was pale beneath smears of dirt on his face. "Are you?"

Derrik gave Tweaks a shaky smile. "Yeah, thanks to you."

"Well, then," Tweaks stood up and dusted off his hands. Then he brushed his hair out of his eyes. Suddenly he stopped, his hands inches from his face. "My lens!" he cried. "It's gone!"

Derrik's stomach clenched. This was all his fault. He frantically looked around on the ground around him, but all he saw were circles of white stone staring back at him, all looking too much like round glass. Desperately, he scooted his hands through the rock, feeling them scrape against his skin. The eyeglass couldn't be far. Tweaks had only slid a few yards. It had to be here. He suddenly shifted his feet, hoping he hadn't stepped on the precious lens. He dropped to his knees, putting his face close to the shale and turning his head so that he was looking across a broad expanse of rock. It seemed hopeless.

"Do you see it, Derrik?" Tweaks asked, patting the ground around him. "Have you found it yet?"

Derrik rose to shake his head, but a glint of light caught his eye. It was by the piece of dried grass sticking up between two stones. He carefully crawled over to the spot and reached in beside the grass. Only it wasn't grass. It was the hard metal of Tweaks's earpiece pushing against his hand. When he lifted it up, he was relieved to see the circle of glass shining up at him.

"I found it!" he shouted. The wires were bent at odd angles, but the fossil lightning was in one piece.

Tweaks grabbed it and tucked it into his pocket. "Thanks," he said. "Now let's go get us a boat."

Tweaks walked down to the contraption of pulleys and wheels and was soon climbing all over the mechanism, examining the workings of the ship-hauling device with great interest. He risked taking out his eyeglass to look at various working parts, but he never took his hand off the wire. His curls lifted and swayed in a breeze that carried the scent of salt and seaweed.

Derrik followed more slowly, scooting on his backside to where Ssaska stood waiting. When Ssaska pulled Derrik to his feet, the boy winced. Ssaska turned Derrik's hands over to reveal a scraped palm with beads of blood welling up.

"Let's find something to fix that," Ssaska said. While he rummaged in his pockets, Derrik noticed spears and axes lying scattered around the flat space like rusted rocks. He moved closer to examine them. They were of curious workmanship, like nothing he'd seen in his village. When he turned around, he was startled to find himself at the very edge of the cliff. He froze, battling the terror that tugged at him, urging him to step back.

His eyes betrayed him. He looked down over the side where three thick ropes drew severe lines to the ship dangling below, its prow pointed upward as though intending to ram Derrik right between the eyes. The blue ocean sparkled so far below it was like looking into endless sky. Derrik swayed, feeling like he was tumbling through space, not knowing if he was up or down. His hands spread out, the sea air stinging against the blood on his palm, and his stomach lurched, trying to find steady ground.

A hand grabbed Derrik's arm and pulled him back. "Hey, brave one, you're leaning over too far for my liking," Ssaska said. "Sit down." Derrik fell to the ground, the fingers of his good hand digging into the gloriously solid dirt and rock. Ssaska sat beside Derrik and upended his water skin over the bleeding hand. The cool water stung but felt good as it dripped off the back of his hand and made a pink pool in the rocks. Ssaska wrapped a strip of soft white cloth around Derrik's palm.

"The cliff wasn't this high when I looked at it from the ground," Derrik said, his voice cracking.

"It just looks higher from up here," Ssaska said, tying off the bandage and fastening his water skin back on his belt. "The ship throws off your perspective, too."

Derrik stared at the thick ropes spilling over the cliff. "Who would even think of doing something like this?" he asked.

Tweaks hurried over to them, his finger pointing back at the pulleys. "The ropes are really thirty-five different ropes wrapped together in a spiral," he announced. "It must have taken a very long time to make, or else a lot of people worked on it." He scampered over to the cliff's edge and looked down. "I'd say those ropes are at least 300 feet long, maybe more." He waved his arm back to the structure that held the ship in place. "I figured out how it works."

"Can you lower the ship?" Ssaska asked.

Tweaks shrugged. "With just the three of us, it would probably smash against the rocks. I'm thinking there had to be a crew of men to haul it up as far as it is."

"I wonder what happened to them," Ssaska said. Tweaks and

Ssaska looked over the edge of the cliff at the ship. Derrik stayed well back.

"It looks sturdy and there are these thick ropes," Ssaska said, "Derrik, do you think you could climb down?" He received no response. "Derrik?" He looked to find Derrik sitting well back from the edge.

"No," Derrik said, glad for the first time that he'd fallen hard enough to draw blood. "My hand hurts too badly."

Ssaska nodded. "Tweaks, do you think you could do it?" He hefted a coil of rotting rope from the rusty bounty left behind. "My leg still doesn't work quite right from falling off the Dremi. Still, I'm fairly sure I can anchor the other end of a safety rope."

"Fairly sure?" Tweaks asked, looking up at the snake man's face. "I'm to bet my life on your word and that threadbare rope?"

"You are the lightest one of us," Derrik said.

"Yeah. Fancy that," Tweaks said. Then he lifted his arms in invitation for Ssaska to tie him up. "I'll go. I'd like to see this ship close up anyway."

After Ssaska knotted the rope around his waist, Tweaks leaned backward over the precipice, his blue eyes wide. Ssaska flicked his tongue. His arms bulged with muscle as he let out rope. Tweaks walked down the side of the cliff. Every slide of Ssaska's hands down the rope released a musty odor of mold into the air.

Tweaks grabbed the center rope that led over the cliff and guided himself toward the bow of the crippled ship. He climbed over the rotten prow and started down the sun-bleached deck, holding tightly to the ship's rail, trusting it more than the musty old rope digging under his arms.

A sudden gust of wind smashed him into the deck, breaking his hold. He swayed back and forth, the old rope sliding against the splintery railing, effortlessly sawing it in two.

"No!" Ssaska yelled as the rope went limp in his hands.

19

SPLINTERS

Tweaks's heart fell faster than his body as he plummeted down the vertical deck and hit the front of the captain's quarters. His weight slamming into the ancient door was enough to burst it open, dropping him hard against a wooden desk. He froze, dazed and sick with fear. He was sprawled against the sideways desk. He could only hope it wouldn't collapse beneath him. But nothing happened. His eyes slid to the desk legs. They were fastened to the floor with large bolts. The ship swayed gently on its rope tethers and the desk held.

Tweaks gingerly straightened up, feeling the pain of fresh bruises on his back. He carefully fished his eyeglass from his pocket. Keeping hold of it, he took a good look around the cabin. The open doorway several feet above spilled light into the square room. Anything that wasn't bolted down was piled on the wall below him. He peered at the pile of debris. Among the items was a wooden chair that looked like it belonged to the desk, a shirt bunched into a corner, a metal "v" shaped instrument with a hinge on top, a wooden box spilling out papers, a coil of rope, and a few books with dark leather covers.

Maybe one of them was the Captain's Log. Could he trust the cabin wall with his weight? First, he searched the desk, but the log wasn't there. So he gingerly stepped onto the cabin wall below him. The desk creaked and the ship swayed. Tweaks held his breath. When the ship settled down, he quickly searched the papers but couldn't find anything that looked like a logbook.

The dinghy was more important than the ship's log. He tucked his eyeglass into his pocket and lifted the coil of rope from the wall. It was in better shape than the piece that lowered him over the cliff, probably because it was sheltered from the elements. He looped the rope around his body and looked up toward the open doorway. Then he pulled himself up onto the desk, which let out a complaining creak. Tweaks didn't trust that it would hold him much longer.

Even without his eyeglass, Tweaks could see something in the corner by the door. It appeared to be a chest that had also been fastened down. *What might be in it?* He scrambled across the desk to the side of the room where built-in shelves offered him a rough ladder. He climbed up to the doorway, feeling every fresh bruise again. When his foot slipped, he clung to his handhold, not knowing if the desk would be less forgiving of another fall. He reached the chest and lifted the lid. It was disappointingly empty.

When he pulled himself out of the cabin, Ssaska shouted, "Are you all right?"

Tweaks looked up to see the snake man clinging to the top of the thick center rope, his anxious eyes on Tweaks.

"I'm fine," Tweaks shouted.

Ssaska hesitated. His tongue flickered out twice. He stared at Tweaks with shining black eyes.

"Go back," Tweaks said.

The snake man slithered up the rope and disappeared over the edge. Then he looked over the side, his worried eyes still on Tweaks. Tweaks carefully made his way down to the end of the ship and looked out over the rail at the dinghy. It hung below the ship like a fat bleached gray tail. Many of the warped planks were split lengthwise. His heart sank when he saw the head-sized hole bashed in the bottom, with spines of wood sticking out in all directions. Tweaks rubbed his eyes. They would not be sailing over the water in the dinghy any time soon.

Heart heavy, Tweaks pulled himself slowly up the deck. His

arms ached and new bruises protested as he strained to pull himself over the edge to sit on the prow. His shoulders slumped and he stared up at Ssaska.

"Are you all right?" Ssaska asked.

"Tired," Tweaks answered. "The dinghy's no good."

Ssaska's face disappeared. Then he came back over the edge. "Can you climb?"

"In a minute," Tweaks said. He dropped his head, feeling the pain of his muscles and heart.

After a minute or two, something touched his shoulder. He jumped and looked up to see a rope of knotted clothing dangling just overhead. Ssaska held the rotting rope at the top, leaning over so far it looked as though he might tip over the edge. His green scales rippled when he shook the rope, which looped down to hold up the string of clothing. "Grab hold."

Tweaks got up on his knees. "You're going to fall!" Tweaks shouted.

"Derrik has my feet," Ssaska answered. "He says he's sitting on rocks and wants his trousers back, so please hurry."

Tweaks grabbed the end of the clothing rope, lifted the good rope off his shoulder, and looped it through the end of a twisted shirt. Ssaska pulled the end of the good rope to the top, then braced it around his body and helped pull Tweaks up. "Thanks," Tweaks said.

"You're welcome," Derrik grumbled, tugging at the knots in his clothes.

"So you can work this?" Ssaska asked, pointing to the pulleys.

"I said I know how it works," Tweaks answered.

"If the dinghy's no good, then let's lower the ship to the water and use it," Ssaska said.

"I don't think it's in any better shape," Tweaks answered. "It's been hanging off that cliff for who knows how long? The bottom is probably scraped away, or as thin as paper. I searched for a Captain's log to see if I could find out why anyone would do this, but I had no luck."

Ssaska's tongue flickered and he nodded. "It is not really important why they did it. I expect the captain was insane. Maybe they all were."

Something hit Ssaska in the back. He turned to see his wrinkled trousers land on the ground. His eyes darted to Derrik, who was struggling with his shirt.

Ssaska bent and picked up his trousers. "Let's get this ship lowered," he said. "Even if the hull is rotten, we can use the wood to build a raft."

Tweaks moved over to the mechanism and took hold of a long wooden lever. "This should do it," he said. He pressed down, but the lever didn't move.

"Must have rusted gears," Tweaks said. "Derrik, help me."

Derrik tugged his shirt down over his belly as he walked toward Tweaks.

"Push down," Tweaks said, boosting himself up so he could apply more of his weight. Derrik grabbed the lever opposite his friend and pushed with his uninjured hand. The lever resisted for just a moment and then gave way, plunging the boys to the ground. A defiant screech of metal ripped the air as the pulleys and gears jerked, jumped, and exploded apart. A sizzle of sliding rope filled the air with a sharp burning odor, and a crack of wood against rock made the boys flinch.

"Get down!" Ssaska roared, diving for the ground.

Derrik covered his head with his arms, and Tweaks turned his head just as the end of a huge rope snapped over the top of them, the frayed ends flying like tentacles. Tweaks let loose a piercing scream. The rope flopped to the ground as though the sharp scream had stabbed it through. Tweaks continued screaming.

"It's over," Derrik said, turning toward Tweaks who was curled up, his knees against his chest, his head bent forward, and both hands cupping his ear. Everything was silent, except for the screaming.

Then Ssaska's boots sounded, the ground vibrating under his feet as he hurried to the boys. He knelt beside Tweaks, and with a voice more gentle than Derrik had ever heard him use before,

Ssaska said, "Let me see."

Tweaks didn't move, except to scream again.

Ssaska took hold of Tweaks's arms and pulled them back from his ear, murmuring, "Let me see. Let me help."

Derrik gasped. Tweaks's ear looked like raw meat. Streaks of bright red blood smeared the side of his head.

"What happened?" Derrik felt like he was in the middle of a nightmare.

"The rope flayed his ear," Ssaska said. "We need something to wrap it."

"Don't touch it!" Tweaks yelled.

Ssaska stared at the raw, red ear.

"Let's just get down," Derrik said, even though it was hard for him to draw breath. "We'll figure something out after we get down."

"Stand up," Ssaska said to Tweaks. "You've got to walk."

Tweaks pushed himself up to his feet, tears running down his face.

"I'll walk beside him," Ssaska told Derrik. "You get the rope."

Derrik didn't question the snake man. Instead, he used both hands to pick up the rope. They headed back down toward the beach, Ssaska keeping pace with Tweaks, his breath coming heavy and hissing as he kept Tweaks so close to his side that he was nearly carrying him.

"I need to rest," Tweaks said.

Ssaska stopped and stretched his back.

"Did it work?" Tweaks asked, his shoulders hunched and his hand cupped over his bloody ear. His voice bordered on hysteria. "Do we have a ship?"

"I don't know," Ssaska said. "But we'll find out."

After a few more minutes, they made their way around the hill back to the beach. Glancing up, they saw the ship hanging crookedly from two ropes, like a broken toy. The dinghy no longer dangled from the back of the boat. Instead of the chain that had held it in place, there was a gaping hole.

Tweaks jumped and pointed. "The dinghy! It fell off the ship! We can salvage it!"

"Let's wash off that ear first," Ssaska said.

"No," Tweaks stepped back from the snake man. "I have a headache."

"You'll have worse if you get septic. Let me look at it again."

Tweaks ducked his head and slowly lowered his hand. He flinched when Ssaska took hold of his head to tilt it to one side. The piece of bloody flesh on the side of Tweaks's head didn't look much like an ear.

"It will heal," Ssaska finally said. "Better to leave it exposed to the air if you can stand it. But we must wash it first."

Tweaks could not protest strongly enough to overcome Ssaska's strength. Only after his ear had been washed in the ocean water, and rinsed with clear water, did they move toward the bottom of the cliff.

Here, the sandy beach was narrow, bordered by cliffs on one side and a huge rock jutting out into the sea on the other. The dinghy had unfortunately hit the rock and shattered into splinters. The biggest piece was one held together by the metal plate and loop that fastened the chain in place.

"None of this is worth the effort," Derrik said, kicking a cracked board.

Tweaks sank to the sand and curled himself up, rocking back and forth with his hand over his ear. Derrik sat beside him and patted his back with his good left hand. Ssaska limped over to stand beside them. "What a fine bunch of adventurers we are," he hissed. "We made it through the dreaded forest, and now we're stopped by a simple expanse of water."

"We'll find a way," Derrik said. "We have to find a way."

20

MISSING

Ssaska moved further down the beach, staring out across the water.

Tweaks grabbed hold of Derrik's hand. "You've got to tell Skippy that I really do love him," he said.

"What are you talking about?" Derrik asked. "Tell him yourself."

"If I don't make it." Tears welled up in Tweaks's eyes.

"Don't be stupid," Derrik said. "Getting your ear skinned isn't going to kill you."

"I just can't stop thinking about how he grabbed my finger," Tweaks said. "It's like he—I don't know—trusted me or something." Tweaks swiped at his eyes. "I just can't die without him knowing I really did care."

Derrik snorted. "He's a baby. He doesn't know anything."

Tweaks turned to Derrik, his eyes blazing. "He knows! He looked right at me and smiled, even though I was thinking all the worst things I could about him." Tweaks turned his back on Derrik and sniffed. "You just don't know what it's like."

"I don't want to know what it's like to be a mooncalf."

Tweaks stared at Derrik through wet eyes, his hand cupped over his wound. "I can't . . ." he took a shuddering breath. "I can't wiggle my ears anymore."

Derrik could think of nothing to say.

"Hey!" Ssaska yelled, his voice high and sharp. "Come here! Hurry!"

Derrik jumped to his feet, alarmed. Tweaks turned his head toward Ssaska and squinted. "What's going on?"

"I don't know," Derrik said. "He disappeared behind the rock." Derrik started toward Ssaska. He heard Tweaks struggle to his feet but didn't wait. He rounded the rock to see Ssaska with his feet in the water, tugging on a round wooden barrel. Several others crowded around him, but some drifted away, bobbing on the waves.

"Where did those come from?" Derrik asked.

"They must have fallen out of the ship's hold when the dinghy tore loose," Ssaska said. "Come on, grab another one."

Derrik waded out and grasped another barrel, struggling to free it from the water, ignoring the sting of salt that seeped under the bandage on his hand. He tipped the barrel and rolled it up the beach so easily that he was sure it was empty. Lashed together, these barrels would make a handy raft.

Tweaks waded in to help. By the time they'd gotten all they could reach, twenty-one barrels stained the sand beneath them dark with water.

"Tweaks," Ssaska called, "Unravel the rope."

"Unravel it?" Tweaks asked.

"It's too thick to tie around these barrels," Ssaska said. "Derrik, come help me position these." Ssaska shoved a barrel across the sand until it bumped into another one. Tweaks sat down and unwound a strand from the huge rope that had mangled his ear. Derrik took the strand from him and moved toward the barrels. Tweaks sat, shoulders slumped, watching him go.

"Unravel more," Ssaska said.

"Can't we finish this later?" Tweaks asked, cupping his hand over his ear. "I don't feel well."

"The tide is rising," Ssaska explained. "If we don't get it done now, we'll have to move all the barrels or lose them in the night."

Ssaska walked over to Tweaks and squatted down. He picked up one end of the chunk of rope and worked a strand free. "Do you need help?"

"No," Tweaks said, reaching out and pulling at another strand. "I've got it."

Ssaska nodded. "Good." He got to his feet. "Come on, Derrik. Let's get this raft put together."

Derrik hesitated and then pulled the snake man's dagger from his belt. "Here," he said, holding it out to Tweaks. "You might want to use this to help separate those strands."

"Thanks," Tweaks said, turning the knife over in his hands and pushing it into the twisted rope.

They worked until dusk, but ran out of rope with four barrels left over. "I guess that will have to do," Derrik said.

"It might not," Ssaska said. "If only we had a little more rope." He looked up at the cliff.

"The ladder!" Tweaks shouted.

"Portina's ladder!" Derrik said.

"I'll get it," Tweaks hurried back along the beach, but in moments, he was back, his face pale, his breath coming hard. He looked from Derrik to Ssaska and back again, and blurted, "Portina's gone!"

"No," Derrik said, releasing a loose barrel and sprinting toward Tweaks.

"I tied her right there," Tweaks insisted. But there was no giant cow looking back at them.

"She must have left a trail," Derrik said, hurrying toward Portina's tether spot. "Something that big can't get away without showing signs." He reached the patch of forest Portina had stripped of greenery. An odd tittering sound from the tree made Derrik snap his head up, but he didn't see anything. It didn't sound like any bird he'd ever known. It was more like the ticking of dry branches hitting one another. He tried to shrug off his unease. He had a cow to catch. When he studied the ground, he saw large cloven hoof prints leading deeper into the forest.

"Marson said she'd find her way back home after we reached the ocean," Tweaks said.

Derrik turned to see Ssaska looking at him over the top of Tweaks's head. "Quiet," Derrik said. "Don't spook her."

He led the way under the canopy of trees. The darkness was deeper in the shade, making Derrik suddenly aware of how late it was. A scuttling sound in the branches overhead made Derrik shiver. If it got full dark before they found Portina, they might never find her.

Derrik hurried along the fresh trail, lifting his gaze occasionally to see if the cow was in sight. A hundred steps into the trees, he saw the movement of a tail, attached as high as a ceiling. It swung around and slapped at a huge expanse of fur.

"I see her!" Derrik whispered.

Portina stood still, her head down to the ground, as Derrik moved up beside her. He grabbed the rope ladder. "And where do you think you're going?" Derrik asked, reaching out to pat Portina's head.

Portina blew out a snuff of air and raised her eyes to Derrik. Something white and grinning on the ground looked up at Derrik, too.

21
Log

The skeleton head looked cheerful as Tweaks, Ssaska, Derrik, and Portina stood in a ring around it.

"Who is it?" Tweaks asked.

"Looks like sailor's clothes," Ssaska said. The shirt was half gone with holes. A tear in the sleeve showed a glimpse of a bony arm crossed tightly over the chest. Tattered trousers ended under a blanket of leaves, which was as far as Portina had managed to uncover the skeleton before Derrik interrupted.

"He could be from the ship," Derrik said. "We could check his pockets."

"What pockets?" Tweaks asked. "There aren't enough clothes left to have pockets, even if he started out with them."

"Shouldn't we find out who he is?" Derrik asked.

"Go ahead," Tweaks answered.

Derrik looked at Ssaska. The snake man's tongue flickered, but he said nothing. So Derrik turned and reached out his hand, quick so he wouldn't have to think about what he was doing. He grabbed a piece of rag the skeleton wore and gave a tug, looking for a pocket opening. The fabric pulled free, letting loose a tiny puff of decaying fibers.

Discouraged, Derrik turned toward Tweaks, ready to admit defeat. But Tweaks's face was even paler than usual against his red curls. Tweaks wasn't looking at Derrik. He stared at the skeleton. Then he pointed and said, "He died holding something."

Derrik turned to see the corner of something sticking out from under an elbow. He leaned forward and carefully took hold of a piece of sleeve. This time when he pulled, the skeletal arm bones stirred before the pinch of fabric tore free. The arm moved, revealing a book covered by old, cracked leather. Derrik tried to read the front of the book, but the other skeleton arm blocked it.

"Here," Tweaks said, handing Derrik his snake knife. "If you're scared to touch it, use this."

"I'm not scared," Derrik said, but before he could do anything more, a green-scaled hand swooped down over his shoulder and grabbed the book's corner. When it pulled free, the skeleton jostled in a brief dance of agitation. "It's all spotted," Ssaska said, smoothing a hand over the sailing ship embossed in the splotched leather, the book's paper edges mottled as well. Ssaska gently lifted the cover, then separated the sticky first page with the slender point of his tail. He squinted his yellow eyes in the deepening dusk under the trees. "The log of Captain Brom VanCorman," he read.

"It's the captain's log!" shouted Derrik.

"Then this must be the captain," Tweaks said. "Do you think the necromancer's army got him, too?"

"He's been dead much longer than that," Ssaska said. He darted a look upward. "Come on, we need to get out of these woods before it gets any darker."

Derrik took hold of Portina's ladder. She followed him readily and then bent to nuzzle his hair when the beach came into view. "Stop that!" Derrik yelled, ducking out from under her huge lips.

When they reached the raft, Derrik said, "I'll tie her up again."

"It's not necessary," Ssaska said. "She's served her purpose. Let's get her unloaded."

The travelers took everything off the cow except her saddle, piling their weapons and leather bags into a small pile on the beach. They could have fit twice as much into one of their waist high raft barrels.

"Now turn her loose," Ssaska said, winding the rope ladder around the last of the barrels, finishing the raft at four barrels wide and five long, with one left over.

Derrik stared at the huge cow, his heart suddenly heavy.

"It's time for her to go," Ssaska said. "Just point her in the right direction." He tightened a knot. "Go home," he shouted.

Portina stared at him with huge dark eyes. Then she turned, waded through the sand to the edge of the trees, and sank down on her belly. While the rays of the setting sun painted the sand red, her jaw worked, chewing her cud.

"She doesn't want to leave us," Derrik said, his mouth curved in a smile.

"I hope she doesn't jump in and swim after the raft," Ssaska said, testing the barrels as they wobbled in the water. "Come on, let's get our things in here."

Tweaks and Derrik piled the weapons into the center barrel, fitting in some ubella fruits and sand berries. Ssaska wrapped the logbook in a leather satchel. "Aren't you going to read it?" Derrik asked.

"It's too dark," Ssaska replied. "There will be time in . . ."

A strange call pulsed out from the shadowy trees. "Waaalooo."

Portina lifted her head and turned toward the sound.

"What was that?" Tweaks asked.

Ssaska's face was grim. "I don't think we want to know."

A dry clacking clattered from the forest, backed by whispers and stuttering words so strange, the hair rose on Derrik's neck. In horror, he watched Portina lumber to her feet and charge into the trees.

"No!" Derrik yelled. He took off running after the cow.

"Stop!" Ssaska hollered. But Derrik kept going, and Tweaks joined in the chase.

Ssaska took a quick look at the barrel raft, growled, and then went after the boys. He caught up just as they reached the place where the dead captain lay. Portina stood over his skeleton, her tail swishing and her ears pricked. Then, with a yowl and crashing that shook Derrik to his very core, the trees exploded with half a dozen creatures, all disjointed bones and partial skin scraps stuck together in strange combinations; a weird blue-green flame pulsed from them at odd joints here and there. The creatures jumped for the giant cow and swarmed all over her.

Portina shook her big head, sending a half-skeletal monkey-like thing whirling through the air. A goat-like skull with a collar of horns growing from its neck and a pointed ridge down its back somersaulted from a kick of Portina's hind leg.

"No!" Derrik shouted.

The four remaining creatures turned their dead blue-green eyes on Derrik.

Derrik pulled his snake knife out of his belt.

Ssaska took in a sharp breath. "That won't do any good," he muttered. "These are the necromancer's mistakes."

Before Derrik could die of fright, something white zipped through the air, spinning toward Portina's face. The creatures swatted at it, but their mismatched limbs made them clumsy. The white thing spun around Portina's head until, as though crazed by a biting fly, Portina took off at a gallop. Her dash to freedom whipped branches across her back, scraping the creatures off. They scrambled up onto their misshapen legs and stood there, swaying, staring at Derrik.

"Run!" Ssaska yelled, turning and sprinting toward the beach. Tweaks was right behind him. Just as Derrik slid the knife back in its sheath at his belt and spun around to run for his life, the white thing flashed past him, spinning like a crazed moth or huge milkweed umbrella. He didn't like it, but he couldn't waste much time thinking about it. He had too many worries behind him.

When Derrik broke free of the tree line, Ssaska was already at the raft and Tweaks ran toward the water, sending up little spurts of sand behind him.

"Hurry!" Ssaska yelled, waist deep in the ocean, his hand holding the raft.

Tweaks splashed into the water without hesitation. Ssaska

boosted him onto the barrels. Derrik heard the stumbling steps and grunts of the horrifying creatures behind him, but didn't dare look back.

"Faster!" Ssaska urged, his eyes wide, his tongue flicking wildly.

Derrik put on a burst of speed, churning water. The deep waves slowed him instantly, so he leaned forward, stretching out his hands and kicking with all his might.

Ssaska flung his arm out and caught Derrik by the collar, dragging him to the raft. Derrik crawled onto the barrels, coughing and spitting. Ssaska pushed them to deeper water before climbing on board. His lungs dragging in air, Derrik saw through his dripping strands of hair that Tweaks had a broken barrel stave over the side of the raft, beating the cold, dark water in a frenzy.

22

STOWAWAY

When the sun rose, the travelers called an end to the restless night and stretched their sore backs, checking the flat horizon. Glad there were no decaying creatures swimming after them, they still wished for a spot of land to aim for.

"Now what do we do?" Tweaks asked, rubbing his eyes.

"It's light enough to read the log," Ssaska said. He reached into a center barrel where they'd piled their things. An alarming dry clatter sounded and Ssaska yanked his hand back.

"What's in there?" Derrik asked, his heart pounding as he scooted to the edge of the raft, which wasn't far enough away for his liking.

"I don't know," Ssaska said. His brow creased, his tail waving back and forth. "Come out!" he shouted.

The rattling stopped. Only Tweaks had the presence of mind to grab a barrel stave and hold it up in front of him for protection.

"Come out now or I'll get you out," Ssaska warned.

The travelers stared at the edge of the barrel. Then it shifted slightly, and three thin bones rose up over the wooden barrel's edge, bent at their small joints, and curled over the lip like fingers. Another bone hand rose up and perched beside the first. Finally an ovoid-shaped head made of pure white bone slowly inched its way up behind the hands.

"Augh!" Tweaks twisted his head away.

The creature let out a hiss through pointy needle-sharp teeth.

In a single leap, it balanced its feet on the edge of the barrel. A lizard skeleton stood before them, with one long arm, one short arm, and wings of thin bone gently rising and falling on its back.

"Get away!" Derrik yelled.

Ssaska pushed his palm out toward Derrik, the skull brand staring him down. Eyes on the skeleton, Ssaska asked, "Who are you?"

The bone creature turned her head around slowly, looking at each of them before answering, "My name is Clatterin."

"You grabbed me, didn't you?" Derrik said, his heart jumping in his throat. "In the woods. You're . . . one of those . . . things."

Clatterin dipped her head in acknowledgement. "I didn't choose this," she said, her wings rising slightly and then lowering again.

"Why are you here?" Ssaska said.

"Because he freed me." Clatterin pointed at Derrik.

"No, I didn't." Derrik shook his head for emphasis.

"When you stood on the stopper of our valley of exile, you opened a narrow passage, as wide as your feet. As long as you stood there, we could escape, but I alone touched you before Portina carried you away."

"Touched me?" Derrik said, his eyebrows shooting up. "You tried to kill me!"

"Not kill," Clatterin said. "I only did what I needed to do."

"How do you know our cow's name?" Tweaks asked.

"I speak all languages," Clatterin said. "Portina wouldn't leave you with the necromancer's mistakes until I convinced her I would see you safely on your way. And . . ." Her bones suddenly collapsed and folded in, and then spread out again in a longer shape, extending their reach with Clatterin's head in the middle. She looked like a giant spider. ". . . I can change my shape." The spider bent its knees and jumped into the air, the legs spinning in a circle in perfect imitation of the white thing Derrik had seen the night before.

"No!" Derrik cried, throwing his hands up.

Ssaska darted to the barrel, reached in, and pulled out his crossbow.

Clatterin circled the raft, then settled back down in an empty corner. "I have no wish to harm you," she said, facing Ssaska.

"You didn't tell us what you want," Ssaska hissed.

Clatterin's bones folded back into a lizard shape. "I want to repay the necromancer for what he did to me, and all the others like me."

"If the others are like you, then why did you have to promise Portina you'd keep us safe?"

Clatterin put her head in her bony hands. "They aren't all like me. My fault is the soul flame permeated into my bones, allowing me to separate into pieces and still function. I can still reason and think for myself, which is not what the necromancer wanted from his followers, so he banished me." She tilted her head. "I also glow blue. You can see it better in the dark."

"We have no reason to trust you," Ssaska said.

"That sounds familiar," Tweaks said, dropping his board with a thump. "Remember Derrik saw *you* as evil just because your skin is made of scales."

Derrik studied his friend. "What do you think of her, Tweaks?"

Tweaks looked at the lizard made of bone. Her eye sockets remained on him until he nodded. "She means us no harm."

Derrik sat up straighter, his eyes on the stowaway. "I'm with Tweaks, then," he said. "She didn't kill us last night while we slept."

"Maybe she has a different plan," Ssaska said, his voice hard.

"There are three of us and one of her," Tweaks said.

Ssaska stared at Clatterin. Then he nodded. "I see no other recourse. You may stay. But I will have my eye on you."

He kept staring at Clatterin while reaching his hand into the barrel again. This time he came away with the satchel holding the book. "Tweaks, you're the best reader," he said, handing the book to Tweaks. "Tell us what the log says."

Tweaks opened the book, put on his eyeglass, and began reading.

Day ten, Month five
Today my crew and I made a good deal of trade in furs at Gymon, for the islanders have not many furred animals there. We also retrieved a good deal of shells and pearl from the natives.

Day thirteen, Month five
Today the pearl we traded for on Gymon proved useful, for the mainlanders at Misyan enjoyed it greatly.

Day seventeen, Month five
We have reached Falk. Not made much profit, but I am happy, for we now head for my home port of Meeya.

Day nineteen, Month five
We have not reached Meeya. I thought good fortune lay ahead today when my men and I spotted a whale. But it may be bad fortune, for the man in the crow's nest says it was not a whale, but some sort of monstrous and evil leviathan. I fear the poor fellow has gone mad.

Day twenty, Month five
We have been at sea too long, for we all saw a blue fire burning on the water! The men think it is an omen. I believe it was just a reflection. I don't believe that superstitious nonsense.

Day twenty-one, Month five
I think we have all gone insane. I've decided to head for the nearest land—a cliff face in the distance.

Day twenty-two, Month five
We have reached the cliff and found it has a pulley system that is well crafted. I wonder if it was used to pull goods up the cliff face for some race that is no longer there, for we found no signs of homes

or habitants. I have a marvelous idea. We can use the pulleys to lift the ship up the cliff face and safely onto land.

Day twenty-five, Month five
The boat is proving very difficult to lift. Some men say I'm mad, but it is they who are mad. I saw the thing in the water. It seemed to be waiting for us. I know that it is drawn to the boat, so we must take the boat out of reach.

Day twenty-seven, Month five
I am writing this so any who find it will not make the same mistake as me. My men are all dead. While working on lifting the ship, they were attacked by a huge creature, neither dead nor alive. All were killed. The beast was unaffected by our attacks. It stank of rotting flesh with a strange green flame burning in its head.

Ssaska gave a sudden low hiss, urgent and frightening. "We have to get out of the water," he said in a voice so tense it was hard to understand. "We're in danger!"

The tale from the Captain's log had sent a cold shiver up Derrik's spine, and Ssaska's reaction only made it worse. "The captain had to be insane, Ssaska. Why are you so worried?"

"Blue-green flame, a creature that is not living or dead, weapons don't have any effect on it. Derrik, it's one of the necromancer's creations!" Ssaska shouted.

"He is right," Clatterin said, her teeth clacking. "The blue-green flame is the sign of a soul flame corpse. We have to get to land!"

Ssaska desperately dipped his board into the water. Derrik and Tweaks grabbed boards to help, flailing at the water with reckless paddling.

"No," Ssaska shouted. "We're not getting anywhere. Work together."

Clatterin spun out her bones and whirred them overhead. I'll try carrying you to land," she said, lowering to touch Tweaks's shoulders.

"Get away!" Tweaks said, batting at Clatterin.

"Stop," Ssaska said. "Listen, Tweaks, we've got to get away from here as fast as we can. If she can help us escape, then we should let her do it."

"I don't want her to drop me in the ocean!" Tweaks protested.

"I won't let you fall," Clatterin said.

"Trust me, she has a good grip," Derrik said.

"All right," Tweaks said. He sat stiff and rigid with his eyes closed and his shoulders hunched.

Clatterin slid long bones under his arms and spun her spider leg bones over his head. Tweaks lifted an inch off the raft, but Clatterin soon dropped him again. "Too heavy," she said, landing on the raft with a click of bone legs. "I'm sorry. I'll try to help another way."

Clatterin formed a fin of bones to help paddle, and Tweaks got busy paddling with a board. After several minutes, Tweaks pulled his board out of the water and slumped over in exhaustion. Derrik anxiously scanned the horizon. "Are you sure about the monster?"

"Yes," Ssaska hissed, his tongue darting in and out. "I know it's out there."

"It is," Clatterin agreed. She stared out across the cold blue water. "But it's possible you'll make it to land before it finds you."

"Only if we keep going," Ssaska said, his voice urgent.

Tweaks bent forward, his arms around his stomach. His tattered ear wobbled when he said, "I'm hungry."

Ssaska reached into the barrel, pulled out the food, and passed it around. The sand berries crunched in their teeth, releasing sweet spurts of flavor into thick, juicy flesh. When the first ubella fruit was down to the stem, Clatterin reached out and plucked it from Ssaska's hands before he could flick it over the side.

"Do you eat?" Derrik asked, eyeing her skeleton.

"No," Clatterin's voice was bitter. "The soul flame keeps me alive such as I am. But the urge to chew remains."

They watched the horizon, each of them taking a different side of the raft, but nothing showed up. As the day wore on, they dozed under the hot sun, letting the ocean current carry them. Clatterin took off on a couple of flights to scout the area, but each time she returned with no news of the sea monster.

The day wore out, but evening brought no rest for the raft crew. The sunset cast a dim red glow across the water. Derrik turned to see what looked like a light off in the distance. It could be the setting sun glinting off the water. But the sunset was red, and the distant light gave off a sickly greenish glow. It moved toward them in a sinuous motion that sent chills of alarm up Derrik's spine. "Sea monster!" he yelled, sitting bolt upright. He grabbed a board and, ignoring the cut on his hand, paddled like a mad man. But where could they go? Where was there any safety from a sea monster in all the vast water around them? They couldn't outrun it if there was nowhere to run, even if they could have moved quickly enough.

Ssaska reached into the barrel and pulled out his crossbow. He fit a bolt to it and aimed at the light sliding toward them with alarming speed. The string sang and the bolt sailed true to its goal. Just before striking its target, the bolt turned to ash and peppered the churning water.

"What happened?" Derrik yelled.

"The water is its sanctuary," Clatterin explained. "Only when it is out of its element can it be attacked."

Ssaska drew his sword and braced himself, facing the enemy. "If we put out the fire, it will die," Ssaska told them.

"A difficult task," Clatterin added. "For it is a fire lit by souls, and the soul flame is housed within his waterproof hide."

A large wave rocked the raft, and then the tail disappeared behind a hideous gray head rising out of the water. They stared in horrified disbelief at a monstrous face. The top of the head glowed a sickly greenish-blue. The bulbous eyes roved over them. Its lips stretched wide, and the smell of rotting flesh blasted from the creature's mouth. Arrows from hundreds of bows and the spears of a thousand dead sailors stuck out of the rotten head in a horrible bristling array. The serpent let out an angry roar filled with the stench of death. Tweaks screamed. Derrik's whole body rocked violently with fear as flecks of foul-smelling water and putrid meat hit his face.

The creature dove under the water, its flaming green head glowing until it blended into the deep green depths. Derrik looked around wildly in the last rays of sunlight, wondering where the creature might break the surface. His frantic eyes caught sight of a shape silhouetted against the sunset, a sharp relief of black on the flat line of water. "Land!" he shouted.

Ssaska whipped his head around and stared at the horizon, his face grim.

"I'll see if I can get help," Clatterin offered, folding her bones and reshaping them to fly. She turned into a spinning nightmare and sped off toward the dark lump ahead.

A sudden bump from beneath the raft sent Ssaska flying through the air. Derrik tried to hang onto the center barrel, but only managed to snag the strap from his leather pack. The barrels broke apart and the sea creature's spiny head burst through the center at the peak of the watery mountain. Its toothy mouth opened as it shattered the raft, eager to grab a warm morsel of bones and living flesh.

23

Beached

Derrik opened his eyes to see a wave curling toward him. He groaned and rolled over on the gritty sand. His muscles screamed in protest and he stopped, shivering and fingering an uncomfortable lump at his waist. Slowly he drew out the snakeman's knife. How it had stayed put when the raft capsized was a mystery, but Derrik was glad to have it. A wave broke over a rock at the water's edge, sending saltwater spray into the air. Memories of the horrid sea creature crowded his thoughts, making him suddenly crab-walk away from the water's edge, ignoring the bruises and cuts that begged him to stop. His heart beat in sudden fear. What if the creature walked on land? Fighting the beast with his knife would be like using a toothpick. Derrik anxiously searched for any sign of Tweaks, Ssaska, or even Clatterin, but all he saw was a vast expanse of beach littered with barrel staves, a water skin, and his leather satchel. Other than the knife, he had nothing to defend himself.

"Twe—" He tried to yell but his throat was too dry. How long had he been here? It seemed like days. Derrik couldn't tell if the sun hovering at the horizon was setting or rising. He was so tired. If only he could find his parents, then he could go home and everything would be back to normal.

Pushing himself up gingerly to his knees, Derrik searched for anything to drink. His water skin was empty, but he tucked it into his belt anyway. Finding nothing to eat or drink, he moved to the edge of the thick rainforest. In the welcome shade, he found leaves holding little pools of water in their cool, green palms. He drank as much as he could find. Then he sank to the ground and leaned against a tree trunk, thinking.

By now he could tell that the sun was rising in the sky. He got to his feet, unwilling to believe he was the only survivor. He walked along the beach close to the trees, bleary-eyed, and doing his best to search for tracks or any sign of his friends.

His heart leaped with hope when he discovered two broken barrels lashed together. He hurried toward the partial raft, but there was no one there. He collapsed in the shade of the barrels, his heart sore. How would he go on alone?

The sun beat down. His scant shade wouldn't be shade for long. He didn't want to believe that Ssaska and Tweaks were dead, but if they were alive, where were they? Maybe he was the one who had died. Maybe this abandoned beach was where the dead went.

He needed water. He pushed himself stiffly to his feet, and stopped and stared at two pair of footprints in the sand, one bigger than the other, leading from the raft into the forest. "Tweaks!" He staggered toward the tree line and then saw a third track, wide and long. He stopped, puzzled. It wasn't possible for the putrid sea monster to have a set of rotting legs. Derrik shivered. He swallowed hard and followed the prints to where they disappeared among thick greenery. Birds chirped encouragement and curious insects hovered near his head. Derrik walked deeper into the trees, but there was no trail to follow.

Discouraged, he sat down against a tree. More insects buzzed at his eyes, wanting to taste the salt from the tears welling up there. Derrik lowered his head to his knees and wrapped his arms around his head.

"Derrik." The voice was faint, as if it had come from inside his head. Was he going crazy? Would he die alone, a babbling idiot at the end? If that's the way it was going to be, he was glad he was alone.

"Derrik!" the voice quavered a little nearer, then faded away.

"Derrik!" It sounded so real.

Derrik lifted his head and swatted at the cloud of bugs around him. He strained his ears, but heard only the rustled laughter of leaves. Crazy people thought they were sane, too.

"Derrik!"

The voice was achingly familiar but as elusive as an insect hovering behind his ear. Derrik stood and walked deeper into the trees until he came upon a clearing. As soon as he saw the people waiting for him there, he stopped dead in his tracks. There were his parents!

24

Lizard Village

Derrik tried to yell but couldn't make enough sound come from his dry throat. His parents stared at him. Derrik ran forward, faster and faster, and then stopped. His mother was yelling his name, he was sure of it, but her lips weren't moving. Her cold blue lips stayed in a rigid line. Her eyes didn't move, either. Mist swirled high enough to block the trees, isolating the three of them. Willan Sparks repeated his son's name, standing rigid as stone. Derrik tried calling out again, but he couldn't make enough noise.

Two more voices added to the cries. Tweaks and Ssaska appeared out of the mist behind his parents. He could hear them plainly, but they didn't move. More and more people called out his name, imploring him as they appeared out of the mist. He wanted to help them, but every time he tried to get close to someone, they seemed to move away. Then he saw why. There were strings attached to each person's arms and legs like strings on a puppet. The strings tightened and the people began moving backward, calling for help, pleading for him to save them. The voices grew louder and louder. Derrik tilted his head back, his gaze following the lines clear up to the sky where a skull-etched silver mask on a tall, skinny figure moved the strings that bound his friends and all the pleading, motionless strangers.

"Let them go!" Derrik yelled.

The mask only grinned its skeletal grin down at him, and the man behind it showed no sign that he'd heard. As he moved all the people away from Derrik, their voices faded, replaced by loud, hollow laughter that sent cold shivers of dread through Derrik's body. He knew the man was after him.

Suddenly more afraid than ever, Derrik looked for some place to hide from the tall masked man, but the man chased after him, calling, "Derrik, come join my family." The man grabbed him and tied strings to his hands and feet. They pinched terribly. Derrik felt himself being led back to the crowd, but he didn't want to go. Struggling against his bonds, he tried to run, but the tight strings held him securely.

"Derrik!" This time Tweaks's voice alone called to him. "Wake up, Derrik. Come on, please wake up."

Derrik opened his eyes and saw a face covered with red scales looking down at him. "Ahhhh!" he screamed.

Tweaks's face appeared next to the reptile's. "Derrik, it's all right. These are friends."

Derrik's panicked gaze slid to another strange face, bright green and baring white fangs that gleamed in the sunlight. Then Ssaska's familiar dark green face appeared. Derrik realized with a start that Ssaska looked rather handsome in comparison to the other lizards. "It's all right, Derrik," Ssaska said. "We're among friends."

Derrik sat up, his head spinning. The dark red reptile scowled at him and raised an alarmingly bright yellow frill that looked like a jagged strip of leather circling his head. The reptile was gripping its upper arm with a clawed hand.

"What's wrong?" Derrik asked.

"You cut Kram," Tweaks said. "You were yelling, and he ran over to help, but you slashed him with your knife."

Derrik looked down to see the snake dagger clutched in his hand, the blade smeared with blood. He dropped it. "I'm sorry," he said. "I must have thought you were the puppet man."

"What are you talking about?" Tweaks asked, his face full of concern.

"In my dream," Derrik said. "It was creepy."

Kram blinked leathery lids over bulging eyes.

"Not that you are," Derrik hurried to say. "I didn't mean you at all, I meant that there was this tall guy with a silver face in my dream. He was chasing me."

"It's all right this time," Kram said in a rumbling voice so low that Derrik felt the ground vibrate. "Just don't do it again."

"I won't," Derrik said.

Kram nodded. "In that case, you'll live a longer, happier life."

The red blood against red scales didn't look like much until Ssaska bound it with a strip of cloth from his shirt. The fabric soon camouflaged itself with red blood.

"I'm very sorry," Derrik said. "I didn't know it was you."

"It's just a scratch," Kram said. "Don't keep going on about it."

"Come on, Derrik," Tweaks said, reaching down to help Derrik to his feet. "There's a village up ahead."

"We're going with them?" Derrik asked, wiping his bloody knife on green blades of grass before sticking it back into his belt.

"They saved us," Tweaks said. "After that creature broke us apart, me and Ssaska grabbed hold of the same piece of raft, but we couldn't see you anywhere. The current carried us here, and we washed up on shore. Those reptile men came and got us." Tweaks clapped Derrik on the back, startling him. "We thought you drowned." Tweaks's voice broke, and he swallowed. "After they took us to their village, we insisted on looking for you, so they brought us back to the beach, and here you are!" Tweaks gave Derrik a smile that would have been brilliant except for the piece of green food stuck in his teeth.

"Looks like they fed you," Derrik said. "I'm glad you left prints for me to follow."

"Not ours," Tweaks said, shaking his head. Then he winced and covered his mangled ear. "We couldn't walk at first," he answered. "They carried us." He jabbed a thumb back at the two lizard men and a snake man who stood around Derrik in a circle. "At least we were conscious. But you were delirious."

"What did I say?"

Tweaks snorted. "That you wanted to live. Then you slashed out at Kram, here, before I could finally get you to wake up." Tweaks looked around at the trees and shivered. "I've got a bad feeling. Let's get out of here."

"Where's Clatterin?"

"We haven't seen any sign of her."

The reptile men carried Derrik through the forest to a tall fence made of thick vines. Leaves twisted up the columns of green and fluttered in the slight breeze as though waving a greeting. The gate swung open to show a village carpeted with grass. Bushes snuggled up against the walls of the city, some dipping leafy branches to the ground, some standing with stiff greenery at attention, and some rounded, looking soft as old yarn. Wooden dwellings, thatched with brilliant leaves, hid behind abundant ivy and climbing trumpet flowers. Small blossoms peeked out from between thick leaves and vines.

A strange assortment of scaly citizens stared at Derrik with undisguised curiosity. Some wore solid earth tone colors, like green, brown, or yellow. Others had patterns on their skin, from spots to mottled gray designs to bright blue diamonds or golden arcs on black. A variety of body shapes ran from slender snake people to thick lizards or round turtles. A crocodile woman with worried eyes pushed aside a curtain of luxurious leaves to uncover the opening of a huge hollow tree. She stood aside while the men carried Derrik in.

"You poor thing," the crocodile said through a permanent smile of sharp teeth. Even though her eyebrows knotted in concern, Derrik tensed, hoping that her method of dealing with injured things was not to eat them and put them out of their misery. The reptile men laid him on a broad bench covered with soft greenery, and then they left the hollow tree. Tweaks and Ssaska stayed behind.

"I'll get some cloths and tonic for your skin," the crocodile said, moving toward a doorway at the other side of the tree. "Ssaska?"

"I'll watch him," Ssaska promised.

Derrik waited until the crocodile was gone before he sat up, his head pounding. "What are you doing bringing me to a carnivore?" he demanded. He moaned and pressed a hand to his head.

"Lie down," Ssaska said. "She's not going to eat you."

"She does have big teeth," Tweaks said, his eyes trained on the doorway.

"And all she does is smile with them," Ssaska said. "Didn't she make your ear feel better?"

Tweaks rubbed at his scarred, misshapen ear. "Yeah, it feels better."

"But it still looks like raw meat," Derrik said.

Ssaska's voice was unusually stern when he said, "There's no call to speak unkindly of Desserin. She's doing her best. It appears that you are judging her by her looks, Derrik. You should know better than that."

"Just don't leave me here alone," Derrik begged.

"I won't leave until it's necessary. But get that look off your face before Desserin comes back or you might hurt her feelings."

"Me, hurt her?" Derrik asked, incredulous.

"Yes." Ssaska's answer was firm. He leaned closer to Derrik, and Tweaks moved in to hear. "Desserin was the youngest in her family, too young to know that her father was a cruel crocodile with little love for her mother and none for his children. When he was banished from town, he took his family and got lost. He forced his older children to fish for him, but a terrible storm washed them down the river. Only Desserin, her mother, and one sister remained. In a rage, her father grabbed her sister and dashed her to the ground where she lay lifeless. Desserin's mother screamed for Desserin to run. The last thing Desserin saw was her father's fist heading for her mother's head. Desserin stumbled into the river and was carried downstream. She managed to crawl out, but would have died if a family of snakes hadn't adopted her and brought her to Lycan Island to live."

Derrik was silent.

"You see, Derrik, she knows what it's like to be small and afraid. She would never hurt anyone, unless it was to defend someone weaker. Even then, she would never intend to kill."

"So, she's like a guardian?" Tweaks asked, his face alight with wonder.

"Yes, the truest guardian you could ever have," Ssaska said.

"She really is nice," Tweaks assured Derrik. "It's just those teeth that made me wonder." Desserin clumped back into the hollow tree, her arms piled with bandages, jars, and bottles.

"I'm leaving to discuss travel plans," Ssaska said. His tongue slid out of his mouth and back in again. "You're in good hands, Derrik." Ssaska gave the crocodile lady a little bow and then disappeared.

"I'm Desserin," the crocodile said. "You need to get out of those clothes."

"What?" Derrik clutched his shirt with both fists.

Desserin's scaly eyebrows raised. "I know, it seems strange to me, too. But your skin is not adapted for long exposure to water, and your clothing is wet. So take it off."

"It's all right," Tweaks reassured Derrik. "See?" He stood up and stuck his arms out, showing off a shirt of thin green fabric that shimmered in the dimness of the tree. His new trousers were made of something thick, soft, and brown. "They make the pants out of pounded bark," he said. "The shirt is from dragonfly wings mixed with milkweed silk and some other stuff. It's really comfy." He flapped his arms. "I'm going to try making some when we get home."

As soon as Derrik was in dry reptilian clothes, which he had to admit felt as comfortable as they looked, he endured Desserin's doctoring with salves and ointments and a dose of some liquid that tasted like stinkweed. With surprisingly gentle hands, she wrapped a bandage around his hand and the half-healed wound on his palm. Her reassuring voice was unfailingly kind.

Once Desserin was satisfied that he was healing properly, she gave him broth with some kind of seeds softened by boiling. As soon as he started eating, his stomach roared that it was too hungry to wait for spoonfuls, and Derrik ended up drinking the soup, swallowing the seeds whole.

"My, my," Desserin said, her voice disapproving, but her smile frozen in an expression of friendliness. "Would you like more?"

"Yes, please," Derrik said, holding out his bowl.

"You don't feel any discomfort?" Desserin poked a green claw toward Derrik's stomach.

"Oh, no, it's very comfortable," Derrik said.

Desserin brought him a chunk of speckled bread with the second bowl of soup. Derrik ate it as quickly as he could while trying to act like he had good manners. The bread had an interesting tang to it, which Derrik thought must come from the generous sprinkling of spices and herbs that gave it its mottled look. When he was finished, he smiled at Desserin. "That was so good," he said. "Thank you."

Desserin's eyes smiled along with her mouth. "I'm glad to see you liked my insect bread," she said, jabbing an elbow toward Tweaks. "He was not so appreciative."

"Insect bread?" Derrik asked, his smile fading.

"Yeah," Tweaks answered, his eyes sparkling. "All those little flecks of black are bits of bugs. I used my eyeglass to check it out before eating, but you're full of protein now!"

"You need rest," Desserin said, pushing against Derrik's chest with her claw until he was lying flat on the bench. Then she pulled an incredibly soft blanket of woven feathers up to Derrik's neck.

"But I'm not tired," Derrik said.

"You must be," said Desserin.

"Maybe a little," Derrik admitted. "But I can't sleep."

"You haven't even tried."

"I want to walk around before I go to sleep," Derrik said.

"I'll watch him," Tweaks offered.

"Well," said Desserin. "It's not typical, but what do I know about your race? You're the first smooth skins I've ever seen."

"We'll be all right," Tweaks said. "Come on, Derrik."

"Thank you again," Derrik said as he slid off the bench and followed Tweaks out the door.

The boys soon came upon a marketplace, full of the sounds of soft hissing as the sellers and buyers negotiated over such delicacies as live mice, roasted eels, and lobsters large enough to feed Derrik's family for a week. The variety of reptile people nearly made Derrik dizzy. Their clothes showed various shades of forest hues, including soft pinks, dusky reds, and deep blues that mirrored forest flowers. Some had tails dragging on the ground, some sported large spines all over, some had heavy brows, some had no chins, some waved extra limbs, and others had thick, bony head plates sticking out over their shoulders like bonnets. A couple of reptile people with brilliant green frills running down their backs glided down a tree trunk and landed gracefully beside a stall to buy some fruit.

As much as Derrik stared at the creatures around him, he met curious reptile eyes looking back at him. He was startled by a tug on the hem of his shirt and whirled around. He had to lower his gaze to see the pale green face of a small turtle-like boy with a moss-green shell fixed to his back and tiny horns growing from his bald head. As soon as the child had Derrik's attention, he asked, "Where have your scales gone?"

"I don't have any," Derrik replied. "I'm a human."

"What's human?"

"I have no scales." Derrik held out his arm. "Feel it."

The turtle boy touched Derrik's arm with one claw. His scaly forehead creased. "Does it hurt?" he asked.

"No. Not any more than your scales hurt you."

The turtle boy gave Derrik a lipless smile, then joined his turtle parents. The father gave Derrik a little wave, and then turned his shell and walked away with his wife and son.

"Derrik! Tweaks!" The boys turned to see Ssaska moving toward them through the crowd. "What are you doing out here?"

"We just wanted to look around," Tweaks said.

Ssaska took them each by an arm and propelled them back

the way they had come. "For your information, not everyone here is as nice as Desserin."

"Why would anyone have anything against us?" Derrik asked. "Well, except for Kram."

"Most reptile lycans would give you the benefit of the doubt," Ssaska said. "But there are some who would have a quarrel with you simply because you are warm bloods."

"Warm bloods?" Derrik asked.

"He means mammals," said Tweaks.

"Oh." Derrik was silent for a moment. "Well, this warm blood is ready to get out of here and find my parents."

"You feel well enough to travel?" Ssaska asked.

"I'd feel better on the road than staying here any longer."

Ssaska let go of the boys' arms and walked between them, casting frequent glances to either side. "We are on an island about halfway across the water to the necromancer's palace," Ssaska said. "As soon as we find someone willing to take us the rest of the way, we'll leave."

"And do you know of any such willing creature?" Derrik asked.

Ssaska sighed. "If he exists, he lives by the water on the other side of the island."

Derrik tensed. So much time had already passed since his parents were stolen. Was there any time left to save them? His words came out in a shout. "Isn't there anyone in this village who will help us cross the water?"

A couple of orange and black spotted lizards glanced at Derrik over their shoulders, shiny black eyes narrowed in disapproval.

"Sh," Ssaska hissed. "There isn't anyone else. This village does not take to the big water. Other lycan species inhabit this island too, each with carefully drawn boundaries, and little trade between them. The mammals do most of the sailing, but they hate cold bloods. If they were the ones who'd found me on the beach, they would have thrown me back to the sea monster. So even if you could find mammals who agreed to take you, they would never let me on their ship."

Derrik's heart dropped. "No other lycans sail?"

"No," Ssaska explained. "There is a boar village with more tolerance of reptiles, but they think sailing is a waste of time. Bird lycans don't bother with it because they fly, and we reptiles don't sail because we swim. The only exception is Flavak."

"How far is it to Flavak?" Derrik asked.

Ssaska flicked his tongue up at the sky. "Two or three days."

"I'm ready to go," Derrik said.

"I can't go with you," Ssaska said.

"What?" It was Tweaks who spoke, staring at Ssaska with unbelieving eyes.

"You don't want to come?" Derrik asked.

Ssaska shook his head. "I can't. We'd have to travel through all the lycan villages. It wouldn't be safe if I'm with you."

"We could walk around the towns," Tweaks suggested.

Ssaska shook his head. "The territories extend to the water, so if we avoid the towns, we'll be suspected of spying. We could be thrown in prison or worse. Believe me, my presence could be the end of us."

Derrik's shoulders knotted. "Please! We need your help to get into the palace."

"I'm sorry," Ssaska replied.

Derrik's brows lowered. "But there must be some way to reason with these lycans."

"There is an annual council of villages," Ssaska said. "That is the only time there is complete peace. But we can't wait for that. And without an express invitation to visit, you're taking chances."

"Then we're in the same danger as you," Derrik said.

"Not quite. The boar and mammal villages should accept you as mammals, and birds get along fairly well with peaceable mammals. I am not welcome anywhere but here."

"How are we supposed to get to the palace?" Derrik's voice was bitter.

"I don't know. Maybe Clatterin will return and help you." Ssaska's eyes closed for a moment, and then he opened them, his gaze fixed on Derrik. "I hope you understand that I will do more harm than good."

"We're dead without your help," Derrik said bitterly. He dashed a hand at his eyes and scuffed his shoe against the ground, coating a pebble with dust. He stared at the little lump of dirt before him, then stood up straight and studied Ssaska intently. "What if we disguise you? We'll cover you with a cloak and say you're sick so no one will get near you."

"We'll rub furs on your skin to make you smell like a mammal," Tweaks added, jumping up and down. "We could even hide a dead animal under the cloak to disguise your scent."

Ssaska shuddered. "I don't know—"

"Come on," Derrik said, heading back toward the marketplace. Tweaks grabbed Ssaska's hand and followed. Using coins borrowed from their rescuers, they ended up buying a couple of dead mice, a fistful of untanned rabbit skins, and a large wool cloak that was especially hard to find. It covered Ssaska from head to foot and had a couple of inner pockets for holding fresh mice corpses and rabbit skins.

Then they took inventory. They'd lost a lot while escaping the sea monster, but they still had a scimitar, Derrik's knife, one crossbow, five bolts, and a water skin for each of them.

The three traveled back to the hollow tree where they sat down at Desserin's table and studied a large wooden plate of bugs and grubs with small fruits here and there. Derrik gave Desserin a grateful smile and daringly picked out several fruits to eat. He soon claimed he was so full from eating before, and now so tired that she hustled him off to bed, leaving Tweaks staring at his squirming dinner.

25

Boars

Their journey across the island started early the next morning. They shouldered lightweight food packs provided by their rescuers. They all carried water pouches. Tweaks wore a soft hat that covered his ears.

"Thank you," Derrik said, eyeing Desserin and the lizard men. "I don't know how I'll repay you, but I will."

Desserin put a claw on his shoulder and looked into his eyes. "Saving your family and your own skins is payment enough. Now go, and find your parents." Tweaks gave Desserin a hug, something he'd never volunteered to do for Derrik's mother.

The travelers started down the road. "We should reach the boar village first," Ssaska said from beneath the deep hood of his cloak, "unless we get lost."

"If they're friendly to reptiles, do you really need to wear your cloak?" Derrik asked, his belly twisting at the sight of the dark-robed form, even though he knew it was Ssaska.

"They're not really friendly," Ssaska said. "They've been known to ally with cold bloods, when it has been in their own interest. I don't think you have time for them to stop and question me." Derrik plodded on in silence.

Suddenly, a familiar whirring sounded overhead, and the travelers tipped their heads up to see Clatterin spinning through the sky toward them. She dropped to the ground and reformed her bones into a lizard shape.

"Where have you been?" Ssaska asked.

"Up there." Clatterin pointed toward the sky. Even if she wasn't already smiling, Derrik could hear the smile in her voice.

"That's not what I mean," Ssaska answered with no trace of humor.

"Well, I couldn't very well drop down into the lizard village to say my 'how do you do's,' now, could I?" Clatterin asked.

"But you're a lizard," Derrik said.

"Was," Clatterin corrected him. "Now I am a pile of animated bones."

"Which is what we may be if we don't all remember that boars are easily insulted," Ssaska said. "Don't stare or plug your nose. They take any challenge, real or imagined, very seriously. Do not test their friendliness." He pulled his hood back and gave the boys a meaningful look, keeping their gazes until they nodded understanding.

After walking a little further, Ssaska whispered, "Can you see that?" He pointed ahead. Derrik looked up to a sign that made him shiver. No words were on the menacing picture of a boar goring some large animal with its tusks. Skulls of several different animal species decorated the sign. Derrik thought he recognized the head of a large cat, a gorilla, many monkeys, and one that looked like an enormous human skull.

"It's the boundary marker," Ssaska said. He pulled up the hood of his cloak. "This begins boar territory. We are required to leave an offering of peace at the sign to show we mean no harm." Up close, Derrik saw that a battle picture on the sign showed a boar fighting a cat with two tails and narrowed eyes. The cat in the picture was much bigger than the ones Derrik had seen.

"Do those creatures really get that big?" Tweaks asked.

"Yes. We were lucky to run across small ones."

"I will not go on with you," Clatterin said.

Three pairs of eyes stared at her.

"I would create more problems." She spread out her arms. "How could you explain me? But I want to help." A half dozen of her smallest bones peeled away from her body and curved around one another, forming a woven half circle as big as a plum. "If I may place these bones over your ear, I will translate what I can for you." The strange earmuff spun slowly in the air, awaiting permission.

"I'll wear it," Tweaks offered.

"Good," Clatterin said. "It will be much better concealed under your hat." The little bone cage disappeared under Tweaks's hat. He stiffened.

"Do not worry," Clatterin said. "It will stay, and will not hurt you. I will meet you on the other side." Then she folded into a spider and spun off into the sky.

"Be quiet now," Ssaska said, leading the way to the sign. He pulled out the largest rabbit skin and placed it at the base of the sign on top of a huge pile of treasures, which included skulls, jewels, pictures drawn on skins, odd stones, and a large variety of shells and offerings from the sea. When they moved past the sign, Derrik almost expected a large boar lycan to jump out and gore them, but nothing happened. Tweaks gripped the handle of his sword.

"Let go, Tweaks," Ssaska whispered through dry lips. "They may take it as a challenge."

Tweaks let go. Several yards down the road, they saw a boar man with matted brown boar hind legs, but a fur-covered waist and torso of a muscular man. Its head was that of a boar, bristling with thick hair, the mouth growing two tusks at least six inches long. The flat brown nose quivered, picking up their scents. Two tiny black eyes seemed to search for the slightest reason to attack the strangers. An axe hung from his belt and he clutched a spear in one hand. The boar man spoke in a voice that was more like a grunt, "I'm Brontis, guardian of the gate," he announced proudly. "As such, it is my duty to question you on your purpose and origin." He gave a small snort.

Everyone was silent, until a voice almost smothered with coughs and sniffles said, "Tell him." Derrik had to look around to assure himself that it was Ssaska who spoke. The snake man was bent over. He waved his cloak-covered hand toward Derrik.

Derrik straightened and faced Brontis. "I am Derrik," Derrik replied, "and this is Gerret," he added, pointing to Tweaks. "This is Efta," he said, motioning to Ssaska. "He is sick and cannot talk."

"That still leaves me with the problem of origin," said the boar. "From where do you hail, human?"

"A small town called Bylon."

"You are far from home," Brontis said. He glared at them, one by one, sniffing the air. Derrik felt a trickle of sweat between his shoulder blades and fought the urge to reach back and scratch it. He remained still, standing as tall as he could.

When Ssaska gave another cough, Brontis's broad face creased with anger. "We want no sickness in our midst!" he raised his weapon and aimed it at Ssaska. "Be gone with you! Go back from where you came!"

Derrik stiffened. The boar man could easily take his head off with one swipe of his axe. Mixed with fear was his despair at the boar's order to return to the far side of the island, opposite from where they needed to go.

Brontis took a step toward Ssaska, his spear pointing out in front of him. If something didn't happen fast, Ssaska was in danger of losing his disguise.

"It is not a sickness that can be shared," Tweaks blurted.

Brontis's eyes narrowed in suspicion. "How is that so?"

"It's enchantment," Tweaks said.

"Magic?" Brontis's eyes grew wide, and he darted a fearful look toward Ssaska's hooded form. "Whose magic?"

"The necromancer's."

Brontis licked his hairy lips. His voice went soft with pleading. "Do not draw the necromancer to this place."

"The only reason we pass through is so we can fight him," Derrik said.

Brontis gave the travelers a single nod, his fearful eyes shifting back and forth between them. "Very well," he said at last. "I find no fault with you, so you may pass. But pass through quickly." The boar man stood aside. They walked beyond him on a path leading through a rough wooden gate, garishly decorated with carved spirals of wood on other wood spirals that curled out and up in a dizzying variety of sizes. In between the spirals, figures of boars showed vicious, open mouths displaying tusks of various thickness and length, including a broken tusk or two.

The village itself was quite different from that of the reptiles'. Instead of a bright marketplace with various colored citizens moving through the stalls, this town was quiet and still. Gray and brown buildings lined the streets where boar people moved slowly, hardly glancing at the swirls and spirals on all sides, which were similar to the ones on the tall village gates.

"Tweaks, that was brilliant," Derrik whispered.

"It wasn't me," Tweaks said. "Clatterin's bones told me what to say." It was strange to think of Tweaks hearing voices from dead bones, but Tweaks was the happiest he'd been since his ear was mangled.

As they walked along the main road, it seemed that every boar stopped and stared at them. Derrik gave his water bag a nervous squeeze. It was nearly empty.

"Tweaks, do you have water?"

Tweaks lifted his water skin. "Just a swallow."

"We'd better get water," Derrik said. "I don't know how long it is until the next town."

"Water?" a gruff voice said from beside them. Derrik turned to see an old boar-headed woman with wrinkly ears peering at them. "Did you say water?"

"Yes, ma'am," Tweaks answered. "But if you want some, we're sorry. We don't have any. We were looking for some."

"I can help you," she said, snorting a little. "You see that tavern?" she pointed down the street to a dusty tavern. "You can get water there."

"Thank you," Tweaks said, touching the brim of his hat.

"You're welcome," the boar woman said. Then she trotted down the road.

Derrik moved closer to Ssaska. "How's your water?"

Ssaksa shook his bag, showing it was nearly empty. "Let's go get them filled up."

"I can't," Ssaska said.

"Why not?"

"The smell. I can barely stand it out here, but inside four walls? That would knock me out."

"It doesn't smell that bad to me," Tweaks said, giving the air an experimental sniff.

"I'd rather wait outside," Ssaska said. "There's an alley beside the tavern where I won't draw attention to myself." He tightened his hood as Derrik led the way into the smoky tavern with Tweaks at his heels. A fire pit sat in the center of the room, its low curb built out with bits of brick. In a far corner, six boars sat at a round table, snorting and squealing over some playing pieces in their hands. The odor of mud mixed with the smoke, and a sickish sweet smell that Derrik couldn't identify swirled past his nostrils. He didn't like it here. The only good thing was that no one seemed to take much notice of them.

At a nearer table sat three boars, puffing on a long spiral pipe that held a smoldering rolled leaf. They regarded the humans lazily through the haze of smoke. Derrik walked past them toward the bar, and was nearly there when two boars jumped up from a gaming table, glaring at each other over the scarred wood. The pure black boar with shiny tusks was the biggest Derrik had seen. He scratched his hoof across the floor with bone-jarring force. "Lantis, you cheat."

The smaller boar's long, bristly brown hairs stood out like quills, and he had only one tusk. "Perhaps the god of the hunt smiles on me, Cutter!"

"No one wins ten times in a row with cubes like yours!" Cutter retorted.

Before Lantis could reply, Cutter lifted the table straight off the floor and brought it down on Lantis's head, breaking the top in half. Lantis staggered and then fell, his hooves scrabbling against the stone floor. Derrik recoiled as a small wooden cube rolled to his feet. He stared down at a colored carving of a red-eyed black boar's head with several small animals running beneath it.

Cutter gave a snort of anger and turned the broken table top upside down, revealing a small tray fixed to the bottom that held five more playing pieces with the same markings as Derrik's. "I knew it—"

Cutter's accusation was cut off when Lantis pushed straight off the floor and rammed his head into Cutter's belly, twisting his head up to gouge Cutter with his tusk. Cutter spun away and then turned back and grabbed Lantis by the ears. He steered him to the door and threw him out. Cutter's hooves clattered across the floor to the bar. "Sorry for the damage, Grufnak," he said. "Keep the money we played with to pay for it."

"Much appreciated," replied Grufnak. "And, Cutter, I didn't know—"

"I understand. You didn't know he was a cheat," interrupted Cutter. He strode over to a different table and sat down with two boars for another game of wooden cubes. Instead of checking under the table, he stared at the other players who swiftly moved their arms to the tabletop, their hands far from the edge.

"Come on," Derrik said. "The sooner we're out of here, the better." Tweaks's knees buckled, and Derrik gripped his arm. "Stand up," he whispered through clenched teeth. "Act like you're not afraid."

"Let's just leave," Tweaks begged. "I'm not thirsty."

"All right." Derrik turned with Tweaks toward the door and headed for it.

"Hey!" Grufnak called. "You don't come in here for a free show without buying something!"

Derrik stopped. His feet felt like rocks, but he managed to turn and look at the grizzled boar behind the counter. "We only came in for water," he murmured.

The boar man put a hairy hand behind his ear. "What? I can't hear you pip-pip-pipping over there like a mouse. Come closer."

Derrik noticed that Tweaks still faced the door, so he took hold of his shoulders and turned him around. They carefully picked their way through the wood slivers and hair on the floor and over to the bar. "Excuse me," Derrik said quietly. He tried a smile, but only got a cold stare in return. "We need water. Please." Derrik swallowed, but his throat was dry.

"Ha!" Grufnak barked. "So, the bare skinned humans come begging for water. What do you take us for? Livestock?" Grufnak leaned forward and jutted his whiskered jaw toward Derrik. "We don't have use for weaklings or water here. We drink Nectar and Hax."

"Sorry." Derrik glanced at Tweaks, who hunched his shoulders and stared back. "I don't know what those are," Derrik said, turning back to face the bristling boar.

Grufnak spoke distinctly, as though Derrik were simple minded. "Nectar, human, is a gift to us from the god of the hunt. Hax is a strong boar-made drink. Those are what we serve here, human."

"We have no money," Derrik said. "Only this dagger." He held out the snake man's dagger.

Grufnak thumped his hairy hand on the counter and shouted, "What use is that to me? I want good boar money, not an ugly reptile knife. And no one leaves my place without a purchase, especially not humans!" His thin lips curved around his tusks in a menacing smile. "You can use that scrap of metal to play for money." Before Derrik could answer, he raised his voice and shouted at the gaming tables, "Make room for another."

Derrik shrank under the scrutiny of all the boar men who looked up at him. His head pounded. He was afraid to play this game of wooden cubes that he knew nothing about. If he lost, he didn't see how they'd get out alive. If Cutter clopped him on the head with a table, Derrik would never survive. If he happened to win, it might put the boar men in such a foul mood that he wouldn't survive that, either.

Derrik picked up his dagger, slid it into his belt, and started toward the back where the remaining players from Cutter's earlier game had reassembled.

"Come here, human," Cutter snorted. "We need a fourth."

Derrik froze. He dared not ignore the black boar's invitation. His feet reluctantly changed direction and he sidled up to the table where three boar men held their strange little cubes of wood.

"Sit," Cutter said.

Derrik sank down onto the edge of a chair, facing a bowl in the center of the table that held wood cubes with different pictures on the sides. Several square coins of dull metal sat in piles of various heights. They radiated from the bowl like sunbeams. Derrik didn't know what to do, so he sat there, avoiding eye contact.

"Well?" Cutter said, his voice coming from a raspy place way back in his throat. "Are you going to play, or sit there like a wart?"

"Excuse me, I would like to play," Derrik said, careful not to stare at anyone.

Cutter spread his hands, palms up. "No one is stopping you, unless you have no money."

"I don't have money," Derrik said, "but he," he glanced at Grufnak, "said to use this." Derrik pulled his snake dagger out slowly enough that it would not appear as a threat, then set it on the table. The boar men stared at the silver dagger and the curved snake head at the top as though it might suddenly come to life and sink its fangs into them.

Finally, Cutter said gruffly, "Where did a human happen by that?"

Derrik didn't know what to say. If he said he got it from a snake man, it could very well ruin his friend's cover. His fighting experience would be no match for this many boars.

Cutter pounded the table. "Tell us how a human came by a wretched necro snake's dagger!" he roared.

Derrik jumped. "I killed it," he shouted, his heart pounding in his chest so hard that it hurt. The tavern fell deathly silent. Cutter stared at the knife and then back at Derrik's pale face. "You killed one of those serpents?" Cutter asked slowly.

Derrik darted his eyes to the side, looking for Tweaks, but

Tweaks stood directly behind his chair. Derrik licked his lips. "Yes," he answered, picturing the dead snake men in the giant's camp. It was partly his fault that they had died.

Cutter's mouth split into a jagged grin. "Maybe there is more to you humans than I thought," he said, slapping the table. He reached out and slid the knife to the center with one finger. "That should do for fifteen flavins." He looked at the other two boars. "Any in?"

"I am," said the silvery gray one, throwing some coins in the center of the table.

"That's fine, Tak," Cutter said, nodding his head.

"I don't know how to play," Derrik said.

"It's very simple," Cutter said. "We each draw ten cubes from the bowl. The ones with an X on them are worthless. The ones with a skull are one point, the ones with two skulls are two points, the ones with a hand on them are worth five points, and the one with the god of the hunt are worth ten points." Derrik recognized the "god of the hunt" cube. It was the same one that had fallen at his feet, so detailed it almost looked like the panicked creatures across the bottom were real.

"Whoever gets the most points wins," Cutter finished. He held out the bowl to Derrik, who counted out ten cubes and looked at them all. He had twenty-six points total, made up of two twos, two fives, two ones, and a ten. The other three showed zeros.

Cutter finished passing the bowl to the other boars. Then he turned to Derrik. "Oh, yes, human, you have to exchange two from your hand for new ones. You pick which two." Cutter rattled the bowl.

That was easy. Derrik would exchange two zeros. So he set two zeros off to the side and reached into the bowl for two more cubes. He drew out a five and a one. Now he had a total of thirty-two points.

"Lay them down," Cutter commanded.

Every player laid down their pieces. "Thirty, twenty, twenty-two, and thirty-two," Tweaks called out from his place behind Derrik's chair. "Derrik wins."

Tak jumped up so fast his chair crashed to the floor. Pointing a grimy finger at Tweaks, he cried, "The human cheated! He looked at our scores before we laid down!"

"No!" Tweaks protested.

Derrik twisted in his chair and saw Tweaks's face pale with dread, one hand on his eyeglass as it tilted off his nose.

"I didn't—please— " Tweaks began, but Tak cut him off.

"Then how did you know them?"

"I added them up when you laid them down," Tweaks said.

"Impossible!" Tak squealed. "No one can do it that fast. Somehow you cheated, you little worm!"

"Is this true?" Cutter asked, his dark eyes fixed on Tweaks.

"No!" Tweaks said. "I can do it again! Just try me!"

"Is this a challenge?" Cutter asked.

"Yes," Tweaks squeaked.

"Good. If you'd said 'no,' you'd be dead." Cutter reached into the bowl. "And if you fail, you will be dead." He pulled out a handful of cubes and laid them out in a row of five cubes, picture up.

Before Cutter removed his hand from placing the last cube, Tweaks spoke up. "It equals thirty-six." Cutter carefully counted the cubes, three boar heads, a hand, and a skull.

"Again," Tak demanded. Cutter reached in and pulled out more cubes. This time he threw them onto the table.

"Twenty-six, not counting the two face down," Tweaks said quickly. Derrik did his best to suppress a sudden urge to smile at the amazement on the boar faces. It took them a little while to calculate the fifteen cubes scattered across the table. Six twos, four ones, a ten and two X's stared up at them, besides the two lying face down.

"It appears that the human did not cheat," Cutter said, not sounding particularly happy about it. "But at least this human has snake killing skills."

Derrik stood and carefully scooped the coins into his hand. Tweaks picked up the dagger and they headed for the bar. "I'll buy Nectar," Derrik told Grufnak.

"Fifteen flavins," said the barkeep.

Derrik took several coins from his hand and asked, "Are these flavins?"

"Yes," Grufnak huffed. Derrik dropped them on the bar and took a bottle full of amber liquid from Grufnak. When they turned away, Grufnak growled, "What is the small one buying?"

Derrik slowly faced the bar again. "How much is Hax?"

"Ten flavins," said the barkeep. Derrik dropped the coins on the bar as Tweaks sidled over to the bar and timidly took a bottle of thick green liquid from Grufnak. Then the boys hurried to the door and nearly ran into Ssaska, who leaned against the carved door jamb.

26

Bird Men

"I heard everything," Ssaska whispered. "I almost blew my cover when that boar accused you of cheating. It's a good thing he thought highly of you for killing a necro snake."

"Then you know we didn't get water?" Derrik asked.

"Yes." Ssaska touched the empty water pouch at his belt.

Tweaks tipped his head. After a moment, he said, "There's water just outside the village gates."

Derrik's brow furrowed. "How do you—? Oh. Never mind."

Tweaks grinned and tugged at the edge of his hat.

Derrik turned and strode down the path, ignoring stares from boar people, and eager to put this village behind him. When they walked away from the boar village gate, Clatterin whirled into view. She landed beside them, but kept her spider shape.

"Thanks for your help," Tweaks said.

"You're welcome," Clatterin answered, stalking along on her long, bony legs. "The water is just inside the forest."

"Why did they settle so far from water?" Derrik asked.

"It runs underground through their village," Clatterin said. "There was water in the tavern. Grufnak just wanted your money."

The travelers filled their canteens and drank deeply. Clatterin waded into the stream as Ssaska wiped the dripping water from his chin. "The bird lycan village is next," he said. "They hate reptile lycans as a whole, but are much nicer to mammals." He pulled his hood so far over his face that Derrik wondered how he could see. "If I keep silent, we should be fine. Everybody ready?"

Derrik replayed the terrifying time he had spent in the tavern. "Are you sure the birds are friendly to mammals?"

"That's what I was told," Ssaska said. "Why don't we go find out?"

Clatterin rose out of the water, her legs spinning, showering the others with drops of cold water.

"Hey!" Derrik cried. Clatterin let loose a crackly laugh, then disappeared into the sky.

They started down the path toward the bird lycan village, walking through deep forest that abruptly ended at the edge of a plain. The travelers paused, staring out over the flat where slender water plants traced the path of the river with a deep green line. Out on the plain stood the gleaming white walls of a city. The path led right to it.

"Well," Derrik said. "At least we can't be ambushed."

Tweaks snorted. "Birds fly, Derrik. We could get attacked from above."

Derrik tensed, casting frequent glances upward as they made their way along the path, but they reached the eggshell-smooth walls of the bird city without any trouble. Two magnificent eagle statues guarded the gate. They each had two muscular arms in front of their mighty folded wings. Tails fanned out from behind their stout legs, and three long talons curved out from each foot. The statues were perfectly matched in size and coloring. As the travelers drew nearer, Derrik was startled to see the statues turn their heads and look over the visitors with round, intelligent eyes.

"They move!" he gasped.

"They're not statues," Tweaks said.

Derrik expected some kind of interrogation, but the eagles simply extended their wings toward the gate and let the three travelers pass through.

"That was easy," Derrik whispered.

"Too easy," Tweaks said, looking over his shoulder at the

large birds. "I have a bad feeling about this."

"They're friendly," Ssaska hissed.

A nearby ostrich jerked his head around and stared at the cloaked Ssaska with a suspicious eye. Ssaska pulled his cloak tighter and strode on.

The birds' village was much like the reptiles', with a lot of activity but full of bright colors more varied than the reptile town. Many different species of birdmen and birdwomen walked through the streets, chatting and buying goods from stalls, such as beads, exotic bird seed, colorful balls, seashell head ornaments, and beak polish. One bird man in particular, with a peacock head and tail, was very stunning.

No glum stares greeted visitors here. As they walked down the street, they actually received several cheerful greetings. There was a lot of entertainment on the streets, not just from the vendors, but also from street performers. Several birds ran on colorful barrels in an amusing performance along the side of the street. Some presented acts on a trapeze strung up overhead. A bird magician stood in one corner of the marketplace, making bouquets disappear and reappear with wide flourishes of his wing. At the edge of the crowd flitted a small man with the head and wings of a hummingbird. As the magician did a particularly complicated flourish, the little birdman darted out a slender arm and snatched a pouch off a crane man's belt before darting away. He was a thief!

"Stop!" Derrik shouted, but of course the hummingbird didn't. He just kept moving away from the crowd.

The crane man turned toward Derrik, his startled eyes looking out from a wrinkled face creased with age and sparse on feathers. "That man took your pouch!" Derrik explained.

"Oh dear, oh dear," said the old man, fumbling with stiff fingers at the place where the pouch had hung, while his wings fluttered feebly up and down. "Is all I have in this world!"

Derrik knew what it felt like to lose everything. "Stay with him," Derrik shouted to Tweaks. Ssaska couldn't run well in his long cloak, and it would be deadly for him to show his scaly flesh, so Derrik took off after the hummingbird man alone. The little man glanced over his shoulder at Derrik, then fluttered his wings and lifted into the air. Derrik kept running as fast as he could through the crowd. A couple of times he lost sight of the hummingbird man, but then he would catch the flash of iridescent blue and be back on the trail of the small body with the rapidly beating wings.

Before long, the hummingbird man darted into the window of a smooth brown building made of mud packed tight and glossy. Its doorways and windows were artfully framed in polished sticks. Derrik dashed in through a door and found himself in a long hallway with closed doors on either side of him.

"Ah," came a creaky voice from behind the door on the right. "Let's see what you've brought me this time."

Still fueled by anger, Derrik pushed the door open. The room was dim. A voice called from one corner, "Millicent, you useless excuse for a cleaning bird! You're early! Come in an hour, when you're supposed to!"

"Excuse me?" Derrik said.

The coat rack in the corner moved when a tall man dressed in black threw his head up from between a pair of hunched shoulders and stared at Derrik in surprise. Derrik gasped when he saw that the coat rack was really a man with the head of a vulture.

"What are you doing inside my home, you rude young man!" shouted the old bird, hobbling toward him.

"Sorry, sir," Derrik said, taken aback by the vulture man's anger. "But I followed a thief in here. You must have seen him."

"A thief in my home?" the vulture waggled his head, making the loose skin sway. "Posh! You should leave, human, before you find more trouble than you can handle!" He was a bad liar. Now Derrik knew that the vulture was in league with the hummingbird.

The vulture stopped just a few feet from Derrik. He was rather frightening, with his sharp hooked beak; bald, wrinkled head; and mean black eyes. Derrik shuddered. He wanted to leave, but the memory of the old crane's tearful eyes made him speak. "Please, sir, I just want the pouch."

"I warned you, human!" shouted the vulture as he drew a small curved stick from inside his long coat. Derrik looked at the stick with a puzzled frown. It wasn't thick enough to do much damage if the vulture intended to beat Derrik with it. Derrik was certain he could snap the stick in two if he got his hands on it.

The vulture raised the stick and shouted some garbled words. A cloud of black smoke shot out of the wand and stopped in mid air. Then it shaped itself into a child-sized head and body with pudgy arms and legs. The cloud receded, leaving a little black demon with long white teeth, claws, and horns, who fell to the floor with a thud. At first it looked rather confused. But then the old vulture pointed to Derrik and cried, "Attack!"

An evil grin crossed the demon's face. It leapt up and ran at Derrik, arms outstretched. Derrik instinctively kicked at the demon, sending him flying through the air to hit the opposite wall. There was a loud *pop* and it disappeared.

"Drat!" the vulture screeched. "I forgot how old that spell was." He shook his strange little stick. "No matter, I have other tricks!" He pointed his wand at Derrik, who dodged, but the stick followed him as the vulture said, "Millipin swa —" before he was seized with a fit of coughing. Derrik dodged the other way, just missing a bright orange light shooting out of the wand to bounce off the wall behind him and singe his shirt with sparks.

"Drat!" the vulture yelled. "I'm getting rusty!" He shook his wand in a frenzy, launching more orange lights with every lunge. "Millipen swaddlein!" he screamed over and over.

Derrik ducked behind a couch. He saw, too late, that the hiding place was already taken by the hummingbird man. Derrik tried to stop, but knocked the birdman over that sent him sprawling into a somersault. Pillows spilled off the couch and a lid popped off a tipped woven basket and rolled across the floor, narrowly missing a bolt of orange light that hit the hummingbird man smack in his chest. He was small to begin with, but when orange sparks shot out through his arms and legs, he shrank even smaller and landed on the floor next to Derek.

"Drat and double drat!" shouted the old vulture. Derrik stared at the hummingbird man in amazement. He'd shrunk to the size of a bumblebee and was bound with tiny ropes.

Derrik crouched, his hands on the floor. He touched something and was startled to realize that it was the crane's money pouch. Derrik grabbed it and fastened it tightly to his belt. Now how would he escape? If he stuck his head out, he might be shrunken in a zap of orange sparks. When he saw a pillow that had fallen partially behind the couch, he had a desperate idea. He grabbed the pillow and threw it out to one side of the couch and then scrambled out from behind the other side.

"Millipen swaddlein!" From the corner of his eye, Derrik saw a burst of orange sparks bounce off the pillow just before it shrank from sight. Derrik made a dash for the open door by the vulture, which startled the old bird so much that he held his wand out in front of him like a forgotten toy.

Derrik suddenly changed course, leaping for the stick. He grabbed it and aimed at the vulture. "Millipen swaddlein!" he shouted. The stick vibrated in Derrik's hand. Orange sparks shot out the end, spraying the vulture. He shrieked and shrank to the size of a kitten, his arms pinned at his sides by rows of tiny ropes. "Drat it all! Confound it! Curse you!" his angry little voice rose from the floor.

Derrik slumped, his breath coming hard. He had the old crane's pouch, which was all he had wanted in the first place. But this wand could be useful. There was something else he needed to know. Kicking the basket aside, he picked up the squirming vulture man and brought him close to his face. "What is the reversal spell?" he demanded.

"Why should I tell you?" the vulture snarled.

"Because I'm bigger than you," Derrik said, raising the wand with his other hand and pointing the end toward the vulture.

"Stop!" the vulture man screamed. "Don't make me disappear! Haven't you done enough already?"

"It doesn't seem so," Derrik said in a hard voice.

The vulture glared at him before saying, "You reverse the

spell by pointing the back of the wand."

"Is that all?" Derrik asked, turning the wand in his hand and pointing the back end toward the vulture. "Do I say the words now?"

The vulture squirmed in fresh panic. "No, don't!" he shrieked.

Alarmed, Derrik nearly dropped the birdman, but managed to hold on. "What is it?" Derrik asked. He moved to the basket and held the vulture over the opening. "Tell me, or I'll drop you in the basket and say 'mil—' "

The vulture man whipped his head to one side and sank his small beak into Derrik's finger. Derrik gasped and opened his hand. The vulture hung on for a second before losing his grip and falling with a *thud* into the basket. He landed on his back, staring up at Derrik. "You have to say the words backwards, you rude boy, or else whatever you're pointing at turns inside out."

Derrik stared at the ceiling, his mind working on the sounds. Slowly, he said, "Nileddaws nepillim?" Pink sparks shot from the wand, striking the small couch pillow on the floor. It bloomed back to its original size. "Thank you," Derrick said with a polite nod. Then he turned away.

The vulture struggled to his feet. Even though he couldn't jump high enough to reach the basket's edge, he jumped up and down, yelling, "Aren't you going to change me back?"

"Since you appear to be fond of picking on those weaker or smaller than you, I think you need to stay just as you are," Derrik said. He bent, scooped up the hummingbird man, added him to the basket and clapped the lid on. The prisoners yelled and thumped, but Derrik wasn't worried. Even if they managed to untie each other, they wouldn't be able to lift the lid. The cleaning woman should have no trouble finding them when she arrived.

"Curses on you, rude young man!" the vulture man yelled.

"Stealing is not a good profession," Derrik answered. "Think about that while you await freedom." Derrik pulled out the remainder of his boar flavins and dropped them beside the basket with a clatter.

The thumping stopped. "What was that?" the vulture's small voice asked.

"Payment. This wand is much too dangerous in your hands."

The vulture sputtered and squawked as Derrik walked out of his house and worked his way through the crowd of colorful citizens. The crane was sitting on a bench beneath a dark green tree that fairly dripped with puffy pink flowers. Derrik saw Ssaska raise one cloaked hand in greeting from his place in the shadow of a nearby tree. Tweaks stood next to Ssaska.

"You got pouch?" the crane man asked, his old eyes hopeful. Derrik laid it in the old bird's lap. "Oh, much thanks, you splendidy boy!" he exclaimed. "How to repay such a deed?"

Derrik's face grew hot and he squirmed. "I don't need anything. Happy to help."

"I not let these go unrewarded, no. Does you have place for sleeping? No?"

"No," Derrik said. "We must go now."

"Go where in the dark?" the crane man asked, bending forward and rising slowly to his feet. "Dark streets are no place for staying. Come home, just for this night."

"Derrik, it's all right," Ssaska whispered.

Derrik turned, surprised to see that Ssaska and Tweaks had moved up close behind them. The crane cast a dubious look at Ssaska. "Him with you?"

"Yes," Derrik answered.

The crane stared at Ssaska's cloak for a long moment. "What's wrong with him?"

"He's a friend . . . who could be misunderstood."

Ssaska spoke in a low voice. "I mean you no harm, kind sir."

The crane bowed his head, then looked up and spread his hands. "If no harm, then you come." He led the way to a tall, thin building with smooth, deep purple walls. Inside, ornate archways led between rooms. Pictures decorated the walls, both paintings and three-dimensional works done with braided grasses, leaves, and sticks in a variety of intriguing designs. The beautiful fabric-covered furniture shimmered in the fading light slanting through the windows.

"Your house is great," Tweaks said.

"Thank ye," the crane answered. "Once was rich, but now is gone. My home is old, but happy for it. Please to sit and feed."

In spite of his bandaged hand, Derrik insisted on helping the crane man get four cups of sweet honeysuckle dew and a plate of ripe berries from his pantry. Tweaks carried the food to the sitting room. The old crane blinked at Ssaska. "You may remove cloak." When Ssaska hesitated, the crane man asked, "You so ugly, then?"

Ssaska answered slowly. "Some think I'm the enemy when they see my face."

Tweaks nodded. "We thought so at first."

"If him good to you, then him good," the crane man said, settling back in a tall backed chair and sipping his dew. "Please, be comfortable."

Ssaska hesitantly raised his hands and slowly lowered his hood. The crane man's cup froze in midair while he took in the snake face. Then he blinked and lowered his cup to a side table. Shakily, he rose to his feet. "Me never smelled you," he said. He glanced at Derrik, then Tweaks. "Good disguise. I go to bed now. You leave first thing in morning, yes?"

"Yes," Derrik said.

Ssaska sighed.

The crane man disappeared behind a polished white door. A lock clicked into place, then all was quiet.

"Maybe we should leave now," Derrik said.

"No," Ssaska said, his voice weary. "We need rest." The travelers found a bedroom with a big bed as round as a nest that dipped down in the middle, and a couch curved like a quarter moon in one corner.

"We shouldn't stay long," Derrik said, stretching out on one side of the big bed. It was as soft as downy feathers. As he stretched out, it molded to the shape of his body. His eyelids grew heavy. "As soon as the sun comes up, we should go."

Ssaska claimed the couch. "That's a good idea. We should leave before the town wakes up."

"Hey, where am I supposed to sleep?" Tweaks said.

"Just climb on the other side of the bed," Derrik murmured. "I'm so tired, I won't even know you're there."

"What happened when you went after the crane's pouch?" Tweaks asked, landing on the bed so hard he nearly dumped Derrik onto the floor. Derrik sighed and sat up. He told them everything that happened and pulled the wand from his pack so they could see it.

"You sure that thing's magic?" Tweaks asked, reaching out to touch the dry, bent stick.

"Appearances can deceive," Ssaska said.

Derrik pushed open the rose-colored glass of their bedroom window and leaned out. He plucked a leaf as big as his head off a nearby plant and placed it on a table. Unsure if it would work again, Derrik aimed the stick at the leaf and said, "Millipen swaddlein!" Orange sparks flew, and the leaf shrank to the size of a fist.

"Wow!" Tweaks said, pulling out his glass and peering through it.

Ssaska leaned in closer. "I see the bindings," he said.

"Me, too," Tweaks said, his voice full of excitement. "Who would've guessed?" He looked at the magic wand with new respect. "I wonder if that old vulture will ever get back to normal size."

Derrik yawned. "I don't know. If he got one magic wand, I suppose he could get another."

"No matter," Ssaska said. "Let's get some sleep."

Before long, Tweaks and Ssaska lay still and quiet. Derrik listened to their measured breathing. He longed for sleep but stayed awake. It wasn't because of the bed, which was probably the best he'd ever laid his head on. He couldn't sleep because he was afraid of what he would see if he did. The memory of his forest nightmare was still perfect, every part so detailed it was like he had actually been in the dark clearing with all those people, his friends, family, and strangers.

Finally exhaustion won, and despite his fears, Derrik slept.

27

Nightmares

A sound almost too quiet to be heard roused Derrik. He turned over in the soft nest and opened his eyes. Ssaska stood in one corner of the room, looking out the brightening rose window. Derrik sighed and rolled over. Tweaks was merely a lump under a blanket on the other side of the nest. Derrik stretched, delighted to find there was no pain or fatigue. He couldn't remember the last time he'd been so rested. Except for village celebration days, he'd never felt so ready to get up in the morning. He sat up and swung his legs out of bed.

"Good morning," Ssaska said. "I was just about to wake you. The sun is rising."

Derrik glanced at the deep, glowing pink of the rose glass in the window. He reached over, laid his hand on Tweaks, and shook him. "Come on, time to get up," he said.

Tweaks didn't move.

Derrik shook him again. "We need to go, Tweaks."

Tweaks remained still.

Derrik's brow creased with sudden concern. He put both hands on Tweaks and nearly rolled him out of the nest. "Tweaks!"

No response. Derrik glanced up at Ssaska, who stared back at him, his eyes unreadable. Derrik grabbed the blanket and pulled it off his friend.

It wasn't Tweaks. A tall, skinny man dressed in blue robes

swirling with rich black designs lay there. He wore a skull-like etched-silver mask. It was expressionless, with two holes where the eyes were supposed to be, but nothing was inside them.

Derrik opened his mouth to yell to Ssaska for help, but before any sound came out, the masked figure raised a skinny black-gloved finger and held it to the stiff mouth on the mask. Derrik felt tightness close around his throat, and he couldn't breath. He couldn't call out or make a sound.

A deep voice laced with evil amusement said slowly, "Shhh, Derrik, you mustn't wake Gerret." Hollow laughter began softly but grew louder as the other hand appeared from the dark robes, holding strings attached to a little puppet that was Tweaks.

"Help me, Derrik," the little Tweaks called, but his mouth stayed still.

Horror coursed through Derrik, and he shivered, still unable to breathe or speak.

Then the masked figure started pulling Tweaks away from Derrik, laughing without moving his masked head in the slightest.

Derrik looked up at Ssaska, horrified to see him tied by strings, and being carried away by a silver masked figure. He looked back at the bed. The figure was gone, the bed untouched.

Ssaska's voice whispered a plea, "Help me, Derrik! Help!" yet Ssaska's face was as motionless as the silver mask of his captor. His pleas slowly faded, only to be replaced with uncontrollable hollow laughter.

Derrik jerked his head back and squeezed his eyes shut in a violent effort to free his throat from whatever power held him silent and breathless. He thrashed so hard he suddenly struck the floor. His eyes flew open. He sucked in breath and sat up, panting and grasping the side of the nest bed with fingers that still spasmed in terror. Through the open rose window, Derrik saw the sun barely peeking over a distant mountain. Derrik jumped to his feet and turned to see Tweak's red curls lying against his pillow. Tweaks snored, his hand curved by his face and his red ear scabbed and bumpy.

Ssaska sat up on the crescent couch and stretched his arms over his head. "Have you been awake long?" he asked.

"No," Derrik sighed, relieved to have woken from the horrible nightmare. "Tweaks, you lazy boy, get up," he said, pulling the blankets clear off his friend. He was half afraid there would be a silver mask hidden somewhere in the blanket folds, but it was just a blanket.

They left their room with their backpacks on. Ssaska had the robe over his shoulders with the hood flung back. They found bowls of toasted grain, flower petal salad, and worm cakes laid out on the table, but there was no sign of the crane man.

"I didn't expect this," Ssaska said.

"Well, he didn't expect you, either, did he?" Tweaks said. Ssaska pulled his hood over his head before stuffing some of the food in his pack. The boys did the same, then carried the rest in their hands, eating as they stepped outside. They pulled the eggshell door closed behind them.

Only a couple of brown and gray bird people hurried along the street as the travelers made their way to the gate at the far side of the village. Both guards standing there had sleek black crow heads. They raised their arms to the visitors in farewell.

As they walked down the path, Derrik's thoughts slid unwillingly to his too-real nightmares. He didn't even notice Clatterin's approach until she was walking beside him in her distorted lizard form.

"You are troubled," Clatterin said.

"I keep having nightmares," Derrik said.

"Of him?"

"Not just the necromancer," Derrik said. "It's other people, too, even them." He gestured to Ssaska and Tweaks. Then he ran a hand across his brow and continued, "Everyone wants me to help them, but I can't do anything. The man in the silver mask always wins."

Clatterin was quiet a moment. Then she said, "He wants you to believe there is nothing you can do."

Derrik shivered. He suddenly felt as cold as if Tweaks had

just shoved a snowball down his back. "The necromancer is in my mind?" He grabbed his head in both hands.

"He can send dreams," Clatterin said. "That is all."

Derrik dropped his arms. "That's bad enough."

"Yes," Clatterin agreed. She took a few clacking steps, her grinning mouth silent. Then she said softly, "Don't let him get your soul, Derrik."

"Thanks," Derrik said. "What would I do without you?"

Clatterin shook her head. "You would be fine. I wish to be gone from here, to truly move on, as death is intended to do."

Derrik regarded her solemnly. "You don't seem dead."

"But I am. What you see is the souls of others forced upon me."

"We're sorry, really," Ssaska said, coming up behind them. "But there's nothing to be done for you now."

"True," Clatterin inclined her head. "We must first reach the necromancer. Then we can do something about it."

"We've been fortunate thus far," Ssaska said. "But we must keep in mind that the furries are far more cautious than the boars and birds."

"Furries?" Tweaks asked.

"All the mammal lycans besides boars," Ssaska said.

"Why don't the boars live with the mammals?" Tweaks wanted to know.

"The mammals see boars as filthy and brutish because they enjoy lots of drinking, fighting, killing, and yelling, whereas the other mammals enjoy a calmer lifestyle with things like sailing and dancing. This mammal village will take a keen interest in finding out as much as they can about us."

Derrik nodded. "I think I've got our story straight."

"You may have to improvise," Ssaska said. "Mammals are strange creatures."

"Hey!" Tweaks said. "We're mammals." He waggled a finger between himself and Derrik.

Ssaska let out a choked hissing noise that sounded strangely like laughter. "I know."

The first sign of a nearby town was the odd smell of fire mingled with wet fur. A plume of smoke rose up, accompanied by the sound of drums.

"Time for me to go," Clatterin said. She paused and reached out to touch Derrik's shoulder. Her hand felt like a tree branch resting there. "The necromancer can only suggest. He cannot truly get inside your mind, Derrik—not unless you let him." Then she was gone, whirring away into the sky.

Ssaska pulled the hood over his features, covering himself completely.

"It's a good thing the odor from the village is so strong," Derrik said.

"I don't think so," Tweaks argued.

"It is," Derrik insisted. "It makes it more likely the mammals won't smell the reptile beneath the fur."

"Don't bet your life on it," Tweaks said.

"Lycan mammals have a greater sense of smell than any other creature," Ssaska whispered. "Quiet now."

They silently approached the city gates, stained dark red with something Derrik was pretty sure wasn't paint. Snake skulls decorated the front of the gate like broken teeth in a giant set of gums. Derrik noticed spots of color scattered on the wall around town. When Derrik looked closer to see what they were, he suddenly drew back in horror from the different colored reptile skins nailed to the red-streaked wood. A large sign declared in bold, black lettering,

NO Scalies or Featherheads Here!

Derrik took a deep breath. If he had ever wanted to circle around a village, it was this one. But he didn't want to arouse suspicion. Ssaska said that going through was safer, and it would be faster, too. He could hardly wait to get off this strange island of townspeople who did not get along with their neighbors

Two guards flanked the gate. One was a female with the head, feet, and tail of a lioness. Two hoop earrings swung from each ear as she turned her yellow eyes on the visitors. A long, silver claymore swayed at her side.

The other guard was an enormous male grizzly bear. His weapon was a huge double-sided axe. He studied the travelers with his hard brown eyes, the fur over his eyebrows twitching as he sniffed the air. Derrik's skin flinched as he passed the bear, with Ssaska beside him and Tweaks on the lioness's side, but they weren't challenged as they entered the village.

In spite of the mid-day hour, a giant bonfire roared in the middle of town. Orange flames leapt skyward as if wanting to join with the sun. Several mammal lycans danced around the flames, fox ears twitching, cat tails swaying, and paws and claws clapping or waving overhead to the sound of drums.

At the far side of the fire, an elephant lycan leaned against a wall, his huge arms folded. Derrik's gaze went up and up until he saw the elephant man's broad face shining in the light of the fire. The elephant must have been nine feet tall. His dark eyes, set in two wrinkled circles of gray skin, studied Derrik with such intensity that Derrik felt compelled to stop and stare at the elephant's huge white tusks, ending in decorative metal guards at the tips. His round legs continued down to feet with three huge toenails each, and his trunk fell down from between his eyes to hang within his tusks past his huge waist. He wasn't fat but he was wide enough that his height would have seemed normal if he hadn't been standing among lycans so much smaller than he.

Tweaks must have noticed the lycan, too, for he mumbled, "And I thought the bear was big."

Derrik didn't answer. Everything else seemed unimportant. The elephant's gaze burned hotter than fire through the flicker of flames. Derrik felt exposed and alone. He was the only one alive besides this massive lycan. The sounds of drums gradually faded into the distance until all sound was gone. Derrik couldn't tear his eyes away, even though he felt the elephant searching, relentlessly probing with some invisible trunk-like thing sliding around Derrik's head, gathering all his thoughts into the center. Then Derrik heard a quiet voice inside his head, low and nasal. "Why are you here?"

Unbidden from his mind, a higher voice replied. "We come for my captured family and that of my friend, Tweaks."

"They are not here," the nasal voice rumbled.

"I know," said the higher voice. "They were taken by force from our village by snake men riding dremi. They took our families and left burning destruction behind. My friend and I followed them into the forest, and there we found one of them, an enemy, wounded when his comrades pushed him off a dremi."

Derrik was horrified at the little voice in his head telling everything, a funnel for all of his thoughts, channeling them through the elephant's probe. Derrik couldn't let the elephant know they'd befriended Ssaska. He desperately tried to stop his thoughts, to pull his eyes away from the elephant's gaze, but he couldn't.

"And what became of this snake man?"

Derrik steered his thoughts toward the giant's capture. The high voice told of hanging upside down, of the snake men's attack, of Ssaska joining in their forces. The high voice was nearing the part where Ssaska allied with the humans, ready to tell that he'd become their friend and was traveling with them. Derrik had to stop it. The elephant could not know. But Derrik stood frozen to the spot, his gaze captured by the huge dark eyes staring at him from the other side of the fire. Tears welled up in Derrik's eyes. Ssaska was going to die, and it was all his fault.

28

Magnus

Suddenly, Tweaks's face popped up in front of Derrik, making him stumble backwards and blocking his view of the elephant man. Tweaks's eyeglass made one eye appear twice as worried as the other.

"Derrik!" Tweaks shouted, his face full of concern. Tweaks reached out and shook Derrik. "What's wrong with you?"

"I'm okay now," Derrik blurted, turning his head and wiping his eyes. He felt the invisible probe weaken and slide from his head.

Tweaks's eyebrows rose, and his eyes clouded with suspicion. "You're crying. Are you hurt?"

"No." Derrik said, carefully keeping his gaze away from the elephant.

"Clatterin's earpiece told me you were in trouble."

"I'll tell you about it later," Derrik whispered. "Come on."

Tweaks reached up one hand to the back of his head and stuck his fingers under the hat to rub his red curls. Where would Derrik be without his friend? If Tweaks hadn't broken the gaze, Derrik could be dead or dying at this very moment, after witnessing Ssaska's death. Derrik shuddered at the thought of a handsome dark green skin added to the collection of reptile skins nailed to the wall.

The village seemed to go on and on as Derrik led the way through. He expected to feel a restraining hand on his shoulder at any moment and flinched at the slightest sound. He hurried faster when he thought he heard the tramp of angry feet behind him, certain the elephant man wasn't satisfied at having his interrogation interrupted. His breath came heavy through his open mouth. His eyes were fixed straight ahead. This had to be the longest village they'd crossed so far. He wiped sweat from his brow. Would it never end?

At last, Derrik spied another gate in the village wall. He burst through, startling the spotted jaguar guard nearest him.

"Halt!" the guard snarled.

Derrik cowered, Ssaska froze, and Tweaks moved to Derrik's side. Standing tall beside his friend, Tweaks faced the jaguar. "What have we done wrong?" Tweaks demanded, his voice only squeaking once.

The jaguar looked over at his guard mate, a fat rhino with a single sharp horn splitting his vision. The rhino tipped his head so he could look Derrik over. Not getting any help from the rhino, the jaguar turned back to the travelers. "You are in a hurry," he said.

"Is that against your law?" Tweaks asked.

"It depends on what you're hurrying from," the jaguar sneered.

Then the rhino spoke, a surprisingly jolly sound coming from his thick gray mouth. "Isn't it obvious, Timony?"

The jaguar whipped around to face the rhino. "What do you know, Borba?"

The rhino nodded at Derrik. "He's been interviewed."

The jaguar's eyebrow whiskers rose a quarter inch. "You mean . . . ?"

"Certainly. Don't you remember the first time Magnus caught you with his gaze?"

Timony lowered his head and stared at the ground. "Some things I wish I could forget."

Borba nodded. "If Magnus weren't our wise man, he'd be a terrible foe." The rhino lycan lifted his huge mace and pointed it at the three travelers. "If Magnus found no cause to stop them, then why should we?"

Timony nodded in agreement. "So be it. You can hide nothing from Magnus, as you well know."

Tweaks looked from one guard to the other, his brow furrowed with confusion. "What are you . . . ?"

Derrik suddenly collapsed to the ground with a moan loud enough to drown out Tweaks's words. His body landed heavy against Tweaks's legs, making Tweaks stumble sideways. "Derrik!" Tweaks called, kneeling beside his friend.

"There's a fresh water stream just past that bend," Borba said, swinging his mace in the direction of the path leading away from town. "Maybe you should take your friend and stick his head in it."

Ssaska glided forward and bent down on the other side of Derrik. Together, Tweaks and Ssaska lifted Derrik to his feet and supported his stumbling steps to the bend in the path. As soon as they were out of sight, Derrik straightened and hurried forward on his own two legs.

"Hey!" Tweaks said. "What are you trying to pull?"

Derrik whirled around and stood with his hands clenched. "If they knew you hadn't had your brain probed like I did, they might have taken you back to that elephant thing."

"Magnus."

"Magnus, then. If you'd looked into his eyes, he would have read your mind, everything that was in there."

Tweaks rubbed the back of his neck. "Everything?"

"Everything," Derrik shouted. "Including everything about him!" he pointed at Ssaska.

"Sh!" Tweaks grabbed Derrik's hand and pushed it down. "They might hear you!"

Derrik lowered his voice. "I didn't want them to know you hadn't had a mind probe, so I collapsed. It was all I could think of to do."

29
Rigor Mortis

Clatterin waded through the water to meet them, her long toes camouflaged against the white stones in the streambed. Derrik dunked his head in the water, scrubbing his scalp with his fingers.

"Are you really all right?" Tweaks asked.

"It feels like he's still in there," Derrik said.

"I felt a disturbance in the bones I left with Tweaks," Clatterin said. "It was as if the necromancer was nearby."

"The guards talked about this mind probe thing," Tweaks said, "and Derrik was acting strangely."

"There's no one in your head," Clatterin said. "It's just a residue of the mind probe. You need to think of something else."

Derrik raised his head, water dripping into his eyes. He blinked, set his jaw, and said, "I'm thinking of getting my parents back. Now let's go find Flavak before the sun goes down."

"Well said," Ssaska whispered. And they set out for the shore.

Further down the trail, they approached a fork in the road with no signpost to tell them which way led to the sea. Two men sat on chair-sized rocks on opposite sides of the road from each other, almost as if they each guarded a different path. Strangely enough, each man had a dark blindfold tied around his head, and they both held long staffs that rested against the ground.

"They're blind," Tweaks whispered.

The man on the right turned his head. "It appears that the wind has a voice today, Mortis."

"Shut up!" Mortis answered. "I should have listened when wiser voices told me to stay away from you, old, lying Rigor."

Ssaska threw back his hood. Derrik stepped forward. "Excuse us," he said, "but do you know which path we take to the one named Flavak?"

"No, I don't," Mortis replied grumpily.

"Hobble wash! You are a liar!" Rigor shouted.

"Ain't no such thing!" shouted Mortis.

"There you go again, ya old bag of bones!" Rigor said.

"No, you're the liar, lying about me lying!" Mortis protested.

Without a word, Clatterin changed shape and went whirring off into the sky, heading down the road past the forks.

The old men fell suddenly silent. Then Mortis shouted, "What was that noise? Did you just pass gas?"

"No," Rigor yelled back. "That was you!"

"I think I would know if I passed gas, you old liar."

"You wouldn't admit to it, would you, old fossil?" Rigor shouted.

"It smells like you!" Mortis insisted.

"You're just an old tub brained, bug biting, bad breathed bathoon!" yelled Rigor.

"Oh, yeah? Take this!" Mortis threw a rock directly at Rigor's head. Rigor yanked his staff up crossways in front of his face. Derrik saw something small and round reflecting a dewy shine on the end of the staff just before the rock bounced off the staff's center mere inches from Rigor's face.

"So you're getting stick fancy, you flabbery, fat faced, farty brain!" Mortis said.

"Excuse us again," Derrik interrupted, "but we need to get to Flavak's house."

"Don't expect that old coot to tell you the truth. He always lies!" Mortis yelled.

"I do not!" Rigor protested. "That old bat over there is the liar!"

"Derrik, let's just move on," Ssaska said.

"Well, which way should we go?" Derrik asked.

"I don't know," Ssaska answered. He raised a hand to rub his forehead, green scales gleaming in the late afternoon sun. "Clatterin should have told us where she was going before she took off, so we'll just choose a path. All this arguing is giving me a headache."

"Excuse me," Derrik said to Rigor and Mortis. "May I ask each of you a question?"

"Fine by me," huffed Rigor.

"You liar," shouted Mortis. "It's fine by me. You're all tangled up about it."

"Am not!" yelled Rigor.

"Okay, just keep quiet a minute," Derrik said. The two men sat and waited. Derrik asked, "Do either of you know which way it is to Flavak's home?"

"Don't listen to him, he will lie, that's all I know," Rigor said.

"Why, you liar, you," Mortis said.

Ssaska flung his cloak back over his shoulder and grabbed the hilt of his sword.

"Ah, Rigor, the serpent man has a sword," said Mortis.

"Ha," Rigor answered. "He thinks that just because we are blind old men he can frighten us with a scimitar, eh, Mortis?"

"You are both liars," Ssaska hissed angrily. "You aren't blind!"

"Ah," Rigor said. "We cannot see as you understand sight, but we can see in our own way."

Mortis clapped his hands. "Well put, Rigor."

"Well, Mortis, I can see that these three are going to bring us no joy," Rigor said. "What say you to a little rest?"

"Ah, Rigor, another fine idea," said Mortis.

In unison, the two men floated up a few inches and rotated on their rocks to face away from the travelers, all without uncrossing their legs. When they landed again, they changed color and grew a knobbly texture. Within seconds, they both had turned to stone.

"That was very odd," said Tweaks.

Derrik stared at the two sentinels of stone. He shivered as

though a chill wind had blown across his neck, even though the air was warm and balmy.

"Let's go," Derrik said. "If we choose the wrong path, we can always come back." He didn't really believe his words, but he wanted to get away from these two strange pillars.

"How will we choose?" Tweaks asked.

Derrik shrugged. "I don't know. Might as well close our eyes and point."

A piece of dark fabric fluttered down from Rigor's stone pillar.

"What's that?" Tweaks asked, looking closer at the fabric. "A blindfold?" Tweaks darted a look at the stone men, but they sat as still as death.

"Here comes help," Ssaska said. Bones whirred. Clatterin glided in and hovered over their heads. "Take the right hand fork," she said in a breathless voice. "I saw a reptile lycan by the water in that direction."

"You got here just in time," Tweaks said.

Clatterin tipped her head. "I know."

The four of them started walking, leaving the blind stone men behind. Clatterin lagged behind as they made their way toward the ocean. "Are you all right?" Tweaks asked.

"Yes," she huffed. "It's just that I'm not used to being broken up for long. If I don't have all my bones together, it takes more energy for me to move."

Tweaks quickly uncapped the bone muff from his ear. "Here," he said. "I think Ssaska will be able to talk to the reptile with no problem."

Clatterin scooped the bones up in her thin white hands and tucked them into her throat.

"Let's just hope I know the right words to say," Ssaska said.

Before long, they heard the *swish, swish* of the ocean. Rounding a stand of trees, they came before an old wooden hut barely standing straight. Three boats sat before it like pupils before a teacher, and out on the water a larger boat rocked with the waves.

"This is where I saw him," Clatterin said. She folded up small and hunkered down in the grass. Ssaska pulled up his hood. When they moved to the door, Clatterin skittered along behind them on the tips of her bones.

Derrik knocked on the door. There was no answer, so he pounded his fist against the weathered wood. "Hey!" he called. "Anyone home?"

A scuffling noise sounded from around the house.

"What's that?" Tweaks asked.

"I hope it's who we're looking for," Derrik said.

Ssaska trailed the other two as they made their way around the house, keeping close to the walls. Clatterin scampered along behind. Derrik peered around the corner and then stepped out into the open. Tweaks and Ssaska moved out to stand beside him while Clatterin crouched in the grass. A reptile lycan with the head, tail, and skin of an alligator stood with his back to them. It looked like he was working to free a net tangled around his foot.

"Excuse me," Derrik said. "Are you Flavak?"

"Eh?" the alligator raised his bumpy green head and squinted down his long nose at his visitors. "What do two humans and a snake want with Flavak?" he asked, yanking the net free of his foot so hard it tore. "I can smell you through the mammal stench," Flavak said. Ssaska threw back his hood.

"Are you Flavak?" Derrik repeated.

"Yeah, yeah, that's me. Curses, you made me tear my net. What are you bothering me for, anyway?"

"Uh, well, we want to hire you and your boat," Derrik said.

"Do I look like I'm running a ferry?" Flavak yelled.

"No. It's just that you're the only lycan who can take us," Derrik explained. "The mammals won't because we're with a reptile."

"What, ya think that just because I'm a reptile lycan I'll help you?"

Derrik shrugged. "We hoped so. You're the only one we know of who sails, besides the mammals."

"I am." Flavak stood up and swung his tail from side to

side. "But like I said, I don't run a ferry here. I sail because I like it."

"We could pay you," Derrik said, sliding off his pack to dig inside. "We have flavins."

Flavak's laugh was harsh. "Ha! Boar money! What good is it to me? What good is any money? I never go to town."

"We could give you food," Derrik said, pulling a bird seed cake from his pack.

Flavak looked at the cake, with its pretty mixture of different colored seeds, as though Derrik were trying to feed him goat dung. "I get my food and everything else I need from the sea. You couldn't possibly have anything that interests me."

Derrik lowered his seed cake and bumped the pack, tipping it on its side, showing the neck of the Hax bottle. Flavak stopped still, staring at the bottle as though he'd been turned into a statue. After several long moments, he asked slowly, "Is that Hax?"

"Yes." Derrik pulled it out so Flavak could see for himself. "From the boar village."

"I know where Hax comes from!" Flavak snapped. His eyes stayed on the bottle. Then he said, "Well, ya know, I might be able to take you for the Hax. It's been a long time since I had that, a very long time." He darted a look at Derrik. "You sure it's boar made?"

"Yes," Derrik replied, not bothering to hide his eagerness. "So you'll give us passage for this?"

"Yeah," answered Flavak, bending to sweep the bottle out of Derrik's hand. He twisted the lid off as easy as if it were made of warm wax. A strong, grass-like scent, though more bitter, filled the air. Flavak took a big swallow of Hax, then lowered the bottle and sighed. "So, friends," he asked. "Where do you want me to take you?" He raised the Hax to his mouth again.

"The badlands," Derrik said.

Flavak coughed and sputtered. "What in the name of everything do you want to go to the badlands for?"

"We have business there," answered Derrik.

"Sorry," Flavak said, pushing the cap back down on the Hax

bottle. "I don't go there for anyone. Take it back." He pushed the Hax at Derrik.

Derrik clasped his hands behind his back. "You said you would take us!" Derrik's voice came out harsh as he battled the rising lump in his throat. He blinked his prickling eyes.

"Yeah, but I never thought you'd say the badlands," Flavak said, shaking his big green head. "You looked sane to me. Why would I want to go to a place full of nothing but rocks and demons?"

Ssaska stepped forward and plunged his hand into the pack. He drew out the other bottle. "Here, we will give you this also," Ssaska said, holding out the Nectar.

Flavak's eyes grew twice their normal size. "Oh, you are cruel. That's Nectar, I suppose." He blinked. "Yeah, no mistaking it. You've got the two things I can't get from the sea," he said, his eyes soft.

"All you'd have to do is drop us off and then be on your way again," Derrik pleaded.

"Just drop you off, huh?" Flavak looked from one traveler to the other. "Then leave you there?"

"Yes," Derrik said. Ssaska and Tweaks nodded. "Then forget us," Derrik added. "We will find our own way back."

Flavak stood a long time, staring and thinking. Finally, he said, "You have a deal. But we must land in the dark."

"Agreed," Derrik said quickly.

Flavak looked at the sky. "We can pack up and go before the day is gone," he said. "Come on. If we're going, let's not put it off."

While Flavak brought the larger boat to the dock, Clatterin scampered inside Tweaks's pack. When Flavak was ready, his three passengers carried everything they had on board. "Is that it?" Flavak asked.

"It's all we have," Derrik said.

"Hmpf," Flavak said. "We might as well go then. There's just one more thing." He extended his arm to a trunk on the deck and reached his big green claws inside. He pulled out a huge bull's head. It dangled in mid air, the horns waggling back and forth on either side of a pair of black, empty eyes.

Tweaks screamed.

"Now, now, little curly one," Flavak said, giving him a look of reproach. "There is no need to afflict my ears with that sound. This is a costume." His other hand dove into the trunk and came out with a pair of furry brown pants, complete with wooden hooves attached to the ends of the legs.

"What is the meaning of the mammal costume?" Ssaska asked, flicking out his tongue.

"In case we meet any furries," Flavak said. "I have lots of disguises." He stood back and waved the others toward the trunk with his thick green arm. "Go ahead. Help yourselves. Better to be ready than ambushed."

Derrik looked into the trunk and was slightly nauseated by the sight of tumbled heads and body parts mixed together. He moved some things aside and pulled out a light colored wolf mask. He soon found the furry brown pants that matched, and pulled them on. Tweaks had a hard time with the larger costumes, but a gray rat head settled onto his shoulders in relative comfort. It took Ssaska the longest to choose. He reluctantly settled on a porcupine mask, complete with wooden quills.

"Ah, the porcupine," Flavak boomed through his bull's head. "Here, this goes with that." Flavak leaned over the trunk and pulled out a shirt with wooden spines attached to the back. Ssaska rolled his eyes and let out a loud sigh.

"Come, come, now, don't worry, it's really rather comfortable," Flavak said.

When they finally got Ssaska into the shirt, Derrik was amazed at how much the snake man looked like a real porcupine. Tweaks scurried around as though the rat costume had become his second skin. Derrik wondered if he looked like a real wolf. From a distance he was sure that no one would be able to tell he was a human.

Flavak adjusted his bull's head. Although the nose on the mask was unusually large, it still seemed a bit small for his long snout.

With their disguises on, the travelers started out for the badlands. It was hot on the ship. The views of ocean and sky were the same relentless blue.

"Can't we take off our masks?" Derrik asked.

"No." Flavak's answer was sharp.

"But there's no one in sight," Derrik protested, "and it's hot in here."

"Then go below decks," Flavak said. His ridiculous bull's head pointed toward the prow as he steered the ship.

Derrik made his way down the narrow wooden stairs. He pulled the wolf mask off, wrinkling his nose at the heavy scent of fish. Breathing shallowly, he sank down on a cot, set in a corner of the dark hold, and lifted off his pack. He leaned against it, grateful to be out of the heat.

Derrik didn't realize he was dozing until an urgent bell sounded. He jerked on his wolf mask and fur pants, then hurried up the wet stairs to the deck. Flavak gave the bell cord a final jerk, waving at a boat of mammal lycans following them. "Just wanted to warn you that we had company," he said, his voice muffled by his mask. "It's probably just a boat of furries that will soon pass." He didn't explain why a boatload of mammals would head for the badlands.

Four or five lycans scrambled all over the rigging in the other boat, pulling on ropes and shouting to one another. Derrik's gaze lowered to the deck, and his stomach clenched. One of the lycans sat behind a giant spear gun—and the spear was aimed at them.

"Flavak," Derrik shouted. "I don't think they're going to pass."

The lycan behind the spear gun motioned to three other lycans.

"They're going to shoot!" Derrik shouted.

"Nonsense," Flavak said, turning to face the pursuing ship, adjusting his bull's head with clumsy fingers. Just then, a long metal spike zipped past him with a *zing* and stuck into the main mast, trailing a long tail of rope that reached to the other ship. "Wha . . . ?" The deck under their feet swayed as Flavak's ship turned broadside. Flavak stumbled closer to inspect the spike. He grabbed hold of the taut rope stretching across the water. "What is going on?" he roared.

With the rope attached, the mammal ship gained on them with alarming speed. Two rat lycans busily gathered up the slack in the rope as their boat drew closer.

"How can they know?" shouted Flavak.

Another spear gun, smaller than the first, rolled up to the prow of the mammal's ship. A small rat jumped on the seat of the gun and turned the spear toward Ssaska.

"Ssaska, watch out!" shouted Tweaks.

Ssaska turned and saw the rat just before he fired. Ssaska pulled off his porcupine head and dropped it over his chest a split second before the spear struck it. He flung the porcupine mask aside as the enemy loaded another spear. This time the rat aimed at the sail. When he shot, he very nearly hit the ropes that kept the sail up, but the spear flew past and sank in the sea.

Ssaska stalked over to the costume crate, ripping off the porcupine shirt along the way. He opened the chest, pulled out his hidden crossbow and bolts, and flung the shirt inside. Then, loading a bolt into the crossbow and pulling back the stock, he aimed at the rat. His bolt hit the mammal with such force that the rat was knocked off his seat and flew halfway across the ship before he landed.

Four other mammal lycans loaded another spear gun and pushed it to the ship's prow. The second rat slid into the empty spear gun seat as the mammal's ship pulled up nearly level with Flavak's.

Ssaska loaded and fired the crossbow again, hitting a horse lycan, knocking him back from the rail. The new rat shot his spear gun and hit one of the sails, making a long tear.

"No!" Flavak screamed. He ran into his cabin, the wooden hooves clacking across the deck, and came back with a long hollow tube and some small red fruits. He yanked off his bull's head and pulled on a thick glove. With his gloved hand, he grabbed a soft fruit and stuck it on the end of the tube. Red juice trickled out, and he stepped back. Flavak brought the tube back, then whipped it forward, aiming at the rat. The berry flew off the end and smashed into the rat's fur. The rat screamed and jumped off the seat, running in little circles, trying to brush the juice off his fur. He turned and headed for the back of the ship, still screaming.

Heedless of their shipmate's troubles, the other mammal lycans shot again, hitting the sail and tearing a longer gash. Ssaska returned fire, shooting two more lycans who soon stopped moving.

A rhino lycan was the only one still on his feet. He calmly loaded the spear gun while Flavak's berry bombs hit his thick hide and slid down, leaving streaks as red as blood.

"His hide's too thick," Flavak muttered.

The rhino shot the spear, which connected with the sail again. The fabric was all but shreds.

"You, boy, run over and pull that long rope on the mast," Flavak ordered.

Tweaks jumped up and ran to the rope, his rat tail sliding across the deck. He gave the rope as hard a pull as he could, and the sail inched up. Derrik ran over beside him and grabbed the rope, adding his strength to help Tweaks raise the sail. Just as they tied it off to a pole sticking out of the mast, the mammal ship hit them, knocking them off their feet. The only one left standing was Flavak.

Abandoning the spear gun, the rhino man lumbered across the deck. He opened a crate and pulled out a hollow, bell-shaped piece of metal covered with big, round studs. He shoved his fist into the bell and ran to the railing. Then, with a cry of rage, he jumped onto Flavak's ship, hitting the deck so hard it radiated cracks out from his huge feet. He lowered his head and turned it side to side, searching for prey. Derrik and Tweaks helped Ssaska up, but Flavak had disappeared.

The rhino's angry eyes focused on the mast. His grim mouth curved into a cruel smile. He lowered his head and charged the mast with thick legs pounding the boat, making it shudder so hard that everyone toppled over onto the deck and Derrik's mask fell off.

The rhino pulled his metal covered fist back and swung it into the mast with such force that splinters shot out in all directions. He looked at the crack for just a moment, then bent his neck and slammed his head into the wood, pushing until the tall mast cracked and slapped into the cabin at the back of the ship, caving in the middle with an enormous crash.

"Use your magic wand on him!" Tweaks yelled.

Derrik swallowed. "It's in my pack."

"Get it!" Tweaks urged.

"It's below deck."

Tweaks groaned. The rhino lycan turned and glared at Derrik through small eyes nearly buried beneath overhanging brows.

Ssaska had his loaded crossbow aimed at the rhino. He pulled the trigger. A long bolt flew out and thudded into the rhino's left shoulder. The enemy jerked, reached up, and pulled out the bolt, leaving a gaping wound that spilled dark red blood down his front. He narrowed his eyes at Ssaska, raised his knobby metal fist, and pounded the deck, cracking it with a loud snap. The rhino let out a snort that made Derrik's hair stand on end and then ran towards his three enemies with his head lowered. They had nowhere to run, nowhere to hide. They stared at the rhino as he drew closer, his blazing eyes growing larger with each shattering stride.

30

Sinking

One stride away from knocking them all into the water, the rhino jerked to a stop, his gaze dropping to a spear point sticking out of his chest. He roared and spun around, the dull clang of his fist guard striking the spear as he made a wild grab for it. Then the rhino tipped sideways and fell to the deck, making the whole boat shiver. His fist guard flew into the air before landing on deck with a *thump*. Then all was still.

Derrik was startled to see Flavak standing on the deck of the mammal lycan's ship behind the enemy's biggest spear gun, water dripping from his snout and shoulders. Flavak glared at the dead rhino, then shifted his dark gaze to Derrik.

Derrik's legs wobbled a little as he walked across the deck to pick up the metal fist. It contained three straps bolted inside for the fingers to grip, and the interior was padded with wool. The outside was scarred with gashes.

Sudden, terrified squeaks pierced the air. Startled, Derrik dropped the fist. Flavak stood on the enemy ship's deck holding a squealing rat that twisted in his grasp. "I'll teach you . . ." he began. Then he stopped and stared with growing horror as his own ship gave a sudden lurch and tilted, groaning as it took on water.

"Come on, Derrik!" Ssaska yelled as he and Tweaks climbed to the high end of the deck and leaped across to the mammal lycan boat. Derrik scrambled up toward the railing, but the ship gave way beneath his feet, tilting more sharply into the water. Derrik crawled as fast as he could, grabbed the railing, and threw his leg over it. He stared down into a gap of roiling sea between the two ships, frothy white peaks snapping like teeth.

"Jump!" Ssaska called. "I'll catch you."

Tweaks stretched his arms out. "Come on, Derrik. Hurry."

Derrik hesitated. If he missed and landed between the ships, their pitching hulls would crush him between their wooden jaws. The ship jerked, and Derrik slipped on the railing. He tried to regain his balance, windmilling his arms, but he could feel himself falling forward as if in slow motion toward the roiling water.

Suddenly, a snake tail lashed around his waist and tightened until he could barely breathe. A scaly hand clamped over his arm and gave a mighty jerk. Derrik flew upward, screaming as the ship he'd been standing on sank with an agonized creak of twisting timbers. Derrik crashed to the deck of the mammal lycan ship and lay still.

"Derrik!" Tweaks yelled, rushing to his friend's side. "Derrik!"

Derrik opened his eyes. Three anxious faces and one angry rat face stared down at him. Ssaska massaged the end of his tail. "You're heavy," he said. "Next time, I'd rather rescue Tweaks."

"Thanks," Derrik said, blinking up at Ssaska. Ssaska nodded, and Derrik sat up. "So one rat survived," he said.

The rat snapped its teeth, a freshly torn ear running blood over an eye, his fur missing in patches where blistered red flesh showed through.

"Leftover mammal scum," Flavak said.

Ssaska let go of his tail and began collecting his crossbow bolts from the bodies of the mammal lycans scattered on deck. He only retrieved four, since the bolt he'd shot at the rhino had gone down with the ship. Then he began pushing bodies overboard.

Flavak shook the rat. "How did you know we weren't furries?" he demanded.

The rat shrank a little and snapped his teeth.

"Tell me!" Flavak roared.

"W-we didn't," the rat answered. "We were told to destroy your ship. That's all."

"Who hired you?"

"It wasn't a hire," the rat lifted his chin, although his whiskers still shook. "It was a mission of honor for the all-knowing elephant, Magnus."

Flavak laughed. "Too bad he didn't know we'd beat you." Flavak shook the rat again. "You are worthless scum, aren't you?"

The rat twisted in his grasp. "My name's Wilfred."

"I don't care. I'm not going to kill you because you may prove useful, but I won't let you go because you know my secret."

"What secret?" Wilfred squeaked. "I don't know any secret."

"You didn't see the bull, the porcupine, the wolf, and the rat on my ship?"

"Oh." Wilfred sagged. "For a minute there, I thought the rat was my cousin Percy." He peered up at Tweaks, his lip pulled back in a snarl. "But when I got closer, I saw I was wrong."

"I can't have you going back to tell all the mammal lycans just how I sail about the sea," Flavak said. "I'm going to lock you up."

Wilfred hung limp in Flavak's grip as the alligator tromped down the stairs into the ship's belly. Finished with the bodies, Ssaska followed, along with Derrik and Tweaks. Flavak stopped at the bottom of the staircase, forcing his passengers to bump into one another on the galley stairs. "Those goons are blocking my light," Flavak growled. "So you tell me, where shall we put you?"

Wilfred lifted a limp paw to point at a doorway on the left. With little hope in his voice, he said, "That's where all the food is."

Flavak opened the door and stared at the shadowy interior. In spite of the bad light, he could make out stacks of crates and barrels. He walked inside and the others crowded in behind him. "By all the gods of the sea, that's a lot of food," Flavak said. "It's a wonder your ship doesn't sink."

The rat shrugged. "Sometimes the Great Elephant travels with us. And sometimes he sends us to follow those who act suspicious when they pass through our village."

Flavak said, "Even if you eat until you burst, which would be doing me a favor, by the way, we'd still have plenty and to spare for our journey." He dropped the rat on the floor. "If you try to chew your way out, you'll drown before the hole gets big enough."

"You're not putting me in chains?" Wilfred asked, his voice thick with suspicion.

"You're not worth the bother," Flavak growled.

Wilfred stared up at him with narrowed eyes.

"Don't try anything," Flavak warned, "or I'll step on you."

"Wouldn't dream of it, oh mighty Flavak, merciless and feared pirate of the sea."

"You are so right," Flavak snarled. "You'd better not forget how mean and ornery I am." Flavak shut the door with a bang.

When they were back on deck, Derrik said, "I'm sorry we put you in danger, Flavak."

Flavak shook his head. "Those mammal scum didn't even know who we were." He patted his chest. "Not only did we get out of it alive, now I'm the owner of a bigger and better boat." His voice was almost cheerful. "And I have a slave to swab the decks." He gave the deck a satisfied stamp with his big green foot.

"Hey, Derrik!" Tweaks shouted from a place by the railing. He pointed into the sea. "Isn't that your pack?"

Derrik hurried to Tweaks's side and saw debris from Flavak's ship floating on the choppy blue water. He spied his pack bumping up against a wooden barrel. Derrik dashed to the rope ladder and flung it over the side of the ship. Before it completely unrolled, he was halfway down. When he got to the bottom, he realized he couldn't keep hold of the ladder and still reach his pack. His eyes darted around the dark, moving sea, but there was no way he could tell if hidden currents waited to sweep him away. Still, the magic wand in the pack was important enough to risk it. He took a big breath, let go of the ladder, and struck out into the cold water, bumping into ropes, wooden boxes, and floating fish that had been intended for their supper.

"Derrik!" Tweaks called from the deck. "What are you doing?"

Derrik didn't waste energy to answer because Tweaks could see perfectly well what he was doing if he had his eyeglass. Derrik reached the barrel and grabbed for his pack. The top flopped open, spilling out a soggy blob of bread. Derrik's heart kicked him in the ribs. What if the magic wand was gone? He stuck his hand inside the sodden pack and felt around until he touched the slender curve of wood. Relieved, he closed the flap, stuck his arm through a strap, and headed back to the ship. Just as he grabbed the waterlogged bottom rung, an explosion of water made him flinch. Thoughts of the sea monster filled his mind, creating panic in his heart. Derrik scrambled up the ladder, his toes tangling in his frantic effort to escape the terror behind him.

"Thought I'd come in after some of that floating treasure myself," Flavak said. Derrik gripped the rope ladder and turned to see a green snout grinning back at him.

"I thought you were the sea creature," Derrik said.

"Never saw a single sea creature, except for me," Flavak said. "And since you're so afraid, I'd have gotten your pack for you, human, if you'd waited. I could swim circles around your sea monster." Flavak disappeared beneath the deep blue water.

"He has a point," Ssaska said when Derrik reached the deck.

"I did just fine," Derrik retorted. "And why is it that the sea creature isn't around here?" Derrik glanced down into the water. "Unless Flavak's lying to us."

"I don't know," Ssaska said. "Maybe he is lying. Or maybe the creature only patrols a certain part of the sea."

"Hey, snake man," Flavak called, his head just above water. "Help me haul this up, will you?"

Ssaska moved to the railing while Derrik went in search of Tweaks. He found him at the other side of the ship, staring down into his own open pack. "Are you all right?" Tweaks asked.

"Yeah," Derrik answered.

Tweaks looked up at his friend and blinked in surprise. "Not you," he said.

Derrik leaned over and saw the pile of bones glowing faintly blue-green in the dim interior of Tweaks's pack. "Oh," he said. "Why didn't you help us?"

Clatterin's skull turned its eyeholes up toward Derrik. "I would have, if you'd been in real danger."

"Real danger?" Derrik's voice rose to a shout. "We nearly died!"

"But you didn't," Clatterin said. "Besides, if they had captured me and pulled my bones apart, I would have been so weak I wouldn't have been able to gather them back together." She rolled her head so she was no longer looking at Derrik. "And if Flavak sees me, he might set all of you adrift on a piece of twine."

Tweaks closed his bag. "She's right. She can just stay there until we land."

After Flavak salvaged everything he could, he rubbed his leathery hands together and growled, "Let's see what else I inherited." He led the way to the captain's cabin and burst through the door. As he strutted inside, one wall seemed to capture his attention. "Well, well, call me master," he said, a big grin spreading across his long face. The wall was covered with weapons, from axes to maces to armaments that none of them had ever seen before. "Help yourself, boys," Flavak said, waving his thick arms toward the wall. "Take whatever you need, especially the armor." Flavak thumped himself on the chest. "I don't need it."

"Thank you," Derrik said. Tweaks trailed behind Derrik and Ssaska. He didn't admire the swords or knives or lances. He hated fighting, which may have been why he wasn't good at it.

"Find yourself some armor," Ssaska said. "You're going to need it."

Finally Tweaks chose some tan colored flexible archer armor

and boots. The fabric mask had a thin piece of metal on the front to cover his mouth. The back of the helmet consisted of lots of little metal plates overlapping, like fish scales, that flowed down the back of Tweaks's neck like spilled coins. The helmet covered his eyebrows, and he had to tip his head back to see through the eye slots. When Ssaska gave him a dubious look, Tweaks snapped, "What? There's nothing smaller." Tweaks turned away and lifted the smallest bow off the wall. He gave the string an experimental pull.

"You need ammunition, warm blood," Flavak said. He lifted down a quiver of arrows and held it out to Tweaks. Tweaks pulled one out. To his surprise, it was not a typical triangular arrow point. He scanned the other arrows in the quiver and saw a large assortment of projectiles; arrows with thousands of tiny barbs on the tip, arrows with padding on the front for setting on fire, and an arrow with five tips that bent back to form long hooks, with a strong cord attached to the back of the shaft. He also found a very odd arrow that had several thin cords wrapped around its thick shaft with small barbs scattered along their lengths. Tweaks couldn't figure out its purpose.

"Ssaska, have you ever seen one of these before?" he asked, pulling the arrow from the quiver.

Ssaska took the barbed arrow. He examined the strings wrapped around its shaft and the small piece of discolored wood that served as its tip. "I have not seen this before," he said, handing it back to Tweaks.

"Maybe the rat knows," Derrik said. "Hey, what do you think?" he held out his arms to show off the bright silver breastplate of the armor he wore. It was shaped like the bare chest of a strong warrior.

"Nice choice," Tweaks said.

"Only choice," Derrik answered. "Nothing else fit me. Look at this," he reached over, picked up a shaggy looking helmet, and pulled it on his head. Then he lowered the visor. His face disappeared, and in its place was the stiff metal face of a bearded warrior.

"That's creepy," Tweaks said.

"Good disguise," Ssaska said.

Derrik turned his head. "It even has hair," he said, showing them the shaggy hairs covering the back of the helmet. "And you won't believe the boots." He lifted his silver feet.

"Who thought of that design?" Tweaks asked, eyeing the stiff silver toes, complete with toenails.

"It could confuse pursuers," Flavak answered. "They might not know they're following an armed man if they're tracking bare feet."

Ssaska snorted. "You look like a very strong half naked man!"

"You'll have to be strong to carry all that around," Tweaks said.

"No, it's really light weight," Derrik said, his voice muffled by the visor. He looked out through the empty eye sockets. He didn't care what they thought; he felt very menacing, and he liked feeling that way. Perhaps Ssaska thought it was funny because he knew that the boy inside the armor was not as strong or menacing as it made him look.

Derrik turned and lifted a broadsword with swirls and curves carved into the handle from the wall. "This is my weapon," he announced. He still wore the snake dagger in his belt, covered now by armor.

Ssaska kept all his own snake man armor and scimitar along with the crossbow and bolts. The only thing he added to his arsenal were spears that could fit into his crossbow.

Once outfitted, they moved onto the deck and stared out across the water. "When will we get there?" Derrik asked.

"This ship is bigger and slower than my old one," Flavak said. "Not that I'm complaining, but it will take another day to get to the badlands."

Derrik sighed.

"Come on, Derrik," Tweaks said. "Let's practice."

In minutes, they had a barrel set up in front of the mast. Flavak tipped the wooden barrel lid up and leaned it against the mast, then painted a circle on it with some of the mammal lycan blood that had spilled on the deck. On Tweaks's first try, he hit the target dead center.

"Beginner's luck," Ssaska said. "Try again."

Tweaks took aim with one of the long tipped arrows, and to everyone's surprise, the arrow thwacked into the barrel lid right next to the first. As he kept hitting close to the target, a wide grin spread across his face.

"Hey," Ssaska said, "you've got some natural skill there."

"My eyeglass helps, too," Tweaks said, blinking a large eye through the clear circle.

"Maybe I should get one of those," Ssaska said. He held out a long recurve bow. "Here, try this one, it's more powerful."

Tweaks took the larger bow and gave it a try. He was almost as good a shot with the new weapon. Before long, he was hitting the target with frightening accuracy, his swift arrows mere blurs until they stopped, quivering, in the circle of blood.

The next arrow he pulled from the quiver was the barbed one wrapped in strings and tipped with discolored wood. "I'm going to see what this does," he said. He pulled the string back and took aim. He let go and the arrow flew to the target. The strings shot forward, each one imbedding in the mast. It happened so fast that the watchers barely saw any movement.

Silently, Tweaks went up to the arrow and inspected it. "What a marvelous piece of work," he said, sounding happy. After a lot of pulling and unwinding, Tweaks removed the arrow and figured out how to wind and tuck all the barbs back into the arrow and set it to shoot again. He pressed the arrow tip against the mast, which triggered the barbs to fly out and embed themselves in the mast again.

"Marvelous," Tweaks murmured.

Leaving Tweaks to his experiments, Ssaska and Derrik checked their supplies.

"I plan to enter the palace through a back way," Ssaska said. "It's never used any more and leads to the dungeons." He cast a sideways glance at Derrik. "I'm almost sure your parents are there with all the other slaves."

In spite of the sun, Derrik shivered. "It's hard to believe there's an unguarded tunnel leading into the palace."

"I don't know if it's guarded," Ssaska admitted. "I haven't actually used it, but I've heard of two terrors that guard it." He shrugged. "I doubt it's true. It's probably just a tale to keep people away."

31

SCALIES AND FURRIES

Tweaks held the ship's storeroom key in front of him like a knife. "Get back from the door," he said, giving the wood panel a kick. He reached back to make sure the flap of his pack hung open. Knowing Clatterin was there gave him courage.

He fitted the key into the lock and twisted. Then he slowly pushed open the door. Wilfred huddled at the far side of the room, as close to a lit lantern as he could be without getting singed. Crude bandages loosely covered his chest and stomach.

"Hello, Percy," Wilfred said.

Tweaks stepped inside the room and locked the door behind him. Wilfred didn't look dangerous but that didn't mean he wasn't. He had sharp teeth, and he was from the enemy's ship. Tweaks stood as tall as he could. "My name's not Percy," he said.

"It's lots easier for me to remember," Wilfred answered. He sat up straighter, and Tweaks tensed. "I could use it for your nickname."

"Nicknames are for friends. You aren't my friend," Tweaks said.

"I could be," Wilfred said, his voice smooth as oil. "Look." He put his paw up to his wounded ear. "I don't know what happened to you, but it appears we've got some kind of understanding. We could be teammates, you know?"

"I don't think so," Tweaks said firmly. "I've just come down for some crackers."

Wilfred's eyes glittered, still fixed on Tweaks. "The crackers are over there," he said, pointing a skinny black arm toward a stack of barrels. "The one in front's been unhammered."

Tweaks moved over to the barrel and lifted the wooden lid, which was circled with little holes where nails had been pried loose. He reached in to scoop out a handful of hard white cracker squares. Then Wilfred's voice came from so close behind him that Tweaks froze, his arm in the barrel. He hadn't heard a sound. How had the rat snuck up on him so quickly?

"So why would you be friends with the likes of that scaly snake when you could be friends with a mammal closer to your own kind?" Wilfred asked, his voice shaking with anger.

Tweaks remained still, scarcely daring to breathe. Any sudden move might send the rat into a frenzy. He didn't think Wilfred was armed. But then, Wilfred could have picked something up in the storage room. There could be boxes of knives or swords or axes for all Tweaks knew. Why hadn't he brought Derrik with him? That was stupid, stupid, stupid.

He felt a crawling sensation at the center of his back. Certain that Wilfred's evil eyes were aimed at that very spot, he straightened. If Wilfred was going to attack, Tweaks would face him. When he whirled around, he saw Wilfred's wide eyes focused on something above Tweaks's shoulder. Wilfred gasped and then stammered, "Wh-wh-what is that?" The rat backed away, fear plain on his face. He darted into the shadows of the hold, his bandages fluttering.

Tweaks turned to see the faint glow of Clatterin's small bones sitting on his shoulder. He grinned and said, "Thanks."

When Flavak heard about Wilfred's behavior, he hauled him up on deck in chains. "Trying to sabotage my crew, are you?" he snarled.

"It's my word against his," Wilfred said. He darted a sly glance at Tweaks. "And the thing he's hiding in his pack."

"What are you talking about?" Flavak said. "You trying to make trouble again?"

"No, no, there's something in there," Wilfred insisted. "Look for yourself."

Flavak turned a questioning eye on Tweaks. "What do you carry in there?"

Tweaks went pale. "Nothing of consequence," he said, backing up a step.

"Hm." Flavak stroked his long, green chin. "It could be that I want to see what you've got in there."

"You don't need to," Ssaska said, stepping forward. "I speak for him."

"And who are you to speak so I would care?" Flavak snapped. "You are a stranger, riding on my ship." He turned back to Tweaks. "I will see what is in your pack."

Derrik moved to step in front of Tweaks, but Flavak pushed him aside. "Now." He held out his big green hand.

Tweaks looked at the scaly hand, then raised his eyes to Flavak. "May I leave the pack on? Let Derrik open it and then you may look all you like."

Flavak narrowed his eyes. Then he nodded. "All right."

Tweaks turned. Derrik moved closer and lifted the flap on Tweaks's pack. Flavak peered inside. "Bones?" he asked. "You carry bones with you?" His head shot up. "Are you a murderer?"

"No!" Wilfred screeched. "It's alive!"

Flavak took another look in the pack. Clatterin's bones lay as lifeless as cold firewood. He stuck a finger inside and poked at the bones. They yielded slightly to his pressure, then settled back when he drew his hand out. "What bones are they?" he asked. "Where did you get them?"

"They were in the woods we came from across the water," Tweaks said.

"Why would you carry dead bones with you?"

"They move," Wilfred insisted. "They climb and clatter and crawl." He shivered.

Flavak took a step toward the rat. "What have you been drinking down in the storage room?"

"Nothing!" Wilfred shouted. "I saw the bones move!"

"It is strange," Flavak said, glancing at Tweaks. "But who can explain humans? It's back to the hold for you." He reached out to grab the rat, but Wilfred scuttled backwards, his chains clanking piteously.

"No," Wilfred said, his ears and shoulders sagging. "I didn't see anything. Please let me stay out here. I'll help you sail the ship, I promise, and I won't see any more moving bones."

Flavak stared at Wilfred for a long moment. "What kind of influence do you think you could have on those sails up there?" He jerked his snout upward.

"A good one, a very good one," Wilfred answered, nodding his head.

"You'd better, 'cause if you don't, I'll throw you overboard," Flavak roared. "You can bet I'm a better swimmer than you, so trying to escape will get you nowhere but eaten."

"I won't," Wilfred said. "Will you take the chains off?" He held out his black paws.

"No."

Wilfred's eyes hardened. "What if I fall in the water?"

"If you're any good as a sailor, you won't fall in," Flavak said.

With a flick of his tail, Wilfred started up the main mast, dragging his chains behind him. "I just love the sea," he hollered.

The next afternoon, Wilfred spied a black smudge on the horizon. "Land ho!" he called out.

"There're the badlands, boys," Flavak called, pointing a green finger. Derrik and Tweaks stood at the rail, staring at the small speck. Derrik felt suddenly cold. "We're almost there, Tweaks," he said. "We've nearly reached our parents."

"Yeah," Tweaks whispered. "And Skippy."

32

BADLANDS

It was dark by the time Flavak reached the drop-off place. "You'll be swimming from here," he said. "She'll run aground if I sail any closer."

"We can't swim in this armor," Ssaska said.

His protest was interrupted by a rattling sound. He glanced down the deck to see a wooden cart rumbling toward them. Flavak dropped into a fighting crouch. The cart rolled to a creaky stop and Wilfred's head popped up behind it. His skinny black arm jerked up in a salute. "A carrier for the armor, Pirate Captain, sir," he said.

Flavak straightened. "What am I going to do with you?" he growled.

"Make me first mate," Wilfred said with a sneer.

While Tweaks helped Ssaska pack the small two-wheeled cart full of weapons, armor, food, and a couple of torches, Flavak pulled Derrik aside. "Hey, now, I've been watching you, and I've decided you're the best one to make a business partnership with."

"What kind of business?" Derrik asked, suspicion pulling a tight band across his chest.

"Salt."

"Salt?" Derrik was puzzled. "Why?"

"Not just any salt," Flavak said. "Black salt. It's valuable."

"But there's salt in the sea," Derrik argued.

"Not so's it can be used. Who wants to dump a barrel of sea water on their plate before eating?" He let out a rumbling laugh. "I heard the badlands has wonderful deposits of salt." He cleared his throat. "But it must be black salt."

"I've never heard of it," Derrik said.

"Ah, it's very valuable, one of the most sought-after substances ever known. You can do lots of bartering with salt." Flavak looked out across the dark landscape. "It's rumored that the richest deposits are in the badlands. I will not risk my life for it, but you are already determined to go, so if you find any, and if you live, bring it out to me. I'll run it through my buyers and we will share the profit." He hoisted a dark leather pouch over Derrik's head and dropped it over his shoulders, criss crossing the straps of his pack.

"Uh, thanks," Derrik said.

"Now go," Flavak said. "I do not wish to be anywhere in sight when the light comes. It's time for you to get wet."

The travelers climbed down the ladder into the cold ocean, leaving Flavak and Wilfred on deck. Ssaska took hold of the wooden cart Flavak lowered over the side, and the three of them stroked toward shore. Since the land and water were equally dark, it was only by feel that the travelers could tell where the water ended and the land began. Once they splashed into the shallows, they turned, but could not see Flavak's vessel in the night.

"Farewell," Flavak's voice called through the darkness. "Good luck."

"Luck is what you make it," Wilfred said. "There are things in the badlands that you won't even know are after you until you're between their teeth."

"Like you'll be between my teeth if you don't get busy," Flavak roared.

When the voices on the ship grew faint, Ssaska spoke. "We must travel by dark." He grabbed the handle of their cart and led the way inland. Clatterin spun overhead, her faint blue-green glow of little use in lighting the way. When the sky finally brightened from the rising sun, the exhausted travelers spread their blankets and slept through the heat of the day. The next night was the same, walking through the darkness on the barren expanse of flat black rock, listening for any signs of danger, and then plodding along through the dismal landscape until the rising sun lit the sky.

"Give me the skin, will you?" Derrik said to Tweaks when they stopped on the second night. Tweaks lowered the water skin from his mouth and handed it to Derrik. Derrik's eyes darkened as he shook the skin. "You drank it all!"

"There's a little bit left," Tweaks said.

"I'm more than a little bit thirsty," Derrik snapped. "I've been pulling the cart."

"Sorry," Tweaks said. "I didn't think."

Derrik dropped the cart handle. "Well, think about doing without your armor or your stupid warped arrows. I'm not hauling that cart any more."

"We'll need those if we have any hope of entering the palace," Ssaska rasped. "We're all thirsty, Derrik. Take what water you can. Then sleep."

Derrik begrudgingly lifted the water skin to his mouth. It only took three swallows to empty it. Only then did he realize he hadn't offered any to Ssaska. His face burned with shame. Ssaska's back was turned as he spread out his blanket under a shrub so darkly green it appeared black. Derrik quietly laid the skin in the cart and fell into a troubled sleep.

It was late afternoon when they woke. "I'm thirsty," Tweaks said.

"I'm sorry," Ssaska said, his voice sounding thick. "I've never traveled this land by foot. I don't know where to find water."

"Don't worry," Clatterin said. "I'll go find some." She flew off into the air, the whir of her bones growing fainter until the sound was gone.

"We might as well get going," Ssaska said, standing up.

Derrik groaned.

"The sooner we begin, the sooner we arrive," Ssaska said.

Derrik and Tweaks pushed themselves to their feet, their

heads hanging. They trudged through the badlands, flat black rock giving way to a pebbled surface that made walking difficult. Then bigger stones got in their way until they had to stumble around rough rocks that reached Ssaska's waist.

When the sun sank close to the horizon, something worse appeared. A wide channel of water sloshed against rock walls that would have slid them down to a watery death if they had the misfortune of going over the edge.

Tweaks grabbed an empty water skin. Derrik dropped to his knees. Ssaska pointed to the far shore, his voice tight with excitement. "That's where the necromancer's palace sits."

"Water!" Tweaks cried, fumbling through the supplies in the cart. "We can lower skins on a rope to the waterline and let them fill." He licked his dry lips. "I'll do it."

"The channel water is salt," Ssaska said.

Tweaks stared at him. "But maybe not here," he said, his eyes wide. "This could be fresh. Maybe the outgoing tide draws fresh water from the land."

"I'm sorry," Ssaska said.

Tweaks slumped. "What . . . what now?" he asked, rubbing his fist across his eyes.

"At low tide, a rocky pathway appears," Ssaska said. "We'll have to move quickly."

For now there was nothing to do but sit in the scant shade of the two-wheeled cart and wait. Ssaska kept his head up, staring at the far piece of land. Tweaks's chin rested on his chest. Derrik shifted his weight, then shifted again. The late sun was hot. Derrik idly thought of chewing on a cracker. He was hungry, but there was no water, so he quickly gave up on the idea. He hated sitting here, doing nothing. *Were his parents thirsty? Were they hungry? Were they still alive?* Derrik shifted again, his eyes open to the bleak rocky landscape. The worst thing was not knowing.

Something moved. Derrik turned his head and narrowed his eyes, trying to see what had caught his attention. Five big rocks sat evenly spaced, as if they were tallies on the side of a die. Maybe something was hiding behind them. He watched for a full minute. Nothing moved. Perhaps it had been a trick of the light. He glanced at Ssaska, but Ssaska still held his gaze to the far horizon.

Then Derrik saw movement again. He sat up and twisted his head to stare at the rocks. Two of them were touching. They hadn't been that way before, he was sure of it. Was something behind the rocks, pushing them forward? He opened his mouth to ask Ssaska what it might be when six slender rods, three on each side, poked out from beneath the closest rock. Derrik was speechless as the rods dug into the sand to move the rock forward. As it drew closer, two rugged black claws peeled off each side and waved in the air, giving a solid *snap* of rock against rock.

"Ssaska!" Derrik yelled.

Ssaska sent Derrik a curious glance before he saw what he was staring at. Ssaska jumped to his feet. "Rock crab!" he hissed. "Get up!" Ssaska seized the cart while Derrik grabbed Tweaks's shirt and hauled him to his feet.

Impossibly, another rock crab joined the first, scurrying across the bleak landscape toward the weapons cart on stubby legs.

"Are they all rock crabs?" Tweaks asked, darting nervous glances at the rocks strewn around them.

"No," Ssaska said. He grabbed Tweaks and stuffed him in behind the weapons cart next to Derrik. "This terrain is their camouflage. Most of the rocks are just rocks."

A third rock rose up and scuttled toward them so fast, it bumped into the second rock crab. Instantly, the bumped crab spun and snapped its claws so hard that flecks of sand flew off into the air. The third crab scrambled backwards until the offended crab turned back toward its prey.

"This isn't good," Ssaska mumbled.

"Can't we outrun them?" Tweaks asked, cupping a hand over his ear.

Ssaska suddenly darted the cart forward to push away the lead crab, then jerked it back before the crab's claw could take a chunk out of the wood. "We can't leave the channel or we'll miss our passage," he said.

"If we're chopped in pieces we'll never make it, either," Derrik argued.

Ssaska turned the cart slowly to the right, keeping it between them and the first rock crab. Then the crab behind it shifted to the left. "They're trying to surround us," Ssaska hissed. His eyes on the crabs, he said, "Run straight back, as far behind me as you can. Go, get out of here before the circle closes."

"But what—" Derrik began.

"Get away!" Ssaska screamed, his head tail swishing them away.

Derrik stumbled backward. Tweaks caught his arm and gave it a tug. "Come on, Derrik."

The boys ran to a pile of rocks, propelled up its rounded sides by fear. When they neared the top, they stopped and watched Ssaska. The three crabs ringed around him in a horseshoe shape, their hard claws snapping as they edged ever closer to a circle. He was taller than them, but Ssaska didn't have rock-hard claws. He lunged at his attackers with the cart, forcing them back, but he wouldn't be able to keep that up for long.

"We've got to help him," Derrik said.

"It won't be any help if he has to worry about us," Tweaks argued.

Derrik started back down the rock pile. "I can't just sit here and watch them chop him from the legs up."

"Derrik, wait!" Tweaks called. He slid down over a large rock, his hand clenched into a fist. Tweaks opened his fist to show Derrik a sharp black rock.

"What's that supposed to do?" Derrik said, his brow drawn down. "Tickle them?"

"It will distract them," Tweaks said. "Don't tell me you can't hit one of those things from here."

"Of course I can." Derrik jumped down the rock pile, landing on the ground. He snatched up a stone, drew it back, and heaved it at the nearest crab. The stone clattered against the shell. The crab spun on its six short legs, its claws clapping in the boys' direction. Tweaks followed Derrik's rock with one of his own.

The crab scuttled sideways. Ssaska shoved his cart at the two rock crabs that tried circling around him and then darted a worried glance over his shoulder at the boys.

"Use your magic wand!" Tweaks shouted.

Derrik fumbled with the straps of his pack. The rock crab scooted closer, leaving a hatch-mark trail behind it. Tweaks spun around and threw a rock at it, but missed. Derrik dropped his pack on the ground and dug through it until his hand closed on the dry stick. He yanked on it, but it caught.

"Hurry!" Tweaks cried.

Derrik gave a fierce tug, and the stick pulled free with a snap. Derrik stared at the cracked stick, hanging together on just one side.

"Derrik!" Tweaks called. The sound of snapping rock crab claws was remarkably similar to that of breaking magic wands.

Derrik didn't know if it would work. He grabbed the break and held it together while pointing the wand at the rock crab. "Millipen swaddlein!" The wand vibrated in his hand. Orange sparks shot out in a spray that sent hard jolts of pain through Derrik's hand and clear up to his elbow. "Ow!" he cried, dropping the wand as sparks cascaded over the rock crab. Derrik hopped backward, his arm burning with pain as the crab grabbed for the wand. It caugh it in a shattering snap that turned it to splinters. The pain in Derrik's arm drained away as the wand splinters scattered to the wind.

"Derrik," Tweaks said.

"What?" Derrik gasped.

"Derrik, it's Ssaska."

Derrik's head whipped up, and he darted his eyes to the snake man. Ssaska shoved the cart forward, running as fast as he could toward the edge of the channel.

"What's he doing?" Tweaks eyes were full of fear. "Is he insane?"

33

Sharp Spires

Derrik abandoned his pack and took a few running steps forward but stopped with an incredulous grin on his face. "Not yet he isn't." He bent, snatched up a stone, and hurled it across the landscape. "He's shoving the crabs into the water."

Ssaska dug in his heels and jerked to a stop at the brink of the channel's sloping sides. Two loud plops sounded from the water below him. Then Ssaska pulled the cart back and turned to face the boys. Several of their weapons tipped at a dangerous angle through a huge U-shaped hole in one side if the cart, but Ssaska didn't seem to notice. He came on a run through the rock rubble.

The rock crab skittered across the dirt, scooting around rocks as fast as its six legs could take it, finally losing itself to their view when it settled down in a section strewn with boulders.

Ssaska reached the boys. Hanging onto the crippled cart, he gasped, "Are you all right?" Derrik and Tweaks nodded. Ssaska darted a look toward the boulders. "It shouldn't bother us again. The tide's out. It's time for us to go."

When the boys walked with Ssaska to the edge of the water, they saw that the setting sun had turned the tide liquid gold where it spilled out of the channel. Ssaska anxiously scanned the wet ground below him, and then shouted, "That way. Hurry!"

The cart bumped along behind as he ran to a section of rock with a cut path leading down to the water's edge. From there, a dangerous ridge of spiny black rocks poked out of the water. Derrik caught up to Ssaska, carrying a cross bow that had bounced out of the cart. Derrik studied the sharp edged mollusks and shellfish clinging to the rock as though their lives depended on it. He didn't like the looks of them. Just below Derrik's feet, a small creature waved a pair of mean-looking claws on either side of its bulging eyes. Derrik shuddered. The creature scuttled around the first point of slick rock on several spine tipped feet, snapping its claws as it disappeared.

"We're going to have to leave the cart and carry the armor," Ssaska said, his voice weary. "Some of it went over the side."

"What?" Derrik started digging through the cart.

"I'm sorry," Ssaska said. "One rock crab's claw grabbed on just as it went over. It took a big chunk of wood and some armor. I couldn't stop it."

Derrik was not happy when he found his leg armor was missing, but there was no time to feel sorry for himself. "I'll wear what's left," Derrik announced, strapping on his breastplate. It was the easiest way he could think of carrying it.

"Good idea," Ssaska said.

The three of them hurriedly pulled on their armor and shouldered their weapons. They stuffed everything that would fit into their packs. As soon as they were ready, Ssaska was first to step out on the rock, gingerly holding the closest shoulder-high spire as he sought footing. Tweaks was next to disappear down the slope, then Derrik, leaving the uneven cart sitting behind on the smooth rock of the badlands.

Crossing the rim of jagged spires was hard going. Their armor was cumbersome, the rock ridge was rough and slimy, and the mollusk shells were sharp, ready to cut into any bit of unprotected skin. At one point, Derrik almost lost his footing when a long, red, segmented creature jumped out of a puddle. It braced its many legs on the rock and brandished two pairs of bright red and orange claws. When it realized how big Derrik was, it seemed to reconsider and scampered back into the water on ten sharp legs. As Derrik watched, a slimy gray arm reached out of a hole, grabbed the creature, and pulled it in. A couple of seconds later, Derrik watched in horror as the claws and shell of the long red creature shot out of the hole and floated away. He held tighter to the sharp rocks when he could and shuffled faster between spires.

While the moon chased the sun from the sky, Ssaska led the way, his head tail flipping like a stringy ghost as it darted out to help steady him. Tweaks nimbly scrambled from point to point, his thick armor flexing with each movement. Derrik struggled along in his metal boots and stiff armor. He tried to close the gap between himself and Tweaks, but when he made a quick grab for the next spire, the edge of his armored glove struck the rock and flew off his outstretched hand.

Derrik instinctively made a grab for it as it tumbled toward the water, but he slipped and fell, hitting his face against rock. "Ahhh!" he cried as mollusk shells dug into his cheek. Hot tears of pain sprang from his eyes and rolled into the wound, making it hurt even more.

Ssaska stopped and looked back along the ridge. "Are you all right?"

"Yeah," Derrik said, wearily pushing himself up. His glove was gone. He was thirsty, hungry, and miserable, but he refused to say so out loud.

Tweaks turned and stared at Derrik, his mouth open. "You're bleeding," he said.

"It's not the first time," Derrik snapped.

Tweaks looked hurt, and turned and moved away. Derrik frowned and stepped to the next spire of rock. There was nothing to do but keep going. The island up ahead seemed to move further away from them in the silver light of the moon. It felt like he spent hours slipping and stumbling over rock. The squelching and cracking sounds as Derrik stepped on the mollusks and barnacles made him feel sick. Derrik moved to yet another pillar of rock, but this time something was different. This step splashed into a wave of salt water that filled his armored boots.

"Ssaska!" he yelled. "The water's rising!"

"Hurry!" Ssaska called back. "Run!" Derrik obeyed the best he could, moving from rock to rock as fast as his cumbersome armor would allow, slipping and sliding, enduring more frequent attacks from increasing waves. The salty spray from each wave burned his cuts, and he felt faint from lack of sleep, food, and water. He hurt all over—outside and in. His body just wanted to give up and sleep, to heal and rest. A constant fear of falling plagued his every step. Derrik could almost feel himself splashing into the cold water, sinking down into the darkness, the necromancer's badlands claiming him forever.

"There is land just ahead," Ssaska called, his voice pulling Derrik's thoughts from the deadly water. "Hurry!"

Derrik wanted very badly to make it to land. He couldn't stop now. He couldn't give up. Da and Mama were waiting for him. He hobbled forward as fast as he could, which only seemed like baby steps. Skippy moved faster, and he couldn't even walk yet. Derrik's vision grew blurry. All his senses seemed to shut down. He couldn't hear the waves anymore, couldn't taste the salt, couldn't feel the pain. When he finally let go, he landed on a spongy bed of wet sand. Something hooked under his arms and pulled him along, a soft voice hissing, ". . . out of tide zone . . ."

34

Blumpers

Derrik heard a sound too cheerful for death. He forced his eyes open. Bright birds darted between green trees, ruffling the leaves as they dove in and popped back out. What was this place? Derrik curled his fingers at his sides. One hand moved easily, sifting through fine grains of sand, while the other felt stiff. He realized that he still wore one armored glove. Derrik lay still on his sandy bed, not wanting to move. He blinked slowly, taking in the soft sound of waves and the welcome smell of fresh fruit filling the air.

Suddenly, his stomach clenched with hunger. Derrik struggled to sit up. His cheek throbbed, a painful reminder of the treacherous spires of rock. He groaned and looked around. Tweaks and Ssaska lay sprawled on the beach. He tried to crawl over to them, but his armor was too heavy, and his one bare hand was full of cuts that burned. Slowly he stood up and staggered over to them, calling their names.

To his relief, they shifted and groaned. They did not open their eyes, but he could see them breathing. Their exposed skin was nicked and spotted with dried blood. Derrik didn't call again. His tongue was too thick; his throat cried for water.

It didn't take long for Derrik to find a small stream running out from between the trees to spill into the ocean. Gratefully he stumbled over to the cool water. He collapsed beside the stream and drank and drank. Then he pulled off all his armor and stuck his hands in the water. It felt nice, like it could wash away every ache and problem from his life. His hand soon stopped hurting. He filled a water skin and carried it over to Ssaska, badgering the snake man until he finally roused himself enough to drink. Once Ssaska got some water in him, Derrik carried another water skin to Tweaks. It took some shaking to get Tweaks to open his eyes, but once he did, Tweaks spilled the entire water skin over his mouth in his hurry to drink. When the skin was empty Tweaks scrambled up quicker than Derrik thought possible and hurried over to sit in the stream, letting the cold water pour over his wounds.

Derrik followed the fruity smell to the stand of trees. Some of the branches jerked and swayed as though disturbed by a giant invisible hand.

"Clatterin?" Derrik asked in a raspy voice.

The trees kept swaying gently, although Derrik felt no breeze.

Derrik tried to clear his throat, and then said, "Clatterin, is that you?" Derrik waited, but there was no response. He stared at the trees for a moment. He saw no threat, but still, he had a sense of being watched. He shifted his weight from foot to foot in indecision—his hunger pulling him forward, his caution holding him back. He glanced back to see Ssaska slowly removing his armor. Ssaska was nearby to protect him if anything went wrong, and how dangerous could waving branches be?

At last hunger won, and Derrik found himself standing beneath a tree with round leaves that fluttered, revealing dark green backs and light orange bellies. The stirring leaves offered tantalizing glimpses of dark blue bulbs of fruit that appeared juicy and inviting. He glanced at the ground, happy to discover some fallen fruit. He chose one that looked plump and juicy, as big as an eyeball. He sniffed it. It smelled fresh, so he took a tentative bite. Sweet juice burst into his mouth and ran down his chin. The flesh of the fruit was firm enough to let him chew, yet soft enough to be soothing. He closed his eyes in delight.

"Hey," Tweaks said. "Save some for me." Derrik turned to

see Tweaks stumbling toward him, his clothes dripping.

"If you can climb the tree, you can eat all you want."

"Give me a boost," Tweaks said, raising his arms overhead.

Derrik boosted his friend up to the lower limbs. "Ouch!" Derrik cried as the pressure flared the pain in his hand.

"Augh!" Tweaks answered. "Take it easy on my feet!"

"I didn't do anything to your feet," Derrik muttered, holding his hand in close to his chest.

When Tweaks was safely in the branches, Derrik spotted Ssaska beneath another tree, throwing rocks and sticks up into the branches until a bright golden fruit with red stripes tumbled down. Ssaska grabbed the fruit, pulled off the red stripes, and ate the remaining golden stripes and inner pink flesh with obvious delight.

"Is it good?" Derrik called as Tweaks disappeared overhead.

Ssaska looked up. "It's what the munkeries eat."

Derrik left Tweaks rummaging in the tree, picked up another blue fruit from the ground, and moved over to Ssaska. "What are munkeries?" Derrik asked.

Ssaska pointed upward. Derrik looked up into the tree and saw a flash of silver. It was gone in the blink of an eye. He searched until he spied another small, silver-furred creature with hands and feet shaped like human hands. Another munkerie swung onto the branch and wrapped its long furry tail around the first munkerie. The first one jumped up and disappeared into the leaves, followed immediately by the second one. Their antics knocked down another golden and red striped fruit.

It must have been their eyes watching me, Derrik thought. He took another bite of his blue fruit, relieved that the dark foreboding wasn't for anything more dangerous than small tree animals.

"Have it," Ssaska said, flicking out his tongue and handing the golden fruit to Derrik. Derrik pushed the rest of the blue fruit into his mouth and then wiped his lips with the back of his hand and took the golden one. It was about the size of three of his fists put together.

"You need to peel the tough parts before you bite it," Ssaska said.

The fruit was so pretty that Derrik turned it over in his hands, unwilling to tear the stripes off as he'd seen Ssaska do. Ssaska took the fruit from Derrik and ripped off the red stripes. "Like this," he said and handed it back. Derrik thought the pale pink flesh between the golden sections looked delicious. He took a small bite of the fruit in his hands. It was soft and yielding to his tongue, and tasted fresh and nourishing with a mild aftertaste.

"You shouldn't eat too many of those blumpers at once, you know," Ssaska said.

"Blumpers?" Derrik asked.

Ssaska gestured toward the tree that shook with Tweaks crawling around its branches. "The blue ones."

"Why?" Derrik took another bite of the golden fruit, savoring the feeling of sustenance.

"They're too sweet," Ssaska warned. "If you eat too many, they can mess up your digestion."

Derrik took off at a run toward the tree where Tweaks sat with a blue fruit in each hand. "Hey!" Derrik called. "Stop! Don't eat that!"

"They taste so good," Tweaks answered, pushing another bite into his mouth.

"Ssaska says too many make you sick," Derrik said. He coaxed Tweaks out of the tree and fed him some golden fruit.

They explored the other trees, some with different kinds of fruit, some growing nut-like seeds, and one that bore a flattish, palm-sized fruit curved slightly up around the edges like a dish. It hung from the branch on a long, slender stem attached to the middle. Ssaska showed them how to break the thin top skin and let the fruit dish well up to the brim with a delicious liquid. They tipped the liquid into their mouths to roll down their throats with a most satisfying sweetness.

At last they all lay on the beach, full and happy. Derrik's question seemed to come from far away. "Where do you suppose Clatterin is?"

Tweaks barely moved, his voice drawn out when he answered, "I don't know."

"Maybe she got hurt."

Tweaks snorted. "She can't be hurt or killed. Someone could only take her bones apart."

Derrik blinked slowly. "Maybe she really was a traitor," he murmured, not really caring. "She may have gone to the necromancer to warn him we are coming."

"I don't think so," Ssaska replied.

"I don't know where else she'd be," Derrik said.

Tweaks yawned. "Me neither."

"Me neither," Ssaska echoed.

Despite the serious concern in their words, it seemed the world held no more problems for any of them.

The next day was spent eating more delicious fruit, drinking palm fruit juice, and playing in clear water. Derrik tried to coax a munkerie out of a tree to sit on his shoulder, but it only threw a golden fruit at him and scrambled higher up into the branches. Derrik laughed. He'd never felt better in his life. In fact, all three of them felt perfectly content to remain in this place of warm sun, mild breezes, food, and water. Everything else faded to the dark corners of memory, practically invisible.

It was only after darkness fell one balmy night when they were curled up under a starry sky that Derrik had a dream which changed everything.

35

Dreaming Awake

Derrik stood under a warm sun at the water's edge. In the distance, two figures slept on the beach, surrounded by various colorful fruit and jugs of water. When Derrik looked closer, he saw that they were Tweaks and Ssaska. His gaze moved to the shadows beneath the fruit trees. With a start of alarm, he saw two skinny figures concealed there, swaying slightly from side to side and stepping lightly on their feet. They were staring at Tweaks and Ssaska. Not only did their alarmingly thin figures make Derrik uneasy, but also the strange, greenish glow that pulsed from their heads.

The figures stepped out onto the beach, and Derrik gasped. He was looking at two skeletons, not those of humans, but an odd assortment of animal and human bones. The greenish-blue glow inside their skulls was dimmed by sunlight. He watched in horror as the bone creatures stealthily snuck closer to his friends. Derrik opened his mouth to call out a warning, but he couldn't make a sound.

Each skeleton grabbed one of his friends around the neck with their bony fingers. Tweaks and Ssaska thrashed and struggled, but they couldn't overcome the skeletons, who dug their white fingers into their victims' windpipes and held on, grinning at each other until Tweaks and Ssaska fell limp and silent to the beach.

Derrik was running, trying to get to his friends, but no matter how fast he sprinted, he wasn't getting any closer. He could only watch as the skeletons each pulled a pipe from a strip of leather around their waists. They placed one end of the pipe at the opening of his friends' mouths and the other end between their own skeletal teeth. Then they started sucking.

A faint blue mist rose from his friends and flowed into the pipes. The fires in the skeletons' heads burned brighter, changing from a light glowing green to a darker greenish blue.

Derrik stopped running, horrified by what he saw. He didn't want to believe it. Then another shape slipped out of the forest. It was a shape he had seen before, a shape wearing a skull-like etched-silver mask. The familiar hollow laugh came out of the motionless mouth and the masked figure pointed at Derrik. "Igon a trat," he cried to the skeletons. Their grinning white faces turned toward Derrik. Sliding their pipes into their leather belts, they ran toward him, rapidly getting nearer and nearer.

Derrik turned and tried to run, but just as before, he didn't seem to be getting anywhere. He tried to yell for help, but he didn't have any breath for it.

The hair on his neck rose and cold chills rolled down his spine. The sound of clacking and rattling grew closer every second as he ran down the beach. Finally he felt something land on his back, dry twigs grabbing his shoulders and thumping into his legs with enough force to knock him down. With his face in the sand, he heard something rattle. Derrik was lifted up and turned around to face the skeleton that held him in its grasp. Helpless, Derrik kicked and grabbed at the skeleton's bony arms, trying to set himself free. The sight of the grinning skull looming over him turned his stomach, and he fought all the harder to free himself from this nightmare.

A pair of hard hands grabbed his arms and held him tight. Derrik tried to twist away from the captor at his back as the grinning skeleton before him pulled the strange pipe from its leather belt.

Derrik heard a click as the skeleton placed the wooden mouthpiece between its teeth. Holding the front of the pipe with its white jointed fingers, the skeleton moved it slowly toward Derrik's mouth.

Derrik clamped his lips shut, taking desperate, frightened breaths through his nose. His attacker's bones dug into his sides as it leaned in, its eye sockets only inches from Derrik's face, the blue-green flame flickering in the otherwise dead eyes. Derrik wanted to scream, but that would give this monster a chance to stick his vile pipe down his throat. Heart thumping in terror, Derrik tried to twist his head away, but his struggles did no good. The pipe drew relentlessly at his nostrils until a cold blue mist started from his nose and drifted into the pipe. Derrik's whole body went limp as his tormenter continued to draw on the pipe, pulling more blue mist into it from somewhere deep inside him. Derrik's vision lost color and the skeleton face started to fade.

"Derrik!" It was his father's voice, calling from far away. "Help us!"

"Please!" his mother called, her voice no louder than a whisper. Her plea caught on a sob. "You're our only hope."

Derrik jerked upright. His wide awake eyes darted from side to side and his lungs panted for air. He struck out, searching for a sword, but there was nothing around him but sand and his two sleeping companions.

Derrik covered his face with his hands. He drew in a deep, shuddering breath, suddenly remembering why they were on this distant beach. He also knew where they were supposed to go. How could he have wasted so much time?

He pulled his hands away and saw the sky lightening in the east. It wouldn't have mattered to him if stars and moon shone above. He reached out and shook Tweaks. "Tweaks!" he called.

Tweaks mumbled and lay still.

"Tweaks!" Derrik shouted. "Wake up! We have to go find our families!"

In the pre-dawn light, Derrik saw Tweaks's eyes open, a confused look in their depths. Then Tweaks's eyes widened, and he sat up. "Mama!" he shouted.

Ssaska sat up. "Is it time to eat?" he asked, his yellow eyes narrowed, his tongue flickering out only as far as the tip.

"No," Derrik said, getting to his feet. "We have to go save our families. Remember, Ssaska? That's why we're here."

Ssaska stood up, his green scaled face solemn. "I remember now." He cast an accusing look at the fruit trees. "Something is odd around here."

"Let's go," Derrik said.

Ssaska turned to give Derrik an appraising glance. "What made you suddenly remember where we were headed?"

"A dream," Derrik said. "Come on, I'll tell you about it on the way."

Ssaska nodded. "The sooner we're away from here, the better."

They packed up and started quickly in the direction of the necromancer's palace. None of them remembered how much time they'd spent on the beach eating fruit and drinking cool water, but Derrik knew that every second was important. So they ran past the forest, with Ssaska leading.

After awhile, they slowed to a walk until they reached a cliff overlooking a beautiful valley full of green trees. Birds of all colors and sizes flitted among the branches and flew in lazy circles over the green canopy. Derrik heard munkeries chattering and thought he saw a flash of silver between the branches.

"I don't want to stop there," Derrik said. He couldn't take the chance that he would be lulled into another sense of security that might delay them.

"We don't have to," Ssaska said. He raised his hand and pointed across the valley. Derrik looked up and saw a huge palace of dark stone in the distance. It was covered with turrets, pointed towers, curved walls, and jagged edges. It appeared to be a confusing mix of architecture.

"We're almost there," Derrik said.

"We'll have to go around the forest in the valley," Ssaska said. "The necromancer has many spies." A bird flew overhead and Ssaska ducked, eyeing it warily.

"What's wrong?" Derrik asked.

Ssaska gave Derrik a solemn look. "Not all the birds and munkeries you see are what they seem."

36

No Way Out

Ssaska led the way along the edge of the cliff. Derrik kept back far enough that he couldn't see over it. When Ssaska took an angled path leading down to the valley, Derrik's heart did a somersault. He let Tweaks go first and concentrated on keeping his friend in sight as he forced himself to walk down. At last they reached the valley floor, where Ssaska led them on a path around the forest. Derrik saw many eyes looking out at them as they skirted the trees, shiny eyes full of curiosity and strange creatures that showed no fear of the trespassers.

Suddenly, the palace loomed before them, presenting a side view of confusing architecture, a mixture of domes, turrets, angled roofs, columns, and windows of every shape. It was unsettling. One half of the palace butted up next to jagged cliffs and the sea, while the other half extended into the forest and disappeared in the trees.

"That's a lot of cliff," Tweaks said.

"We have to climb down out of sight, then make our way along the beach so no sentries spot us," Ssaska said. "Keep your eyes open for the secret door and for danger."

Derrik grudgingly followed Ssaska and Tweaks toward the cliffs. None of the cliffs stood at the dizzying height of the one with the hanging ship, but Derrik was thoroughly sick of high places.

They followed the edge of the forest until they reached a cliff face made from the same dark jagged rocks that gave them passage across the channel.

"The secret entrance is along the beach at the bottom of this cliff," Ssaska said. "If we try to climb with our armor on, we might fall. And if we throw it over the side, it may be damaged beyond repair. We've got to stagger ourselves and throw it down person to person, in a relay. Who wants the bottom?"

"I do," Derrik said. He was sure he wanted to get to the bottom more than anyone else.

Ssaska nodded. "Get yourself about two thirds of the way down," he said. Derrik swallowed, but his throat was dry. After pulling off what armor he had, he stepped out over the steep stack of rocks, biting his lips, and worked his way down one clump of rock at a time. When he thought he was in the right place, he looked up to see Tweaks already in position and Ssaska waiting with Tweaks's soft brown armor in his hands.

"Ready?" Ssaska called.

"Ready," Tweaks answered, then held out his arms.

Not every piece of armor made it from hand to hand. The things that clattered to the bottom of the cliff suffered the most. When Derrik finally reached the ground, the black, ashy sand underfoot surprised him. From the top, it had looked like the same black rock they'd traveled in the badlands. He stumbled over to his man mask and picked it up. There was a deep dent in the head and on the chin of the visor as though he'd fought in mortal combat.

While Tweaks pulled his soft brown armor back on, Derrik decided it was too hot to wear his. He slung it over his shoulder and carried some in his arms while Tweaks only carried his weapons. Derrik walked unsteadily on the fine-grained sand, feeling as though he might sink into the ground at every step. Ssaska kept them close to the base of the cliff, darting glances upward every so often. Derrik glanced up once to see what Ssaska was looking for, but all he could see were clumps of grass hanging over the top of the cliff like hairy little spies.

A flock of ash black birds suddenly burst from their dark

sand camouflage in front of them, wings rattling as they took to the air. Derrik was so startled, he stepped back and fell, his armor and weapons scattering around him. The impact stirred up a cloud of sand, and Derrik came up spitting.

"Shush!" Ssaska warned, ducking behind a rock.

Derrik held still, his mouth puckered from the bite of alkaline. A cut on his hand was stinging so badly from the black salt that tears leaked from his eyes. Once the birds flew out of sight, Tweaks and Ssaska came out of hiding. Derrik shook his stinging hand in the air, then bent to fill Flavak's pouch with scoops of black salt.

"Were they spies?" Tweaks asked, his voice trembling.

"I don't know," Ssaska answered. "It's likely. There's just no way to tell for sure." He stared at Derrik. "What are you doing?"

"Gathering salt for Flavak."

"That's not true salt."

Derrik shrugged. "It tastes like salt."

"There are other things in it, things not meant for man or beast."

Derrik patted the heavy pouch. "Flavak says it's valuable."

If Ssaska had had eyebrows, he would have raised them. "To some, perhaps." He turned away. "Come on. The coast is clear. Let's get out of sight."

Ssaska searched along the cliff face for the entrance. Derrik looked, too, even though he didn't know what he was looking for. He felt a renewed sense of urgency, as if danger drew closer by the second. He missed Clatterin. He wondered again what could have happened to her. If she were here, and on their side, she could spot any necromancer spy, even if it was a mouse in high grass.

"There it is," Ssaska said, his voice low and urgent.

Derrik looked but didn't see anything that could be a cave. "Where?"

"Right there." Ssaska took a step toward the cliff and disappeared.

Just then, a ripple of movement shifted Derrik's foot. Startled, he looked down at the sand. A small river of collapsing black grains weaved away from him. "There's something here!" He shouted.

Ssaska's head reappeared. "Where?" he asked.

"Right here!" Derrik stabbed a finger toward the sand.

Tweaks let out a little "yip" and danced across the sand on his toes. Derrik saw a small white fin sticking up from the black sand before it sank out of sight in a tiny ripple of black grains.

"Something's out here," Derrik said.

"Then you two should be in here," Ssaska said, extending a hand toward the boys. "Hurry."

Derrik took a single step toward Ssaska when the sand before him boiled. Out of the roiling black grains swam a school of fish, sand spilling off their gleaming white bones with sharp teeth snapping. Startled, Derrik fell backward and the fish bones converged on him, swarming over his feet, biting at his shoes, and ripping pieces of fabric from his trousers. "Augh!" Derrik screamed, swatting at the bones with his helmet.

Tweaks ran forward, kicking at the bone fish. One clamped onto his pant leg and chewed with determination.

Then Ssaska was there, sweeping his tail across Derrik's legs, clearing them for the few seconds it took Derrik to scramble to his feet. "Run!" Ssaska hissed, giving Derrik a shove. Derrik tripped, then caught his balance, crushing a fish underfoot. Incredibly, he felt the gnawing of little teeth at the bottom of his shoe. He scooped up his armor and weapons in one armful and ran for the seam that Ssaska said held the secret entrance. Once his feet felt rock, the fish mercifully fell behind, undulating at the edge of the sand as though they'd reached shore, watching him with their dark eye holes, and snapping their teeth like small, hungry traps.

Tweaks waded toward Derrik. The fish were piling so thick around him they were chewing at the pants around his knees, catching flesh every now and then. Ssaska grabbed Tweaks, lifted him up, and shook him soundly. Fish bones clattered and rattled like sticks in the wind before finally falling to the ground. Then Ssaska tucked Tweaks under his arm and ran for the cave.

As soon as Derrik rounded the lip of rock, he got another surprise. A huge black door blocked the way. It looked as old as the rock itself, but there was no rust or salt corrosion anywhere on its metal surface. Ssaska dropped Tweaks onto his feet, shook the fish bones from his pant legs, and then pushed Derrik aside. The fish bones flopped helplessly on the rock floor. Ssaska twisted the door handle with his scaly hand, and the door swung open easily. Too easily. Derrik felt a rush of apprehension.

"Do you have a key?" he asked.

"No," Ssaska said. "It was unlocked."

Derrik's stomach twisted. This was wrong. A door that led to the palace of an evil necromancer should have been locked.

"I have a bad feeling," Tweaks said.

"There is no other way," Ssaska said. "Unless you want to go up against the bone fish?" He looked back at the small fish bones clicking aimlessly against the black rock and then stepped through the doorway with Tweaks at his heels. Derrik risked a peek around the entrance-way toward the black beach. The ridges and ripples of dark sand lay still as frozen water. He turned and followed his companions more slowly. He didn't want to go in this dark place, but he knew he had to.

Sunlight grew sickly in the dark cave. Ssaska pulled a torch out of his pack and lit it with a sulfur stick. When he struck it, a burst of suffocating stink crowded the confines of the cave. Tweaks gagged. Then the torch burst into flame and the sulfur stick went out.

A loud slam reverberated through the cavern. The meager daylight instantly disappeared. Derrik spun on his heel to see the metal door closed. Ssaska held the torch higher.

"What happened?" Tweaks asked, his voice shaking.

"Maybe it was the wind," Derrik said. He strode over to open the door, but there was no knob or lever of any kind.

"Let me try," Ssaska said. He lowered his shoulder to the metal. With all his pushing, the door didn't budge. No matter what the three of them tried, the door was solidly shut. Even though they didn't intend to leave this place through that door, it was unsettling to have it closed so definitely.

"Let's keep going," Ssaska said. He led the way deeper into the cave, his torch aloft. His feet echoed eerily. Derrik tried putting his feet down more gently, but nothing he did diminished the echo of footsteps. It was unnerving.

After several hundred yards, they reached another door, larger than the first. It was housed in a frame marked with a series of odd angular etched lines. Ssaska moved the light closer to the symbols and interpreted for them. "Any who enter are doomed to stay, to no more see the light of day."

"We've already figured that part out," Derrik said. "Does it say anything else?"

"Yes." Ssaska tilted his shiny head to take in the marks on the other side of the doorway. "You have made a serious error, you must now face the first terror."

He turned to the boys. "I don't think there's really anything there," he said. "The warnings spring from old tales of people who died in the caves from their own foolishness. Then rumors began about a terrible beast." He looked back at the door, then spoke slowly, as though he made up the words one after the other. "People get trapped and panic because the doors lock." He gave the boys a tight smile. "But we aren't panicked, so we'll be fine." Ssaska bent over, the torch lighting up the final marks written close to the floor. "It also says, "The first terror lies beyond this door, to chew you up, 'til you are no more.""

37

THE FIRST TERROR

Ssaska straightened and reached toward the door handle.
"Wait," Derrik said.

Ssaska turned, his tail twitching from side to side.

Derrik tried not to look at the nervous tail. "Don't you think we ought to wear armor in case there's anything inside?"

Ssaska dropped his hand from the handle and nodded. They pulled their armor on by the light of the torch. Derrik slung his pack over his back and held his weapons at the ready.

Ssaska checked on his companions with a single backward glance, then flung open the door. He walked into the dark room slowly, torch in one hand, sword in the other. The room was rough rock, just like the passage they'd walked through. The shadowy corners were littered with boulders, some as small as a dit, a few almost as tall as Derrik. Nothing moved, and there was no sound.

Tweaks and Derrik cautiously followed the snake man into the room. After a moment, Ssaska headed toward the far wall, which was so far down the long cave that Derrik could barely make out a dim rectangle that could be a door.

In the silence, Derrik had to wonder if perhaps Ssaska was right, and the threat of monstrous death was all stuff of legends.

A sudden *slam* made them jump. They whirled around and stared in disbelief at the door. It was shut tight. Derrik knew it would be futile to try to pull it open, and what would be the use? That was when Derrik noticed a large group of glowing spores, like mushrooms or some other fungus, growing on the wall beside the door. He turned away and continued toward the far rectangle, anxious to get to the palace.

Then a grunt sounded behind them. Derrik stopped, "Did you hear that?"

Tweaks covered his scarred ear with one hand and turned his head, listening. "I hear breathing."

Derrik gradually realized it wasn't him, since he wasn't breathing at the moment. He slowly let air out of his lungs.

"What is that?" Ssaska's sudden hiss made Derrik jump. He stared at the snake man, whose round yellow eyes were fixed on a place behind the boys. Derrik whirled around, horrified to see the mushrooms rising into the air.

"What's happening?" Tweaks asked, trying to stick his hand under his armor to get his eyeglass.

"I don't know," Derrik said, barely louder than his pounding heart.

Ssaska stepped toward the rising apparition and thrust the torch forward. Derrik let out a gasp. The spots weren't mushrooms at all, but large glowing boils that had erupted on the back and arms of a gigantic gray-skinned monster.

The creature turned to face the intruders, its huge, powerful arms reaching nearly to the floor. Its angry eyes glowed green. There was no hair on the thing to cover its cracked skin, which was as rough as the rock it lived in. It opened a mouth full of uneven teeth and roared from a terrifying height. Flecks of vile spit hit Derrik's face. He trembled, a cold shiver running down his spine. The breath was so foul, Derrik's stomach heaved.

The creature stood staring at them. Derrik felt hypnotized by the glowing eyes with no pupils—just pure green eyes that gave you no idea of where it was looking. The creature grunted and let loose another bone-jarring roar. It gathered its muscles and ran toward them, using its arms like a pair of front legs. Derrik watched its gray flesh move up and down and heard the sound of pounding and cracking from its huge frame with each stride.

The first one to act was Ssaska. He drew the crossbow from his back and loaded a spear. Aiming at the beast's chest, he fired. But when the spear hit the rugged gray flesh, the tip bent and the spear clattered, useless, to the ground. The monster didn't slow down.

Then Tweaks pulled out his recurve bow and aimed one of his arrows at the craggy head. When he let the arrow fly, it struck the monster's forehead, snapped, and fell to the rocky floor.

Derrik trembled. What if this cavern became his grave? His parents would never know what happened to him. And how could they ever escape? This beast seemed unstoppable.

"Aim for the eyes!" Ssaska yelled. That seemed impossible, since the small eyes moved up and down with each stride the creature took, bringing it closer to its victims. But Ssaska's words were enough to break Derrik free of his stupor of fear. He pulled his sword from the scabbard just as the monster raised a rocky fist and took a swipe at Derrik as it lumbered past. Derrik instinctively raised his sword to block the blow. The blade rang out sharply against hard skin, sending a jolt of pain up Derrik's arm and into his shoulder. His muscles cramped, his fingers spread, and he dropped the sword like it was red hot, flexing his hand to get the feeling back. When he stooped to pick up his sword, he was dismayed to see that it was badly nicked.

As soon as the beast reached the far end of the room, it turned, roared, and charged again.

"Try hitting the sores," Ssaska said. "They're probably softer than its skin, and there are so many, we have a good chance of hitting one."

Derrik took another look at the hideous boils. The skin was stretched taut, like a blister ready to burst, nearly transparent with the green cores jiggling whenever the monster moved. Tweaks and Ssaska each took aim. Derrik raised his sword. Tweaks's arrow flew just ahead of Ssaska's bolt, but each weapon hit its mark. Two boils burst one right after the other, spattering the cave walls with an unearthly green glow. The beast's knees buckled, and it staggered, roaring in pain. Derrik trembled, raising his arms to shield his face. The monster stretched back an arm, twisting around and grasping at the arrow shaft without finding it.

As the creature faltered beside him, Derrik gritted his teeth, gripped the handle of his nicked sword, and lunged to make a desperate stab at a sore. The tip of the sword punctured a boil before the beast lurched sideways, screaming. It swung back to grab its tormentor. Derrik ducked, but the creature's claws caught his pack, jerking him backward. Derrik fell to the ground, struggling to wriggle free of the pack's strap. With a roar, the beast flung his rough gray hand that was still caught on the pack, jerking the strap free of Derrik's upraised arm and sending the pack flying across the dark cavern to land with a soft plop on the stone floor beside the entry.

The beast let out an angry grunt and then whirled to face its attackers as it backed slowly away, moving toward the entrance with its body shielding the boils.

"We don't have enough bolts to keep this up for long," Ssaska hissed. "And if the creature gets his hands on one of us, it will be over. Maybe we can make a run for it." He moved toward the far door. The creature's breath quieted and his small green eyes followed him. Then it stooped and patted the ground around its feet in wider and wider circles until it found a rock. It straightened up and drew the rock back.

"Look out!" Derrik called.

Ssaska crouched behind a boulder just as the monster let the rock fly. It zipped past the place where Ssaska had been a moment earlier and shattered against the floor. The monster stood, arms hanging long, its head turning from Derrik to Tweaks to the boulder where Ssaska hid.

"That's not going to work," Derrik said.

Tweaks nodded sadly. "I think he'll be able to stand there for a very long time."

"Is it looking at me?" Ssaska called.

"Its head is turning toward you," Derrik said.

Tweaks gave a sudden start and twisted around, clutching at the rim of his quiver. "I have an idea," he said. He slid the quiver off his back and sorted through the arrows. "You two go toward the far wall," he said. "Attract the creature. When he runs past me to get you, I'll have a clear shot at his sores."

"Wait a minute," Derrik said. "You want me to act as bait? What if it doesn't work?"

"Then we'll be no worse off than we are now," Ssaska said. "Come on, Derrik." He gripped Derrik's shirt and pulled him out into the middle of the cave. "Run!" They hadn't taken three steps before the beast roared and lunged toward them.

"Wait!" Tweaks said. "I didn't nock the arrow!"

"Quit talking!" Ssaska yelled. "Just do it!"

The beast pounded across the cave with such fury that rocks fell from the ceiling, clattering to the floor. Some shattered and pelted Derrik and Ssaska with flying rock shards. Some of the falling rocks landed on the creature's back. It roared and stretched up to its full height, writhing in pain. Then its furious eyes fixed on Derrik and Ssaska. It curled its claws and closed in on them. Murder lay in the shining green depths of its eyes.

When it passed Tweaks's hiding place, nothing happened. Derrik's stomach clenched in fear, and his heart squeezed tight with disappointment. It was too late now. Everything would be over in seconds. His eyes stung with tears. He hadn't freed his parents. He had doomed Ssaska and Tweaks. With all the anguish in his heart, Derrik screamed, "Tweaks!"

The arrow sailed quietly into the air, hitting a hard gray spot in the center of the creature's back. The arrow burst apart, sending barbs out in all directions, popping most of the boils. Glowing green goo spattered like blood from a mortal wound, while blue-green mist rose up from the creature's back toward the cave's ceiling. The creature twisted around, screaming in rage and pain, a horrifying sound. Tweaks froze, flattened against the side of the cave.

Ssaska shot another spear, bursting the last boil. Derrik picked up one of the fallen rocks and threw it at one of the burst boils. The creature fell to the floor, but the attack didn't stop. More rocks and spears landed on the gray creature until it lay motionless.

Tweaks slid slowly around the cave with his back to the wall until he joined his companions. "I don't see it breathing," he said. "I think we're safe now."

The three moved closer to the creature. It didn't move. Ssaska tugged at a nearby spear. It took some effort, but he managed to pull it free. The creature remained still. "It's dead," Ssaska said.

Tweaks eyed the glowing goo on the end of Ssaska's spear. "What if it's poisonous?"

Ssaska pointed to a blob of glowing green on the back of his hand. "It's not killing me," he said.

"But you've got scales," Tweaks said, shuddering and moving back a step.

Derrik moved closer to the creature, inspecting its face. For the first time, he noticed two short tusks in its mouth. The monster's dull eyes, gray now, were open in a death stare. Slowly, Derrik reached out to touch the rocky gray skin. He hesitantly pressed his fingers to the hard, coarse flesh. Then he pulled his hand back, shuddering. What was this thing? He walked around to the back of the creature, wondering at all its sores.

Then the torch went out.

"Hey!" Tweaks called. "That's not funny!"

"I didn't do it," Ssaska said. "The torch is spent."

"I can still see you," Derrik said.

"I can see you, too." Tweaks's voice was puzzled. "But you look green."

"Green light is better than none," Ssaska said. He plunged the torch into a mass of green goo and twisted it, coating the end. When he lifted the torch up, the end glowed. "I've got another torch in my bag," Ssaska said. "But I'm all out of sulfur sticks." He handed the green ooze torch to Tweaks, who nearly dropped it. Derrik darted in and grabbed it before it could fall and splatter them all. As Ssaska dipped the other torch, Derrik moved across the floor, searching for his pack. He found it, crumpled and torn, but still usable. He picked it up.

"Let's get out of here," Ssaska said.

38

The Second Terror

They held up their torches at the next door. It looked similar to the other two, only smaller, and without the strange writing on the frame. Ssaska bent to twist the door handle open and ducked when he walked through. Derrik had to go through the door sideways to make his armor fit. Tweaks fit through the doorway like it was made for him. The door slammed behind him. Tweaks jumped, turned, and tried the handle. It didn't surprise anyone that the door wouldn't open, and Tweaks soon gave up.

A soft yellow glow lit the room, showing a door of equally small size on the far wall. "Where's the light coming from?" Derrik asked.

"Up there," Tweaks said, pointing to a line of bowls set into the walls near the ceiling. The bowls were too high to see what created the glow.

The room was not as crudely carved as the one they'd just left. The rock walls ran smoother, the floor spread out before them in a series of diamond patterns that formed a triangle design all the way across the room. At the halfway mark, the design was repeated in a mirror image, leaving a straight line from one wall to the next. The strangest thing of all was a pedestal set on the floor, halfway between them and the midline, with a little white egg sitting on top.

"What's that?" Derrik asked.

Tweaks lifted his hands, palms up, toward the object. "It's an egg," he said.

Derrik let out a huff of breath. "What's it *for*?"

"Maybe it's for eating," Tweaks said.

Ssaska stepped toward the egg. "I've never seen this before," he said. "Keep a look out."

Derrik and Tweaks looked all around the room, but there were no glowing mushrooms and no movement. They followed Ssaska to the egg stand. Ssaska slowly reached out his spear tip and poked the egg. He drew back quickly, but nothing happened. He darted a look at the boys and then reached out to to pick the egg up, but it wouldn't budge.

"Maybe it's just a statue to honor an egg," Tweaks said.

"This is nonsense," Ssaska said. "We must be on our way." He walked toward the door across the room while Tweaks hung back, studying the egg intently. Derrik started after Ssaska just as the snake man stepped across the midline. That's when Tweaks yelped.

"It's moving!"

Ssaska pulled his crossbow to the ready, and Derrik drew his sword. Tweaks stepped back when a vertical crack materialized on the egg. The halves tipped apart as though the bottom of the egg were hinged. A small black thing about the size of Tweaks's palm appeared over the edge of the eggshell. It was vaguely round in shape and looked like it was made out of a jelly-like substance. There was no visible mouth, but it looked at the visitors with two round innocent white eyes, the black pupils in the center dilating with interest.

Suddenly, the thing jumped out of the egg and landed on the floor, rolling so quickly towards Derrik that he didn't have time to step away until it was up against his pant leg. It made a soft purring noise and followed Derrik as he stepped back.

"That thing's not a bit dangerous," Tweaks said. "What do you suppose it's doing here?"

"Don't let it fool you," Ssaska said.

Derrik had to agree with Tweaks. He couldn't imagine a

single way that this creature could harm them. Surely it couldn't be the second terror.

The creature remained cuddled against Derrik's leg. Derrik wasn't sure what to do.

Tweaks bent down and put a finger out toward the black thing. "Come on, fella, do you want to come see me?"

The thing blinked its eyes at Tweaks, but turned them up to give Derrik an adoring stare. Derrik felt his heart melt under those captivating eyes.

"So why does he like you and not me?" Tweaks asked, rising to his feet.

"Come on, let's go," Ssaska said, and moved toward the door.

Derrik slowly took a step to follow Ssaska. The thing rolled along the floor ahead of him and got under Ssaska's feet. "Hey!" Ssaska yelled, trying to keep from stepping on the thing and nearly losing his balance.

"What are you doing?" Tweaks called, bending down and putting out his hand. The thing looked at him and rolled in front of Derrik's moving feet.

"Stop it!" Derrik said, jerking to a halt. "Do you want to get stepped on?" He waited for the thing to cuddle up to his leg, but it stood away, it's white eyes rolling from one to another of them.

Ssaska regained his balance and headed for the door. The thing rolled in front of Ssaska's feet so quickly that he couldn't keep from stepping on it, slipping and throwing out his arms to catch his balance.

"No!" Tweaks cried, his eyes full of horror as Ssaska yanked his knee upward. The thing rolled out from under his foot, its innocent eyes blinking up at them.

"I don't think it wants us to reach the door," Ssaska said. "It gets in the way of whoever is in the lead."

Tweaks and Derrik soon realized this was true. They all proceeded forward with slow, shuffling steps, never taking the soles of their shoes off the ground in order to keep the thing from tripping them.

When Ssaska made it to the door, he reached out to grab the doorknob. The thing gave a squeal and its eyes grew wider. It leapt up into the air and smacked into the door handle, instantly thinning and coating the knob with its slippery body. Its two little white eyes stared up at them, as if the doorknob itself had eyes.

Annoyed, Ssaska reached forward and tried to grasp the back of the doorknob to turn it, but the thing spread itself out more. The knob disappeared in Ssaska's fist and he twisted with all his might, but the thing just slipped around in his hand and the knob didn't move at all.

"Let me try," Derrik said. He tried twisting the knob, but it was too slippery. The thing blinked at them with placid eyes, its jelly-like body gleaming in the light, seeming to be completely unharmed by their efforts. They tried to peel the thing off the knob, but it was too slippery to get hold of.

"Come on, little thing," Derrik said. "Just get off of there so we can go through the door, okay?" The thing blinked at him. Derrik drew in a deep breath. As cute as it was, this creature was deliberately keeping him from his parents. Derrik reached out to twist the knob. His hand slipped easily around in a helpless back and forth motion. When he pulled his hand away in frustration, the creature's eyes stared up at him.

"It's hopeless," Tweaks said.

"I don't think so," Derrik answered. He drew out his nicked sword and scraped the edge against the thing, trying to get it off the knob. As soon as the sword blade touched it, an arm shot out of the creature's side with a sword of its own that lashed out. Derrik jumped back, startled as much by the attack as the sight of the little nicked sword in the creature's new hand.

"Perhaps you didn't use enough force," Ssaska said, taking a slice at the creature with his scimitar. Another arm shot out of the thing, scaly and with claws holding a scimitar that looked suspiciously like Ssaska's.

Growing arms wasn't the only feature that changed. The eyes on the thing no longer looked wide and innocent, but glared at the three with narrow, angry white slits as it brandished miniature replicas of their own swords.

Tweaks pulled out his bow, nocked an arrow, and tried shooting at one of the thing's arms when it popped out of the creature. As soon as the arrow hit the jelly, another pair of arms identical to Tweaks's came out of the back of the creature, holding a bow just like his, nocked with an arrow. The arrow flew from the bow and stuck like a pinprick in Tweaks's hand. He jumped back in surprise, jerked the arrow from his flesh, and rubbed vigorously at the wound.

"What should we do now?" Derrik asked.

"I don't know," Tweaks said.

"Every defense we use becomes its weapon," Ssaska hissed, his eyes on the thing. "There is no defense for that."

Just then, the creature slid off the doorknob and came toward them, swinging swords and shooting arrows at the intruder's legs and faces. They all jumped back in surprise, blocking the attacks the best they could. Whenever they defended themselves against the creature, a new arm shot out, brandishing another small weapon.

"We've got to stop hitting it," Tweaks panted. "We're just giving it more power."

"We can't stop fighting, or it could kill us," Ssaska replied, his thin tongue darting in and out of his mouth.

It was true. The creature was growing steadily larger with every new arm it gained and every weapon it held until it was as big as Derrik. If not for their armor, they could have been dead. Its white eyes had disappeared in a mass of swinging limbs, blades, shields, and bows. It still had no legs, so when it moved, it pulled in all its arms, rolled forward, then all the arms sprang back out, facing its enemies with their backs against the wall.

"What are we going to do?" Tweaks squeaked, fending off a sharp blade aimed at his throat.

"I don't . . . know." *Thwack, thwack.* Derrik parried against several sharp arrows, knocking them to the floor in a clatter loud enough to wake the dead.

"We . . . should . . . split . . . up and . . . run," Ssaska hissed, his dark green arm flashing in defense against several wicked scimitars.

As the three sped off in different directions, the creature spun into a blur of black and flashing silver. Derrik shot out on a right angle, horrified to see the creature split a piece of itself off and race after him, slicing at his leg. Derrik felt a bruise spreading under his skin. He didn't allow himself the luxury of limping, but dashed across the patterned floor like a rabbit with a fox on his tail. The center line was a blur beneath his feet as he ran headlong for the far door where they'd come in.

"Augggh!" Tweaks yelled. Derrik turned to see Tweaks stumble over the flailing arms of a separate piece of the creature that had followed his retreat. Tweaks landed on the floor and curled up in pain, rolling to stop on the center line. Derrik skidded to a stop. If he didn't do something now, Tweaks was dead.

Derrik headed for his friend, but Ssaska reached Tweaks before Derrik got there. Ssaska bent, grabbing Tweaks by the shoulders and pulling him back.

Derrik darted a fearful glance at the black-armed thing. To his surprise, the pieces of black rolled together and formed one creature again. The thing stood still, arms drooping at its sides, weapons still clutched in its many hands, hanging there like a weapon display. It was strange to see the thing so still, not swinging metal or shooting arrows.

"Look," Derrik whispered, half afraid that a loud voice might make wake it up so it could try to kill them again.

Ssaska raised his head, still dragging Tweaks. "What's it doing?" Ssaska hissed, his steps faltering.

"I don't know," Derrik answered. "Sleeping?"

Ssaska stopped and Tweaks sat up. "Why?"

"I don't know." Derrik cautiously took a step closer to the thing. It remained still, as if it were dead. But what could have killed it? He took another step, then another. His next cautious step took him over the center line. As soon as he put pressure on his foot, the thing raised its arms, swinging swords and shooting arrows. Derrik jumped back, raising his own sword in defense. As soon as he stood on the far side of the center line, the thing's arms drooped back to its sides and it stood there, waiting.

Ssaska suggested trying to distract it with noise, so they took one of the glowing green ooze torches and threw it past the creature. To their surprise, as it soared past, a long black string of slime shot out, grabbed the torch from the air and pulled it into the body. Within moments, a couple of other arms shot out, holding green tipped torches that cast a sickly green glow on the walls.

"We can't cross the line," Derrik said, his voice heavy with defeat.

"But we have to," Tweaks insisted. "We can't go back. The door's locked."

Ssaska regarded the thing with his yellow eyes, his tongue flickering in and out of his lipless mouth. "We appear to be perfectly safe as long as we stay on this side of the line."

"Isn't there any way to get through?" Derrik asked. He pointed his sword past the waiting thing, silent, armed, and patient, to where the door stood, waiting just as patiently.

"I don't know," Ssaska said, his voice heavy with fatigue. "I'm too tired to think." He sat down and slumped his arms over his knees, closing his yellow eyes and lowering his green forehead onto his arms.

Derrik stood staring at the many-armed thing. His heart beat harder and harder until it hurt his ribs. His dark, angry eyes bored holes into the ugly black blob and its many arms. He looked like some sort of demented spider. It didn't seem to feel his hateful glare. It merely waited, as he imagined it would for all time if he didn't do something.

He glanced at his companions who sat slumped, their eyes down, paying no attention to him in their despair. Derrik couldn't just sit here, waiting for death. He studied the distance between himself and the far door. He would reach it because he'd run his heart out. Even if that thing got him, he'd go down with his hand on the knob, twisting it open for Ssaska and Tweaks, so they could go through and rescue his parents. There was no other choice; he'd rather die than give up.

Derrik edged his way down the mid-line, careful not to step over it as he sidled as far from the sleeping thing as he could get. He eyed the thing, the door, the thing. He gripped his sword. He would make it. He toed the floor. He tensed his muscles. Before he lost his courage, he sprinted across the line.

Before he even took two steps, the thing animated into a whirling black ball of weapons headed straight for him, the glint of steel plain in the muted light. How could it move so fast? Derrik felt panic well up in him as the thing bore down with sickening speed. He ran for all he was worth, but the thing was gaining on him. He would never make it to the door. He would never make it back across the line. The thing was going to kill him.

In spite of the horror bearing down on him, Derrik kept running, his eyes focused on the far door as well as they could see through the tears. *Mama. Da. I tried.*

"Derrik!" Tweaks screamed, just before the blade slashed out and cut Derrik's hip. He stumbled, feeling the agonizing burn of sliced flesh. But he wouldn't fall. He grit his teeth. He'd die with his face toward the door. He stumbled on, the flesh on his back twitched as he waited for the thing's killing strike.

An eerie squeal echoed off the walls of the cavern, rolling around to Derrik's ears, sending him trembling as he lurched the last few steps to the door and leaned against it. The hair on the back of his neck rose in cold spikes. Breathing hard, he turned to see the thing curling in on itself on top of a trail of black powder. Derrik was puzzled, until he felt the unbearable sting of salt in his wound. He let out an anguished yowl.

"Derrik!" Tweaks called, hurrying to his friend and grabbing his shoulders as he slid to the floor.

Derrik kept his eyes fixed on the thing. It writhed in a pile of black salt as its many arms shriveled like strips of meat jerky. Its small weapons pattered to the floor like metal leaves. A sickly greenish-blue smoke rose from the shriveling thing as though a flame inside it was going out, a flame like the one Derrik had seen inside the skeletons in his dream.

Derrik made a sudden grab for his salt pouch, finding a few grains trickling out of a clean slit in its side. The thing suddenly fell silent.

"Is it dead?" Tweaks asked.

Ssaska walked over and gently nudged the small, shriveled black mass with his foot. It rolled slightly, black grains dribbling from its side before it fell back into place. "It's dead," Ssaska said.

He hurried to Derrik and bent to examine the wound, but Derrik said, "No. Let's get through the door. I can't stand staying in this room one more second."

Ssaska grabbed the doorknob, wrenched the handle, and the door squeaked open.

39

Dungeons

"Come on," Ssaska grunted, grabbing Derrik under the shoulders. Tweaks tugged on Derrik's left arm, trying to be helpful but mostly getting in the way. Ssaska dragged Derrik through the doorway before letting him go, Derrik sprawled on the floor.

"Augh!" Tweaks gasped, raising a hand to his nose. "What's that smell?"

"These are the cells," Ssaska said. He bent to examine Derrik's wound. "Hundreds of prisoners from the mainland and islands have been kept here over the years."

The door they'd come through swung shut with finality, cutting off the little light that seeped in from the last room.

"You're cut, but it's not fatal," Ssaska said.

"It hurts," Derrik moaned, raising his hand to cover his nose in an effort to block out the dirty, wet stench of the cells.

A scuffling noise sounded down the narrow hallway that stretched into the darkness before them. Tweaks raised the remaining green torch, but the sallow glow didn't reach all the way down the corridor. "Useless!" Tweaks grumbled, tossing the torch to the side. It rolled into a corner, leaving a faint glowing green track behind it. The dark air around them was ominously silent. If there were prisoners here, why wasn't there any noise? Even if they slept, the sound of breathing would stir the air. Instead, the space around them was as still as a covered grave.

"Who's there?" Ssaska called.

Heavy silence. Then a light bobbed far down the hallway. It moved up and down and side to side, like a restless ghost. *Tap, tap, tap.* Footsteps headed their way, and the light drew closer.

Ssaska pushed himself to his feet. "Seffa soo sayor!" He demanded.

Tap, tap, tap.

Ssaska drew his scimitar and stood between the boys and the approaching light. Derrik sat up, wincing with pain. When the figure drew closer, Tweaks shuddered. "It's a ghost," he whispered, pointing at the white reptilian face floating above a lantern that was throwing off yellow light.

Ssaska hissed and dashed down the corridor. The ghost also hissed and kept coming. Then Ssaska reached out and embraced the specter.

"Derrik?" Tweaks's voice quavered. "What's happening?"

Both snake men turned and headed back toward the boys. "It's all right," Ssaska called out. "This is my friend, Sessafa. He was with me when the necromancer spoke his plans to create an army of skeletons. He didn't think it was right, either." The strange white-scaled snake man took in both boys with his pink eyes, then moved past Ssaska and inspected the boys closely, his strange eyes never blinking. Derrik was surprised at how bright and shiny his scales looked compared to Ssaska's dark green ones, even in the dark light of the corridor. Then the albino hissed.

"He says welcome to the dungeon," Ssaska said.

"Why doesn't he speak like you?" Tweaks asked.

"He didn't care to learn anything other than his native snake language," Ssaska said. "Come on, let's go find your families." Ssaska held out his green hand. Derrik took it and struggled to his feet while Tweaks gave him a helpful push from behind.

They moved down the corridor, passing jail cells made of metal bars and thick metal doors. As they passed each cell, Sessafa held up the lantern so the travelers could see inside. All the cells were bare. Derrik's heart quickened. Where were his parents? They couldn't be dead. He wouldn't believe it. But as they passed cell after empty cell, his fear grew, reaching through his body and making his hands and feet cold. By the time they reached the end of the corridor, there was no question that every cell was empty. His parents weren't here.

"Where is everyone?" Tweaks asked.

At the edge of Sessafa's lantern light, Derrik saw the bottom step of what looked like a flight of stairs leading up and out of the stinking dungeon. Sessafa said something in his unsettling language.

"All the prisoners have been moved up to the palace grounds." Ssaska's face was grim. "It appears the necromancer is impatient at the slow harvesting of souls. He's working a plan to forcefully remove them."

Derrik gasped. "How?"

Sessafa hissed some more.

"It appears that the souls must be harvested at just the right time to be useful in building the skeleton army," Ssaska explained. "The prisoners must feel fear, or a complete loss of hope, or else their souls aren't potent enough."

"Then Skippy can't die," Tweaks said, his voice high. "He's always happy." He giggled—a high, unnatural sound. "It's annoying how much that baby laughs."

Ssaska grabbed Tweaks by the shoulders and gave him a shake. "Tweaks, pull it together," Ssaska warned. "You won't be any good to your family if you aren't thinking straight."

Tweaks stared into Ssaska's yellow eyes, then dropped his head. "I'm sorry. I'm just so tired." His voice trembled. "And scared."

"That's what the necromancer is counting on," Ssaska warned, letting go of Tweaks. "He captures souls just as they leave the dying prisoner's body. That way, they don't travel on to the next world, but are forced to animate the necromancer's horrid skeletons."

"We have to stop him," Derrik said.

Ssaska nodded. "Sessafa was sent down to make certain there are no prisoners left. I'll put on armor and take you two up in chains."

"How is that going to help?" Tweaks asked, his voice sharp.

"We will be among the necromancer's prisoners," Ssaska said. "We'll figure out what to do when we get there. I almost forgot, I will have to keep my face covered, or the general will recognize me for sure, so I'll be wearing a snake man's helmet. Now take off your armor and leave your weapons."

Derrik was glad to be rid of the heavy armor, but felt insecure without the sword, even if it was bent. Sessafa provided a strip of cloth, and Ssaska cleaned and bound Derrik's wound. Derrik dropped his shirt over the bandage circling his hips. Now was the time to save his parents.

They stored the armor and weapons in a cell. While Ssaska dressed in a suit of snake man armor, complete with helmet, Sessafa put metal rings around the boys' wrists. When he threaded a chain through them, he did not lock it shut. Last of all, he tucked an empty sack into each of their waists.

"What's that for?" Tweaks asked.

The albino hissed something. Ssaska explained, "The humans are slaves here, expected to do any tasks the snake men command. The sack helps when there are many things to carry."

"I'm no one's slave," Derrik said hotly.

"But you must look like one," Ssaska said.

When all was ready, Sessafa remained in the dark, and the boys followed Ssaska up the stairs, chains clanking. As they worked their way out of the dungeons, the light grew painfully bright. Derrik and Tweaks squinted, but the snake man seemed unbothered by the light.

"What kind of torture is this?" Derrik asked, putting his arm up over his eyes.

"It's not torture," Ssaska said. "It's sunlight."

"It's too bright," Derrik said.

"You've been underground for a considerable amount of time. Your eyes need to adjust to it," Ssaska said. "Give yourself a minute."

They walked beneath a big arc and entered a courtyard. A group of about five hundred humans huddled in the center. The air stirred. Derrik squinted against the bright light, scanning the human bodies, desperate to find his parents. But all he could see were the backs of prisoners in ragged, filthy clothes, their hair tangled. Even if his mother and father stood right in front of him, Derrik wasn't sure he'd recognize them. He tried to swallow his disappointment. A breeze blew past with a sigh of sympathy.

Snake men guards strutted around in bright silver armor, some with long blue capes and others wearing light brown robes. An orange and brown snake man with a heavy brow poked a prisoner so roughly that he staggered. It was pure meanness, since the prisoner seemed to be in no condition to escape. A mottled green snake guard laughed and drew his hand across his throat. A shiny black snake man with bright yellow patches turned to stare at Ssaska, the high ridge on his helmet wide enough to hold a leathery frill. "What are you staring at?" he hissed.

Ssaska raised his head and squinted at two dremi that sat on the walls on either side of the courtyard, a snake man astride each one. "Checking out the dremi patrol," Ssaska replied. Then he turned and led the boys closer to the wall, where snake men stood high overhead, holding large animal horns at their sides.

The most terrifying sight was two creatures standing before the humans, their wide bodies curiously laced of pieces of bone that stood twice as tall as a man. Their spindly arms reached down past their knees, with long fingers that flexed slightly in the breeze. Was it the wind blowing them into motion? No other parts of their bodies moved, not even the round white heads that seemed precariously balanced on top of their shoulders.

When they made no further movement, Derrik turned his attention back to finding his parents. But there were too many heads, too many hair colors the same as his mother and father. Derrik tried to calm his anxious heart, telling himself he would find them, no matter how long it took.

At the front of the gathering, several sacks sat on a large stone platform, guarded by a line of snake men and decorated with a mix of jumbled architecture just like the palace. When two muscled snake men walked out and picked up a sack, it rattled with an ominous sound.

40

Traitor

"Skeletons," Ssaska hissed.

A snake man striped red, black, and white turned to give Ssaska a curious look. "What are you doing with those prisoners?" he asked.

"Brought them up from the dungeon," Ssaska answered, his voice cold.

"You must be a new recruit," the guard said. "You don't have to stand so close to them, you know. Just shove them in with the other vermin and watch for any who try to get out of line." The guard hefted his sword with a grin. "Then you get to put them back in line. That's fun."

Ssaska gave the snake man a salute and walked around the edge of the crowd, pulling Derrik and Tweaks along behind him so fast they had to run to keep up. When they were out of sight of the helpful guard, Ssaska stopped and jerked his chin toward the platform. The snake men carrying the bags dumped them into a center pit. Not only were there human skeleton bones, but some with horns and others with beaks.

"He's got skeletons from different species," Ssaska muttered. "This isn't good at all."

"Then let's stop it," Derrik said, barely moving his lips.

Ssaska darted a look at the snake guards surrounding them. "Not yet," he warned.

Two more snake men appeared, crossing the platform with a

huge sack, twice as large as the others held, between them. They set it down by the pit, each grabbed a bottom corner, and heaved it up to dump it. Some of the bones spilling from the extra large sack were almost as big as Tweaks. The last one to fall out was a huge human-shaped skull, far larger than any human head that Derrik had seen. When all but one of the sacks were empty, the snake men stood at attention, unmoving. The snake men on the courtyard walls looked at each other, nodded, then raised their horns and blew. A low, hollow sound reverberated through the courtyard. Derrik felt the eerie sound run through him that sent a tremor down his spine and turned his knees to jelly.

He felt Ssaska shove him from behind and Derrik fell to his knees. He looked up at Ssaska, anger sparking in his eyes. Ssaska gave him a warning look. When Derrik looked around, he saw the snake men guards moving among the prisoners, pushing them to their knees if they didn't go down fast enough. Then all the snake men turned and lowered their heads as a tall, blue-robed figure walked though the archway at the opposite end of the courtyard. His silver skull mask gleamed in the full sunlight. The necromancer stopped at the edge of the platform and raised two gloved hands.

The snake men forced everyone back to their feet. Ssaska pulled Derrik and Tweaks up. The necromancer gestured to two of the snake men who spilled the final sack of bones onto the floor. The necromancer lifted his black-gloved hands over the pile, making the bones twitch, then shiver, and then raise up on their ends. Derrik watched the eerie movements, a cold chill running down his back as the bones fitted themselves together into a square seat, raising chair arms on either side and knitting themselves into a backrest with lacy openings between slender white bones. The necromancer moved his hands again. Black mist rose up and intertwined with the bones, sticking them together into the shape of a large throne.

Absolute silence fell over the crowd. Even the snake men stood still as stone. The necromancer walked to the front of the huge chair, his robes swishing. He stopped and looked out over the crowd, his silver mask moving slowly from one side of the courtyard to the other. Then he sat down and pointed to a snake man with a bright silver cutlass hanging from a belt outside his long, red robe. A silver helmet with a bright red crest running down the tail plate shadowed the snake man's features. "Speak, Ransser." The necromancer's voice was slow and sharp, like poison. "Tell them."

Ransser turned to face the crowd, his red crest rippling. "Today you will witness the great emperor's plan to conquer all the lands," he said. "The great emperor will create an army of the undead, one so large that no one could possibly oppose it." Ransser stabbed a scaly finger at the assembled prisoners. "We're using the souls of these pathetic humans as fuel to animate these great new warriors. I will now demonstrate the power of the necromancer's magic."

Ransser walked to the front of the throne and bowed down. The necromancer reached his gloved hand into his robe and pulled out a tube with decorative carvings and inlays of sparkling stones. It winked and flashed colors in the sunlight as he placed it in the snake man's hand. Ransser stood in one fluid motion and walked over to the pit of bones. He raised the pipe's mouthpiece to his lips, aimed it down into the depths of the pit, and blew hard.

"I don't like this," Tweaks whispered.

"Hush," Ssaska said, giving Tweaks's chain a tug.

A faint blue mist flowed from the tip of the pipe. It feathered back and forth like a leaf drifting downward, slowly lowering until it settled down into the depths of the pit.

"Quickly," the necromancer ordered. "Add the traitor bones."

Ransser swiftly straightened up and moved to stand by the throne while several snake men ran forward, each one holding a bone with a faint blue-green glow. They tossed the bones into the pit, the last snake man throwing the ovoid skull of a lizard in as though it were a piece of garbage. The lizard skull had its mouth open in wordless horror.

"Clatterin!" Tweaks whispered, taking a step forward.

Ssaska grabbed his shoulder and yanked him back. "There's nothing we can do for her now."

There was an agitated clatter of bones, and the ground shook. Derrik leaned in toward Ssaska, the hair on his arms standing straight out as he stared at the pit. Tweaks whimpered, and Ssaska didn't even shush him.

At last, a tip of white showed at the opening of the pit. It rose steadily higher and higher, until out burst a horribly twisted skeletal creature. It was followed by several others, each more horrible than the last. It was as if the mix of bones came alive at the touch of blue mist and stuck to the nearest bones. A few faintly glowing blue-green bones showed at various places in the different creatures' frames. Derrik's stomach turned to see Clatterin spread out in so many pieces. She'd never get her skeleton back together. He blinked hard and glared at the creatures' eerie skulls, each one glowing a sickly blue-green.

The creature closest to Derrik was strange indeed, made of the giant's skull with several bones sticking out at odd angles from his back. Hands stuck onto his head in half a dozen places, waving fingers like thick strands of hair on a drowned man. A collection of skeletal bones as thin as mice tails fanned out from the back of the giant's neck.

Derrik's heart skipped down his ribs and he turned away, his stomach churning, but it did no good. His eyes fell on a skeleton monster with a sharp beaked skull that must have come from a birdman. Five arms had attached to the creature, four sticking out the sides of the bony torso while one reached up from in between the shoulder blades and over the head like the tail of a deadly scorpion.

Ransser stepped forward and shouted, "Now I will show you their power." He beckoned to two snake men soldiers standing off to the side of the stage. They staggered over to him, carrying a crate between them. As soon as the box touched the floor, the soldiers jumped back, pressing themselves into the crowd. Ransser lifted his scaled hand and chanted, "Blist mah repah, blist mah repah, blist mah repah."

"What did he say?" Derrik asked.

Ssaska leaned over and whispered, "I don't know. That was not the language of the snakes."

With shaking voice, Tweaks said, "He told them to arm themselves."

"How do you know?" Derrik asked.

"I think Clatterin's telling me."

"How could she?"

Tweaks shook his head slowly, his eyes bright with tears. "She talked to me before, and her bones are here now, and she's talking to me again. I don't know how."

The skeletons moved to the box, and their bones click-clacked like tapping sticks as each hand or moveable tail of bone grabbed swords, maces, and sabers. When they drew back, every hand brandished a weapon. The skeleton creatures stood in a line. The five-armed creature had enough hands to hold two bows along with a huge two-bladed ax in its top arm.

The smallest skeleton was only about the size of Derrik, but it was horrifying. It had lizard-like ovoid skull with a row of cracked and broken teeth. When it turned its head, a fierce triangular skull jutted out the back, ending in sharp, pointed fangs. Bones of various sizes stuck out on either side of the neck in a grotesque pair of flapping, creaking wings that didn't actually lift their owner off the ground. The four limbs beneath the skeleton were made of various thicknesses of bone and ended in bony claws that flexed each time the creature took a step.

Ransser shouted, "Nixit agrave!"

"Step forward," Tweaks said, his voice wobbling so that he was difficult to understand.

The creature with the large skull came forward, brandishing two spears. The blue-green essence trailed slightly behind him as he moved and then caught up when he stopped.

"Igon a trat!"

"A-a-attack," Tweaks chattered.

The giant skeleton raised a spear and threw it with all his might. The crowd shouted as the spear soared, gleaming, over their heads. It struck a pillar at the end of the stage with such force that the tip of the spear stuck out the other side.

Ransser pointed to a skeleton holding a sword and shouted, "Igon a trat!"

It leapt forward through the air and landed on the pillar, clinging to it with its bony feet. The skeleton lifted the sword with both its skinny white arms, brought the sword tip down, and stabbed hard enough to bury the blade up to the hilt.

With what looked like a grin on his face, Ransser shouted an order to the five-armed skeleton. It dashed forward and chopped the pillar clean in half with its tail arm. Before the pillar could separate, the bone warrior drew two arrows with its bottom arms, shot from its double bows, and pinned the pillar back together with two arrows angled in from opposite directions.

The next command brought forth a warrior that ran forward and in a blur of movement, cut the pillar in five pieces with flashing sword blades. The ruined pillar fell at last, pieces rolling to the edge of the stage and off into the dirt.

A moment of shocked silence filled the air. Then a loud cheer erupted from the snake men. Ransser let it go on for a moment, and then raised his hand in a fist. The cheering stopped. Ransser held up the decorative pipe, flashing blue, green, and red reflections on awed faces. "Each of these mighty bone warriors will be equipped with one of these pipes of our leader's design," Ransser explained. "When they defeat the fearful, hopeless enemy, they will use these pipes to remove the dying person's soul. Then they will harvest the bodies after the flesh has rotted off the bones. Our forces will grow until there will be no one who can stop us." He looked at the crowd with an evil grin. "But first we need more skeletons. Snake men, you are to give your lives for your emperor. Igon a trat!"

Bright orange flame shot overhead as the dremi mixed the liquids in the backs of their throats. They took off from the wall, flapping and swooping down toward the courtyard. One of them rolled sideways, tipping the snake man off its back. He fell, hissing and flailing, to the hard stone floor below.

Bone warriors sprang forward and jumped into the crowd. The humans screamed and fell to the ground. Some had their arms around each other. But the skeletons weren't after the humans. Their misty bluish green eye sockets were trained on the snake men.

"What is this?" a snake man shouted as a skeleton warrior leapt into the air. It clacked to the ground behind the snake man and took a swipe with his sword that sent the armored snake's head rolling.

"The necromancer coward!" Ssaska hissed, pulling Tweaks and Derrik behind him. "He won't kill with his own hands, but he orders death for his soldiers in order to steal their bones."

41

Followed

Metal on metal echoed throughout the courtyard, the snake men drawing their swords in self-defense. A row of snake archers formed a line and let loose a huge shower of bolts, but the arrows only glanced off bone or went right through the skeletal bodies.

The crowd panicked, everyone running in whichever direction they thought would get them to safety. When the necromancer rose from his throne and turned toward the archway, Derrik yanked at his chains.

"What are you doing?" Ssaska hissed.

"I've got to follow him," Derrik blurted. "Let me go."

A huge snake man staggered into Ssaska and knocked him sideways. Derrik lurched away just as Ransser dropped to one knee before the necromancer. He raised his face and spoke, but his words were lost in the sounds of battle. The necromancer shook his head and swept his arm around to point to the high wall beside the archway. Ransser bowed and strode toward the wall, his cape billowing around him. He climbed the wall. At the top, he stood straight, seeming to take his stand to oversee the battle. The necromancer moved toward the archway without another glance at his captain.

Eyes on his quarry, Derrik fought his way through a crowd that was too busy fighting for their lives to stop him. Derrik pushed past a snarling snake man spinning in a circle with his hands over his face, blood coloring the spaces between his fingers. Something grabbed his ankle, but Derrik kicked free. Another body fell in front of him, and he leaped over it. A bone warrior aimed an axe at his head. Derrik ducked beneath a bench and rolled out from under it just as it broke in two from the bone warrior's strike. He scuttled on hands and knees between scaly legs, then darted upward, his eyes on the necromancer, who was nearly under the arch. He had to reach him. Derrik pushed through the last few men in his way, his eyes forward. An elbow slammed into the side of his head. He staggered, catching his balance by grabbing onto a snake man's tail. The snake man yelped and twisted, slicing his sword through the air. Derrik leaped for the platform, catching it with desperate hands. The sword whistled in the air behind him.

The necromancer moved under the archway, seeming to pay no attention to the battle raging behind him. He moved slowly down a hallway, not looking left or right. When he reached a door, it opened for him, and he walked through. Derrik was at his heels, breathless from running and so close he nearly trod on the swishing robe. As soon as Derrik crossed the threshold, the door slammed shut.

In sudden darkness, Derrik followed the sound of the necromancer's steps. Suddenly, the whisper of fabric against rock quieted. Derrik stopped and crouched, ready to run or fight.

Then a familiar voice sounded through the darkness. "Your new friend, Ssaska, seems to have more potential than I thought."

Staying low, Derrik turned, trying to find where the voice came from, but it echoed from everywhere.

"I have been watching you and your friends' progress toward my palace, but I didn't expect you so soon. If you had been a day later, you would have been too late. The skeletons would have been set free and all the humans would be dead."

Derrik's anger brought him upright. "Why humans?" he spat. "Why not use snake men's souls? Why not use your own?"

There was a long silence. Derrik felt the hairs on his arms rise, as though a bolt of lightning was preparing to strike. Even as he wondered if he could make his way out of the building and get Ssaska's help, he knew it was hopeless because he'd lost all sense of direction in the darkness.

At last, the voice said, "Your timing is most unsatisfactory. It's inconvenient to have you killed right now, so I'm afraid you'll have to wait for one of my warriors to finish killing all the snake men. Oh, such lovely, fresh bones they will make." The necromancer shuffled his feet, and Derrik turned toward the sound. "It would amuse me to answer your question," the necromancer said. "Soul stealing is not as easy as it seems. I've spent more than one hundred years studying it, along with skeleton animation. For some reason, which may be your race's sheer stubbornness or maybe its stupid willingness to die for one another, human souls create the strongest reanimations, and they last the longest."

A reedy laugh rippled through the darkness, cold enough to cover Derrik's heart with ice. "It was such a puzzle," the whispery voice continued. "Why wouldn't all human souls work on reanimation, when the ones that did were the fastest, most tenacious, fiercest, and best of any other race? I grew to loathe the humans. Their fleshiness sickened me, so I surrounded myself with snake men. Now even they have grown too fleshy to bear. But knowing the secret of harvesting only the fearful and despairing human souls, I can now surround myself with sharp, clean bone warriors."

Derrik's heart recoiled, but he had to ask. "And you really think your warriors are unconquerable?"

"Ah, an interested pupil. So refreshing. You will like this, young Derrik. Now tell me, how can you kill something that's already dead? Hm? I see you have no answer. No matter. You are too late. Today's demonstration will fill my prisoners with terror so I can harvest their souls."

"It will never work," Derrik said.

"You have no hope of defeating me," the necromancer said.

Derrik stood straighter. "I refuse to give up hope. My friends and I will not stop until we have freed everyone."

"But Derrik, you cannot free the others. You don't stand

a chance against my power," the voice said, sounding slightly amused.

Suddenly, something white appeared in the darkness, flying toward Derrik with such speed that it was a blur. When it drew closer, Derrik saw with horror that it was some kind of rodent made of bones. Skeletal wings beat the air as it swooped down. Derrik ducked, but the skeleton followed him and landed on his head to bite his hair and claw his scalp until Derrik yelled in pain. He smacked at the skeleton, but it rattled away out of his reach, its flapping wings creating a breeze that Derrik felt on his hand.

A hollow laugh echoed through the darkness. "You see, that creature is but a small taste of what I can do. I create life from the dead. I am far more powerful than you ever imagined."

The flying skeleton swooped at Derrik and clawed his head again. Derrik made a wild grab, but before he could get his hands on it, it dug its bony talons deep into his scalp and pushed off into the air to fly away. Derrik cried out in pain and pressed his hands to his head. The pressure made it hurt worse. In a rage, he dropped his blood-streaked hands to the sack at his belt and yanked it free. He swung it over his head like a net, aiming for the bone thing. It clacked and fluttered overhead before the sack caught it on the fly. The thing dove to the ground and burst apart, thin bones scattering across the floor.

42

Piles of Bones

"What does he think he's doing?" Tweaks hollered, staring after Derrik.

"Revenge," Ssaska answered.

"Can you see him?" Tweaks asked, standing on tiptoe and trying to see over the heads that ducked and weaved all around them. Screams made it hard to hear Ssaska when he said, "No. You must hide."

"Where?" Tweaks hollered above the din of war and a rising wind.

"In the dungeons," Ssaska shouted.

"Are you insane?"

"They won't look for you there," Ssaska said. "Now go!"

Tweaks glanced behind him and flinched. "Come with me."

"No. I must fight. Tweaks, go now!"

Tweaks reluctantly backed away from Ssaska. Ssaska turned away but glanced over his shoulder to give the boy his strange, lipless smile. "You are a brave one, Tweaks Manning. I'm proud to be your friend." A hissing blast of flame from overhead made Ssaska fall to his knees and aim his crossbow. He let the bolt fly, striking the passing dremi in its belly. The dremi let out a high shriek and flew over the wall. Ssaska reloaded and shot a bolt into a bone warrior. The warrior staggered back, jerked the bolt out, and hurled it into a snake man's back.

Ssaska darted around a pillar. Most of the humans were

huddled on the ground, as still as death. A few of the men stood, looking about them as if unsure what to do. One thin, bearded human made a grab for a snake man's spear. The panicked snake man whirled and stabbed the man, who fell to the ground. With wild eyes, the snake man yanked his spear free and turned to thrust the bloody tip into a bone warrior. Ssaska started toward the fallen human, but the lacy bone golems got there first. One of them shifted its loosely joined bones and bent over the fallen man. It curved long finger bones around the body and scooped it up, holding it against its wide torso.

A woman jumped up from the human huddle, screaming and shaking her fists at the bone golem. It seemed not to notice, but strode away, the man securely in its arms. When the woman chased after it, the other bone golem stuck out a bony foot. The woman flew through the air and skidded along the ground, face down, until she crashed into a pillar and lay motionless. In one stride, the bone golem was beside her, lifting her up with its long fingered hands, cradling her against its lacy body like she was a baby. Then it carried her away, following the first bone golem.

Suddenly, a bone warrior loomed up before Ssaska's face. Ssaska swung his sword, cutting its head off. It rolled away, and the body crouched down, moving its hands over the stones as if looking for its lost head. Ssaska gave it another swipe with his sword, splitting the body in two. Then he looked around and saw another bone warrior pounding on a snake man with its bony fists. Ssaska snuck up behind it, raised his sword, and hacked the bone warrior apart. The bones skittered across the ground, spreading out in an arc. While the injured snake man crawled away, the bones twitched and wobbled. Then they slid toward one another in rapid jerks, clicking back into place, sounding like rain.

Ssaska backed away from the newly formed warrior, a look of horror on his face. His mind struggled to think of a way to kill these creatures. Everywhere he looked, pieces of bone warriors were falling to the ground, then reconnecting. How could they possibly defeat an enemy who wouldn't die?

The skeleton creatures became better at avoiding attacks, jumping from place to place like giant white grasshoppers and effortlessly swinging their weapons and firing arrows before leaping away for another attack.

The smallest skeleton warrior ran a long knife through a snake man, snapping the savage canines of its wolf skull in the air. Then it turned its oval head toward Ssaska and stared at him with wavery blue eyes. Its permanent, broken-toothed grin was chilling. It slowly advanced toward Ssaska, one shoulder wing hunched higher than the other, bristling with spiny bones. It walked in a crouch, its blue eye sockets never leaving Ssaska's face.

Ssaska drew his sword and held it in front of him. If he could cut the creature apart, it might give him time to escape. The skeleton paused, watching Ssaska with intense hollow eyes as it gathered its legs beneath it. Then it jumped.

Ssaska slashed out with his sword, making the creature shift its attack, striking his shoulder instead of his head. The blow unbalanced the snake man, knocking him down as the creature flew past and landed on legs bent in positions that would be impossible if it were alive. The wolf face turned toward Ssaska, its deep, swirling blue eyes watching the snake man struggle to his feet. Then it circled him with its pointed nose in the air as though trying to catch a scent. Ssaska turned with it, his sword at the ready. The bone warrior crouched, settling its haunches down close to the ground. Then it was perfectly still for a heart-stopping moment before it suddenly sprang again. Ssaska raised his sword and blocked the attack, but the canine teeth struck him so hard that his sword flew into the battling crowd.

Ssaska retreated from the advancing skeleton. He backed into a short flight of stairs and climbed up onto a slightly raised platform. The creature walked through the crowd like it wasn't there, punching aside anyone in its way. Its oval face watched him with hollow eyes. All too soon, Ssaska found himself backed into a corner. He risked a glance up at the wall and saw with a sinking heart that it was too steep for him to climb. He darted a desperate look from side to side, looking for any means of escape, but could see no way out.

He turned to face the skeleton. It was horrifying to think that his own bones were meant to turn into an animated monstrosity like the one trying to kill him. How could this bone warrior fail now? Ssaska was weaponless. But that didn't mean he'd go down without a fight.

He darted one more desperate look around, searching for anything he could use to defend himself. There was nothing. He spun back to face his attacker, flexing his hands. If that was all he had, that's what he would use. As he crouched to take the attack, his half-full water skin bumped against his leg. He paused. It was not what he hoped for in a weapon. It would only delay the inevitable. But a minute more of life was worth a chance. He pulled the skin off his belt, grabbed the straps, and began swinging it around his head like a slingshot.

The skeleton did not hesitate, but kept its relentless advance on Ssaska. Apparently a flying water skin wasn't very scary. When the creature was close enough to touch, Ssaska lunged forward, swinging the water skin with all his strength, hoping he might knock the bone warrior aside long enough to run past and lose himself in the crowd.

The skeleton swung its knife and slashed the water skin, splitting it in two. The water splashed the skeleton while the two skin halves fell to either side. As soon as the water hit its skulls, the skeleton chattered its teeth together, dropped its knife, and grabbed at its wolf head, trying to wipe the water away with skeletal fingers. Bright, greenish-blue smoke flared out of the eyeholes, showing a green flame inside the center of the skull. The skeleton spun around and its canines clashed together as it fell forward toward Ssaska, aiming for his throat. Ssaska pressed back against the wall, turning his head and squeezing his eyes shut as the skeleton warrior hit him. Then it fell apart, its pieces clattering to the ground.

Ssaska opened his eyes. A pile of bones lay at his feet. He sagged against the wall, his strength spent. Then, to his horror, the oval skull wobbled. Ssaska jerked upright as the skull rolled toward Ssaska's feet like a lopsided child's ball. Dark eyeholes turned up toward him. "Ssaska?" came the faint voice of Clatterin.

Ssaska froze, staring down at the disembodied head. Then he reached down and scooped up Clatterin's skull. He cradled it in his arms. "What happened?" he hissed.

"They captured me when I flew over the palace," Clatterin said. "They separated my bones and broke my teeth. I'm sorry about attacking you. I did not want to. It was the soul flame lodged in the other skull that forced me along. I'm not very strong with just one bone."

Ssaska glanced at the pile of bones that made no move to reassemble themselves. Then he looked into Clatterin's hollow eyes. "Why is the rest of the skeleton so still?"

"It's dead," Clatterin said. "Water releases the soul flame from the bone warrior bodies, making them just a pile of bones."

"But you're alive."

"Because my bones are saturated with soul flame, I only die when the necromancer dies."

Ssaska noticed a movement and turned to see half a dozen snake men gathering around him, staring at the pile of bones in awe. He grinned and yelled, "Water!"

The snake men soldiers took up the cry. "Water! Use water on the soul flame, and it kills the bone warriors!"

As the snake men rushed off to spread the word, Tweaks limped to Ssaska's side. A smear of blood streaked one side of his face. "Give her to me," Tweaks said.

"What are you doing out here?" Ssaska hissed. "You're hurt!"

"It's nothing," Tweaks said. He gave his outstretched hands an insistent shake in Ssaska's direction. "Give her to me so you can fight."

Ssaska placed Clatterin's skull in Tweaks hands. Tweaks tucked the bone close in to his body and disappeared through the crowd.

Once Tweaks was gone, Ssaska beckoned to the pair of snake men closest to him. "Come with me!" he called. They followed him to a large barrel half full of rainwater. The three of them hefted the barrel in their hands and moved towards the giant skeleton head bobbing up and down as he knocked snake men from side to side in the courtyard below. The three snake men tipped the barrel, dumping water onto the head. Some of the water splashed into the skull, making the blue flame flare before it nearly disappeared. But it didn't go out. Once the water evaporated, the flame brightened until it was an intense blue-green again.

The skeleton warrior lumbered around to face its attackers, raising one deformed arm. The snake men scattered as the giant picked up the barrel and flung it behind him, knocking down a group of snake men and a few humans who had strayed from the center of the courtyard. His other arm darted out, longer than it should have been, and snatched the snake man on Ssaska's left, raising him toward its white head.

Sizzles punctuated the roars and screams of combat. The giant bone warrior stopped, the squirming snake man halfway to its mouth. The giant skull turned upward. Dark, heavy clouds dropped rain into its huge eye sockets. Its giant teeth chattered like a rockslide, and it scampered toward a nearby balcony, stuffing itself beneath the overhang, holding the snake man against itself like a comforting toy.

"Let's get it!" Ssaska roared. Snake men and humans alike charged toward the giant-headed bone warrior. The skeleton picked a chunk of rock from the closest pillar and hurled it at the attackers. Then it threw the snake man across the courtyard and began breaking off chunks of rock with all three of its hands and one of its feet. It hurled them into the crowd until the balcony collapsed onto its head, breaking the skull and letting in the rain. The bony limbs scrabbled against the courtyard floor, and the teeth chattered so hard that bits of enamel flew out and struck the nearest combatants like gravel. Then the pile of bones was still.

The other bone warriors chattered and hopped into hiding under gables and alcoves all around the palace's courtyard. Those with bows shot arrows into the crowd. The others, not learning a thing from the giant skull, pried tiles and pieces of building to throw at their victims along with rocks and pieces of armor. Another overhang shuddered. "It's going to go!" Ssaska yelled, trying to get a good look at the crooked roof through the falling rain. "Get away from it!" Snake men and humans scrambled to get away, but the roof collapsed before they were all clear. Screams of pain rang through the courtyard.

Before Ssaska could check for survivors, the bone warrior who'd been hiding beneath the overhang emerged with a shield over its head, swinging an axe on one side then to the other and making blood fly into the rain.

"Hurry!" Ssaska called, ducking behind a wall. Several snake men followed him and watched as he lifted his shirt in both hands and tore at it until a piece ripped free. "We need more fabric," he called as he bunched the torn fabric around the tip of a crossbow bolt and tied it tight. Then he dunked it into a puddle of water at his feet and brought it up dripping.

A couple of snake men got the idea and ripped their shirts in pieces. Ssaska turned to the others and shouted, "Come! We need everyone!"

As soon as the snake men had assembled their strange projectiles, they lined up and aimed their bows and crossbows at the rampaging bone warrior. "Go!" Ssaska shouted, letting his soaking arrow tip fly. It struck the side of the bone warrior's head, making it turn toward the ready snake men. Several arrows bounced off its face, but one landed in each eye. The bone warrior dropped its axe and shield, scrabbling at its eyes with frantic white fingers. Then it fell apart in a heap of bones that dripped with rain.

"There's another one!" Ssaska yelled, pointing to a skeleton warrior who'd stuffed itself under the roof eaves so that it looked very much like a thick white spider web. "Ready!" Ssaska shouted. "Aim . . . fire!"

More soggy shirt arrows flew toward the bones, which shifted and rattled, trying to avoid the wet fabric. In spite of its best efforts, a few arrows struck its head. One entered its eyehole. Teeth chattering, it clattered and shifted positions until at last it was still. A pile of bones rolled out from under the eaves and fell onto the courtyard with soft clatters.

43

Necromancer

Derrik sagged, his head throbbing, staring at the remains of his tiny fallen enemy.

Then, to his amazement, the bones rolled across the floor toward each other and reconnected. More horrifying was that they didn't fasten to their original joints. A grotesquely deformed bone creature lurched into the air and began flying in erratic jabs around his head.

The voice from the darkness let loose an evil laugh. "You see, Derrik, these creatures can't be stopped. There's no way you can defeat me, you pitiful, fleshy human. This place is full of nothing but pathetic people, like Gerret's parents. They were so weak they died on the journey before even reaching the palace."

Another voice broke out of the darkness.

"That's not true!" Tweaks shouted, his voice shaking. "My parents aren't dead!"

More laughter and the hollow voice replied, "I don't know how you got in here, Gerret, but it doesn't matter. Your soul will soon be mine. It will make up for the souls of your parents, which did me no good at all. It's your fault, you know. They died happy because their son escaped me. If they had only known I would have you in the end, their fear and hopelessness would have fueled my bone warriors. Such a waste. But I won't make that mistake again, now that I know to create fear before the harvest. You must know now that I cannot be defeated."

A cloaked figure wearing a silver mask slipped out of the darkness and stood in the wide gap between the two friends. Derrik was suddenly filled with such anger and hatred that he ran for the figure. The necromancer calmly raised a hand and made a motion with his fingers. A large wall of pale white bones popped out of the floor, blocking Derrik's path. "You see, Derrik, I have control over the dead. I can summon their power to use for myself any time I want, which is a particularly useful ancient art."

Derrik tried to break the wall down so he could get to the necromancer, but the necromancer just laughed. The flying creature of bone descended to scratch at Derrik again, driving him away from the wall. The bone wall collapsed in on itself and sank back down into the floor.

"I must be going," the necromancer said. "I'm sure the skeletons are almost finished with their task in the courtyard." He swept past Derrik.

When Derrik lunged to attack, another bone wall burst up from the ground. Derrik crashed into it and fell backwards. He sat on the floor, dazed, watching through the lacework of white bone as the necromancer walked toward the door. He'd nearly reached it when Tweaks jumped in front of him.

Sounding amused, the necromancer said, "Now, Gerret, you wouldn't be trying to stop me, would you?"

Tweaks held his ground

The necromancer swept an arm to one side, his robe writhing as though in pain. In a voice harsh as broken ice, he said, "Move aside."

Tweaks didn't move.

"I will have you killed later, Gerret," the necromancer said, his words black with hate. "Now move aside or I'll be forced to move you, and I promise, you won't like it."

Tweaks's voice was strange to Derrik, low and angry, when he said, "I'm not afraid of you."

The flying skeleton swooped in to stab at Derrik again. Derrik rolled away. His bandage had worked loose. He grabbed an end and pulled it free of his body. Then he tied it to a corner of his sack and swung it into the air in a huge arc. It caught the skeletal thing and smashed it into the floor, pieces scattering. Before it could reassemble itself, Derrik fell on its bones and scooped them into his sack. As soon as he wrapped it up in his bandage and tightened the knot, the wall collapsed with the ticking sound of bone on bone as it sank into the floor.

The necromancer turned to stare at Derrik in astonishment. Tweaks leaped up, landing on the necromancer's back. He reached around, grabbed the silver mask, and ripped it off the necromancer's face. Derrik's heart shriveled as he stared at the mottled skull sitting on the necromancer's shoulders with a row of cracked teeth grinning a yellow, mirthless smile over the missing bottom jaw. Black spots of decay dotted the skull while white flame burned through the eyeholes.

The necromancer spun around, knocking Tweaks off. He grabbed his mask from the boy's hands and shoved Tweaks into the wall. He swept out into the courtyard and stopped dead still, raindrops hissing into spurts of steam a few inches from his decaying skull. When he saw his bone warriors hiding from the rain, with others scattered in lifeless piles, he yelled in fury.

Everyone in the courtyard turned to stare at him. The snake men gasped when they saw the necromancer's face. A spinning thing descended from the sky, and Clatterin's white face appeared in the center of the whirling bones that stopped in front of the necromancer.

"You!" he shouted, his black-gloved hand stabbing the air. "But you were scattered, you didn't have the strength—"

"You invented a monster when you made me," Clatterin said through broken teeth, her voice cold. "Your bone warriors were so intent on fighting that when they broke apart and were re-assembling, they didn't notice if a faintly glowing blue-green bone rolled away, to be gathered by one of my friends."

"You're the one who let that Tweaks person into my chambers!"

"Yes, because he put me back together. I owed him a favor."

"You wasted your favor," the necromancer sneered. "You can do nothing to me."

"Maybe not," Clatterin agreed. "But I can make you stand alone." Clatterin lifted into the air and flew toward Ransser.

A chant rose from the snake men when they saw where Clatterin was headed. "Away the traitor, away the traitor."

Ransser brandished his long curved scimitar, but it was hopeless without bone warriors to obey his commands. Clatterin's attack pressed him to run along the wide wall toward the necromancer's quarters. Clatterin spun relentlessly before him. Ransser pressed himself against the stone wall, his scimitar flailing in wild swings at the bone thing, but missing every time. He screamed in frustration and then tipped his head back to follow Clatterin's rising form. Rain filled his mouth. He gargled, stumbled, then fell backward with the rain, off the wall and into the ocean far below.

While Clatterin battled Ransser, Ssaska yelled at Tweaks, "Use water!"

Tweaks pulled out his water skin and hit the necromancer hard on the side of his skull. The water skin exploded in a burst of steam and flame.

The necromancer turned, white flame burning brighter in his skull. "You foolish boy, don't you know that my soul flame is stronger than a water skin? My soul is intact, It's never been ripped from my body like those disgusting excuses for warriors." He pointed at the skeletons hiding their blue-green soul flames.

"You really aren't very smart, are you?" Tweaks said.

"You could not have done better!" The necromancer screeched. "I learned with each battle, starting with the first where the useless souls died hoping they would win the fight."

Every living thing in the courtyard stared at the ranting skeleton.

"Only human souls shriveled by fear stayed and obeyed me." He moved his skull face closer to Tweaks. "So, are you afraid now, boy?"

"No," Tweaks answered, folding his arms. "I am disgusted."

"Then you don't understand my power!" the necromancer screamed. He pointed a bony finger toward Clatterin, who still battled Ransser. "I was the one who saturated her kind with soul flame, but letting them keep their own bones made them far too independent." He turned back to Tweaks. "It was stupid of you to help her escape her banishment. You've ruined everything! All the wars, the tedious bone gathering, all the souls taken to get so close! But you have ruined it!"

"You were ruined before you began," Tweaks said.

With a cry of rage, the necromancer lunged forward and seized Tweaks by the throat. Tweaks's arms flailed, knocking the necromancer's mask away. It clattered to the platform as he lifted Tweaks so high that Tweaks's feet cleared the floor.

44
A Good Place to Be

"You insolent youth!" the necromancer snarled, his mottled skull leaning in so close it nearly touched Tweaks's dark red face. "You will die just like your parents—weak and helpless. But I will enjoy killing you!" He raised his other hand, dark fingers curled into a claw that darted toward Tweaks's head at the same instant he released Tweaks. The slap didn't quite make contact, but some unseen force sent Tweaks flying across the platform. He crashed into the doorway and flopped to the ground where he lay deathly silent. Even his curls were still.

The rain stopped.

The necromancer shouted in triumph. A sudden clatter of bone silenced him. He turned his astonished face toward the courtyard. All the bone warriors hiding on roofs and under ledges crumbled into piles of bone and rolled to the ground before his eyes. Blue-green soul flames slipped from their eye sockets and lifted into the air, turning white as they rose higher.

"No," the necromancer breathed, suddenly realizing what he had done. He ran to Tweaks's side and dropped to his knees. "I'm sorry . . . I didn't mean . . . no, it can't be," he stuttered. He tugged at the lifeless boy's shoulders, trying to lift him up.

With her battle won, Clatterin fluttered overhead to land on Tweaks's other side. "No," she cried. "Not him." She fell to her knees, her skeletal hand pressing against Tweaks's cold, wet curls. In a voice harsh with grief, she said, "You killed him." She raised her empty eye sockets to stare at the necromancer. "You stole his life with your own hands, necromancer." Her voice shook. "Can you feel your soul's power weakening?" Her voice grew louder. "As it drains from you, it leaves every one of your creations. You no longer have an army or monsters to fight your battles." Clatterin stood, extending one arm to point an accusing finger at the necromancer's skull. "You have nothing."

The necromancer raised his head, which no longer burned with white light. Instead, dull, dirty yellow eye sockets watched Clatterin collapse into a heap of lifeless bones.

A huge swarm of white souls, like smoke, drifted out of the scattered skeletons. More came out of the soul pipes that lay around the courtyard, forgotten in the fight. The necromancer grabbed his mask and pressed it to his chest like a shield while souls filled the courtyard with white mist. Suddenly, they all turned bright blue and flew towards the necromancer's head.

"No!" The necromancer screamed. He leapt to his feet and ran into the dark doorway that led to his chambers. He would have looked like a frightened child except for the yellowed skull bobbing along in the darkness. The souls drifted in after him, catching him just under the archway. One after the other, they darted into his skull, smothering the yellow flame. When there were so many it seemed his head could hold no more, other souls added to the light, turning into a huge twisting column of blue and white flame spinning brighter and faster until it was a blur of light. The necromancer yelled and clawed at the whirling flame with his skinny fingers, but he could not stop it from engulfing him. Once he was covered in whirling blue and white flame, it slowed almost to a standstill, then burst apart into small white puffs that floated skyward. There was nothing left where the necromancer once stood but a slightly burned expressionless mask made of silver and etched with a skull.

Derrik stared at the fallen mask, tears for Tweaks mixing with the rain water still running from his hair into his eyes. He wiped the back of his soaking wet sleeve across his cheeks and moved over to kneel beside his friend's body. On the other side of

Tweaks, Ssaska gathered Clatterin's bones into a leather satchel. His head lowered, he turned away.

Derrik caught a movement from the corner of his eye. He barely turned his head, his grief weighing him so heavily he felt like stone. Then he stared in amazement at three familiar figures standing in a cloud of fine mist under the archway next to the silver mask.

"Tweaks!" he yelled, jumping to his feet and rushing forward, his heart full of joy.

Tweaks watched him with a half smile on his face. He stood between his mother and father, each with an arm around their son.

"Don't be sad, Derrik."

Tweaks's words stopped Derrik cold. Five feet from his friend, Derrik stood, his heart beating painfully in his chest. "I'm all right," Tweaks said. "When the necromancer tried to take my soul, he lost his own. So it's really better this way."

"But . . . Tweaks." Derrik's eyes burned.

Tweaks's eyes filled with compassion. Then he turned his head. "Look, I've got my ear back," he said, wiggling it.

Derrik let out a strangled laugh. "You mooncalf," he muttered.

Tweaks grinned. "I'm happy, Derrik. I'm back with my family. Well, except for Skippy."

"Skippy?" Derrik felt his heart beat faster. "Where is he?"

"With your Ma and Da. You be a good big brother to him, okay?"

"Tweaks!"

"We will see each other again," Tweaks said. "You're my best friend, Derrik. My brother." Then Tweaks and his parents faded to white puffs of light that joined the stream of souls lifting up into the sky.

Derrik stood, staring upward, tears rolling down his face. He watched a spinning cloud of white that moved just like Clatterin zoom in and nudge the white puff that was Tweaks. What would he do without his friend? He couldn't imagine life in Bylon without Tweaks running around creating things that no one ever thought of before. Why did the necromancer have to take Tweaks, of all people? Someone else could have died instead.

Suddenly ashamed, Derrik bowed his head. So many others had already died, and they had people who loved them, too.

"Derrik!" Derrik turned to see his mother hurrying toward him, her arms outstretched. Right behind her was his father, with little Skippy bobbing up and down in his big arms. Mali's matted hair flopped up and down on her head as she drew closer, her bright smile even whiter against her dirt-streaked face. Derrik couldn't have said what color her dress was supposed to be, but he didn't care.

"Derrik, we thought we'd never see you again!" his mother cried. Derrik grabbed her up in a hug so fierce, it lifted her feet off the ground. His father was at his side in moments, his leather apron gone, his shirt ripped so it hung off him like fringe. Willan Sparks wrapped his free arm around his son's shoulder and clamped on hard enough to start hurting. Skippy leaned over and thumped Derrik on the head with his hand.

"Hey!" Derrik said, pulling back with a grin. He stared up into the little round face, cleaner than his mother's, which didn't surprise him. He'd felt enough of her spit washings in his younger days to guess the reason.

Once Mali was on her feet again, she looked up at Derrik with sad eyes. "Derrik, there's something I need to tell you." She glanced at Willan and then blinked at Derrik. "Tweaks's parents didn't make it." Her eyes welled up with tears.

Derrik felt the too-familiar sting of tears in back of his eyes. "I know, Mama," he said. "Tweaks didn't make it either. So we've got to take care of Skippy. He's going to be my brother now." Mali smiled through her tears and nodded.

"We're glad you feel that way, son," Willan said, his voice gruff with emotion. He ruffled the baby's strawberry blonde hair.

Derrik held out his arms. Skippy's somber green eyes looked at Willan, then Derrik, and then Willan again. Suddenly, he grinned, let out a squeal, tugged on Willan's beard, and reached his arms out to Derrik. Willan let go of the child and popped his knuckles. "Son, it's mighty good to see you again," he said. He grinned at Skippy in Derrik's arms. "Both of you."

None of the surviving snake men challenged Ssaska's authority when he ordered them to feed the humans and arrange bathing facilities for them. Rooms in the palace sheltered wounded humans and snake men alike while they rested and had their wounds tended to. Another detail of snake men were given charge to bury all bodies, including Clatterin's bones. They dug holes for snake men, humans, and the necromancer's mistakes side by side at the foot of the cliff, high above the tide.

When the humans were well enough to travel, Ssaska summoned several dremi to take everyone home. While snake men helped his parents and Skippy climb on one of the dremi, Derrik faced Ssaska. "Thank you," he said.

Ssaska touched the scar on his cheek. "I must thank you. And Tweaks."

Derrik glanced over at the new graveyard where a sea breeze set Tweaks's armor dancing on a stick set at the head of his grave. They'd decided to bury Tweaks right here, with his armor as his grave marker, since there was no family in Bylon to visit his remains.

Derrik checked his pack and pulled out Tweaks's cap, leaving the empty eyeglass staring up at him from the bottom. Derrik closed the pack and glanced at Ssaska. "Well, it's time to go."

Ssaska reached out a green hand and placed it on Derrik's shoulder. "I will see you again," he said, his yellow eyes steady.

Derrik nodded. Then he tugged Tweaks's soft cap over his head and ran for the dremi.

Derrik felt no fear as he looked down over the jagged ridge of black rock marching across the channel where he'd lost his glove. His heart softened at the memory of Tweaks's concern over his bleeding face. As the dremi swooped over Lycan Island, Derrik studied each of the villages from the air. They looked much smaller than he remembered. Across the wide water, he spotted the ship hanging crookedly, swaying over the edge of the cliff on two ropes. Below, on the beach, lay the fearsome sea serpent, its fire gone, its hollow eyes covered with seagulls.

At last, they landed in the field beside Bylon. No one walked the cleared streets. Willan Sparks got off the dremi and shouted, "Hello, the town!" A cloud of sparkling insects scared up from a flowering bush fluttered in panic before flying over the village and disappearing in the scarred trees.

Everything was still. Then a small wooly head peeked out over a clump of grass. The rovo's eyes scanned the curious visitors before fixing on Derrik. It limped out into the open, heading toward Derrik at a steady pace, its torn ear flapping crookedly. Derrik bent down, encouraging the rovo to come closer. He patted the rovo carefully on the head. The rovo closed its eyes and leaned into his hand. Skippy clapped with delight and gurgled at the rovo.

It took two more shouts before any person dared show himself to see who'd arrived on the fearsome beasts. Once explanations were given, the town survivors welcomed the former prisoners home, casting frequent nervous glances at the dremi.

The snake men escorts stayed to help lay foundations for new buildings and re-plant crops in the fields. The dremi stayed close, lighting cooking fires and flying out for supplies when needed.

One morning, a shout of alarm rose from a village guard. Derrik ran to the call, shading his eyes to see approaching strangers, fearsome on their giant bovine steeds, their heads reaching half a tree high. One of them wore a pointed hat.

"The giants!" Derrik whooped, and took off at a run toward the newcomers.

"Derrik!" his mother cried.

"Son! Get back here!" Willan roared.

"Don't worry!" Derrik called back over his shoulder. "They're friends!"

Willan took off after his son, but Derrik had swift feet and a good head start.

Marson's mouth split into a grin when he saw Derrik coming. Without any urging, Marson's mount, Portina, broke into a gallop and dashed ahead to meet Derrik. She skidded to a stop in front of him, knocked off Tweaks's soft cap, and nuzzled Derrik's hair.

"Get away from him!" Willan yelled, holding a fist up in front of him.

Marson glanced at Willan, and then back at Derrik. "Isen him's a wilder man?"

"My father," Derrik said. He turned and held out his hand to stop his father. "Da, these giants helped us when we were in the forest. This is Portina," he patted Portina's giant muzzle. "She saved my life."

Willan stopped beside Derrik, his breath coming in gasps and his wary eyes on the giant cow. "Son, it looked for all the world like she was trying to eat you head first."

Marson slid from the saddle. "No worryin, wilder mans." He pulled off his hat and gave a little bow. "We've comin' to helper yous fixin' yer housers," he said with a giant smile.

"How did you know we needed help?" Willan asked.

Marson pointed upward. "Birdies tellen us things whast we wanter know."

"That's great!" Derrik said.

Willan stared at the giant for a moment, then put a protective hand on Derrik's shoulder. "You can put on the roofs," he said.

"Yesen," Marson said. He popped his hat back on his head. "Yous havers such smallen housers." Marson's forehead creased and his eyes moved beyond Derrik, scanning the ground between him and the village. He spread his huge hands. "Where'n's smallish curly one?"

Derrik looked up at Marson's face and got a good view of his chin and nostrils. Marson tipped his head down to give Derrik a puzzled look. Derrik had to swallow twice before he could get the words out. "He's with his parents." His voice broke, but he clamped his mouth shut so that only his chin wobbled.

Marson regarded Derrik for a long moment. Then he nodded, his eyes solemn. "Thater's a goodin place to be." Then he bent and reached toward Derrik. Willan tried to draw Derrik away, but he wasn't fast enough for the giant's long reach. Marson picked Tweaks's hat up off the ground. It looked like a fly wing in his huge fingers. He dropped it awkwardly on Derrik's head. "Now letter's goen and buildin' youse a good place to be," he said.

Then Willan, Derrik, and Marson led the giants into town.

Glossary

Blumper—juicy and sweet, this deep blue, round fruit is the size of an eyeball.

Bone Fish—fish made of bones that swim in the black salt shores of the badlands.

Bone Golem—a hulking mass of reconstructed bones from various sources, animated by a spell and used by the necromancer as a work force to gather dead bodies and do any other difficult tasks.

Bone Warriors—creatures made by the necromancer of various bones that are brought to life by human souls devoid of hope and full of despair.

Carnor—black and brown rodentlike creature as long as a man's thigh and favored as food by snake men.

Cow Cavalry—a group of giants who ride enormous cows and inhabit the forbidden woods.

Dinghy—a small lifeboat used on larger ships for emergencies.

Dits—domestic birds about two feet tall with black feathers and long, bright orange legs and beaks. Their eggs are used for food and their feathers for insulation, stuffing, and decoration.

Dremi—a large snakelike creature with two sets of wings.

It can fly and breathe fire when it mixes two liquid chemicals combined from glands at the back of its throat.

Drunf—mossy green or brown spotted herbivore about three and a half feet tall at the shoulder with small, round hooves. Lives wild in the woods and is hunted for food and leather.

Golden Fruit—three fists big, it has tough red stripes that must be pulled off before eating the nourishing pink center.

Lycan—a being who has evolved to enjoy the best characteristics of both humans and animals.

Munkeries—small, tree-dwelling animals that resemble monkeys.

Necromancer—a being with magic power enabling him to communicate with the dead or bring them back to life.

Palm Fruit—dish-shaped fruit with a long, thin stem fastened to the center that hangs from a tree branch. When the thin top skin is broken, a soft, sweet liquid seeps into the palm and fills it to the brim.

Rovo—about one foot tall, a domestic animal with long hanging ears; a wooly head; long, thin tail; and four prehensile feet.

Sand Berries—small, tart, pale, crunchy berries that grow at the edge of beaches on low-spreading ground cover.

Ubella fruit—long, orangey-red fruits with a firm, nourishing center.

Book Club Questions

1. When Derrik finds out his parents have been taken, he reacts by planning to look for them. If your friends and family were taken, what would you do? How would you do it?

2. When Derrik sees the dead snake man, he is revolted by its appearance and feels scared, but still plans to go against them in order to find his parents. Would you continue with your plan after realizing that you faced such great odds? Why or why not?

3. After Ssaska saves the boys from the burning grove, Tweaks trusts him, but Derrik is still hesitant. Why do you think each one of them has the opinion that they have? What would you think if you were in their situation?

4. When they first encounter Clatterin, they assume from her appearance and location that she is an evil monster ready to kill them all. Do you think it's wise to judge people or things by how they look and where they come from? Why or why not?

5. In the boar village, the boars hesitate to let Derrik and Tweaks play to earn money to leave the tavern. Cutter gives them a chance because they say they killed a necro snake and he admires that quality. Should you give people a chance without knowing about them?

6. Do you think it's a smart choice for the different types of

lycans to live separate from each other? Do you think they should try harder to live peacefully together? Why?

7. When they arrive at the second terror, they find at first that it's a cute little innocent creature, but when provoked, it becomes very dangerous. Have you ever been provoked to the point that you feel almost like a different person? Are there things in your life worth defending as strongly as the second terror defended the door? What are they?

8. Why do you think Tweaks makes the choice to step up and stand between the necromancer and his friends? Would you have done differently in the same situation?

9. The giants come to help rebuild Derrik's village without being asked. Have you ever volunteered to help anyone? How did it make you feel? If you haven't, would you like to volunteer the next time you have a chance? Why?

About the Author

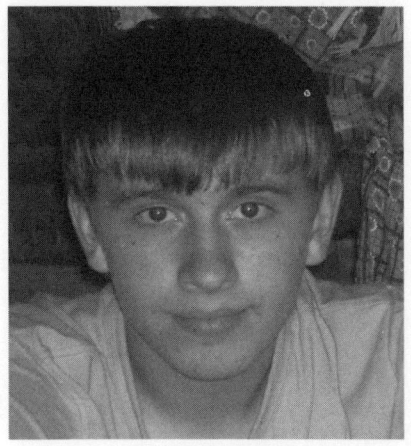

Bron Bahlmann is the fifth of six brothers. While in third grade, he wrote the mysterious *Grave Digger* story, which is still waiting for an ending. He started *Bone Warriors* when he was eleven years old and finished it at fourteen. He has several other books he works on—between walking on stilts and making swords in the backyard.

You can email Bron at bronbooks@yahoo.com or visit his web site at www.bronbahlmann.com.